NEXT DOOR
DOOR
Nympho

C.J. HUDSON

Life Changing Books in conjunction with Power Play Media
Published by Life Changing Books
P.O. Box 423 Brandywine, MD 20613

Library of Congress Cataloging-in-Publication Data;

www.lifechangingbooks.net .
13 Digit: 978-1934230312
10 Digit: 1934230316

ACKNOWLEDGEMENTS

Once again I start at the top, where I thank the Almighty Lord and Savior, Jesus Christ for allowing me to work on this project.

To my wife, Margo Murphy Speight, for having my back and supporting me in my writing projects. Being the wife of a writer can be challenging because I spend so much time writing, but you have had my back and I truly love and appreciate you for it!

To my mother, thank you for telling people about my book. I love you, Ma.

To my in-lawz, Marilyn and Melvin, thanks for all your support. To Uncle Bo-Bo, Uncle Mickey, Andre and Billy, thanks. To Auntie Val, (the horseshoe trophy is still here. lol) To my brother-in-lawz, Anthony, Jason, and Brian (I told you I was gonna spell it right this time bro) and my sister in Lawz Monica, Mo-Mo, and Lissy thanks for helping me promote my books.

Another special shout out to Brian. A lot of people don't know this but if it wasn't for you, I wouldn't still be writing. I was fully prepared to stop after this book, but you convinced me to keep at it. Thanks.

To my fellow writers K'wan and Erick S Gray, thanks for all the advice and support. To Holliwood Chucky and Terry Crumpton, thanks for the support and the advertisement! I'ma holla at you! Everybody keep tellin' me about the commercial.

To my publisher, Azarel... Damn, Boss Lady, you really held my feet to the fire on this one! I almost fell out of my chair when you told me over the phone not to f**k this up! Lol! Thanks for all that you have done for me! I've learned a lot from you and Leslie during my short time at L.C.B.

To Leslie, Kellie, Aschandria, Tonya, Virginia and anyone else who had a hand in this project. Thanks!

To my L.C.B Crew!! Azarel (V.I.P- Confessions of a Groupie), Carla Pennington(The Available Wife), Kendall Banks (One Night Stand), Jackie D (Married to A Balla), Tonya Ridley (Money Maker), Miss KP (The Dirty Divorce Series), Capone(Marked), Danette Majette (Bitter), Mike Warren (Sir,Yes Sir), Jay Tremble (Bedroom Gangsta), VegasClarke (Snitch), Tiphani (The Millionaire Mistress Series), and Erica Williams (A Woman Scorned) L.C.B!! F**k what ya heard, we run this!

To my East High School affiliates. Sir Von-Von, Nae-Nae, James, April, Kim, Arin, Bird, and all the rest of my Blue Bombers!!

To my Midwest forge co-workers, Ervin, Lil Dave, Derek, Steve B, Cross, Steve G, Dennis, Charles, Smokes, Scotty, Leon, Bam-Bam and anybody else who I may have forgotten that supported me.

To the Dogg Pound Lounge on St. Clair for letting me have book signings there.

To Teese and Jerome, Thanks for supporting me!

To Novel Tees, Horizon books, Black and Nobel, Urban Knowledge, and all the Urban book stores who support our genre, I sincerely want to thank you!

To my Facebook Assasinites, Rhea, Kendra, Gloria, Mz La La, Brandie, and everyone else that's supporting me on FB! Request me at my 2nd FB page "CJ Thewriter!"

Well, that's it for now. If I forgot you, I'll get you on the next go round!

The Keyboard Assassin is out!
Peace!!

PROLOGUE

POW! Diamond's back slammed against the wall. The impact of her vertebrae crashing into the drywall caused her framed, autographed pictures of basketball player, Darius Jones to shatter onto the hardwood floor. Diamond's life flashed before her eyes as she thought back to all the lives she had ruined; all the marriages she had wrecked in her short time on earth; twenty-five years to be exact. The loud thunder clapping through the skies drowned out her agonizing screams.

Her deadly moment had come. The red hot slug from the .357 Magnum ripped through her right shoulder blade, shredding tissue and bone along the way. The crumbling drywall was no match for the angry bullet as it tore through speedily. It destroyed everything in its path, and caused Diamond to fear for her life. Her heart pounded as she tried desperately to reach the .25 automatic tucked down in her purse. To her surprise, it wasn't there. Suddenly, she looked up through tear soaked eyes and saw her assailant holding the missing pistol.

"Looking for this?"

The shooter's haunting laugh sent chills up and down Diamond's spine. Bleeding profusely, she struggled to stand up.

"Who the fuck is you? What the fuck is this shit all about?" Diamond asked hysterically.

"You've stolen something from me that I can't get back, and now its time to pay the piper," a cold voice whispered.

Diamond was sure that she'd heard the voice before but couldn't quite place it. The shooter was dressed in black jeans, a black pullover hoodie, and black boots with a black fedora hat pulled down over one eye. Diamond looked at the floor in amazement as the .25 automatic slid across the floor to her.

"Go ahead, bitch. Pick it up."

Foolishly, Diamond snatched the gun up, pointed it, and pulled the trigger. The hooded gunman's sinister laugh resonated throughout the room.

"And all this time I thought you were smart. But you're obviously a dumb bitch. You really think I would give your ass a loaded gun? All that cum you've been swallowing has made your ass semi-retarded."

Diamond threw the gun down in disgust.

"Fuck!" she shouted.

"Yep, bitch! That's exactly what you are! Fucked!"

As hard as she tried, Diamond just couldn't get a clear read on the voice that was coming at her. Whoever it was sounded very well educated. There was no slurred speech or slang to connect them with the hood.

"What the fuck is that 'spose ta mean?" Diamond asked.

"It means, it's payback time and there's nothing you can do to stop what's about to happen to you."

Diamond's eyes bulged.

"You've allowed your over-active vagina to ruin your life. You fucked the wrong guy, baby. You took away my life and now I'm gonna return the favor."

Diamond tried to think back, but she'd fucked so many men that she couldn't be sure who the shooter was talking about. Diamond flinched when her assailant pulled something from her back pocket. With a flick of the wrist, a picture sailed across the floor toward her feet. Reaching down with her good arm, she picked it up and stared at it.

"I don't even know this fuckin' kid!" she wailed.

"Well, maybe you should meet him then. The assassin walked stealthily toward Diamond with the barrel pointed at her head. When the hat and glasses were removed, a look of confusion spread across Diamond's face. Then it hit her.

"Wait a fuckin' minute! It's you! But why? You..."

"Your worse fuckin' nightmare, bitch! I would tell you to say hello to him, but he's in heaven. And you're on your way to hell."

Light flashed in Diamond's face as several hollow point bullets were fired. For the first time in her life, Diamond began to pray, and hoped like hell she would survive.

C.J. HUDSON

1

Diamond

How it all Began

"Where the fuck these bitches at?" I yelled to no one in particular.

They always crampin' my style with this bein' late bullshit. Most bitches like to be fashionably late so they can make an entrance, but not me. I like to get there and scope out the product. That way, if I'm not feelin' the spot, or the men then I got time to go somewhere else, and it won't interfere with my dick searchin' time. I thought about drivin' myself and just tellin' Essence and Angie that I would meet them at the club, but then I came to my senses. Gas in Cleveland had soared to damn near four dollars a gallon. *Why the fuck should I drive and use my gas? Fuck that. Let them hoes drive their own shit, I told myself with a smirk.*

I stopped to laugh while checkin' myself in the mirror for the fifth time in the last twenty minutes. No doubt, I was a sexy bitch. I slid my hand across my short, pixie cut, hair style wondering why people couldn't see a touch of Halle Berry in me. Besides our similar hairstyles, we were both curvaceous, same height, same complexion, just different sized wallets. The only other difference was the fact that Halle once had a sex fanatic on her hands, and I in turn craved sex daily.

It was never hard to get my daily dosage 'cause niggas go crazy over Dream, the nickname I'd given my pussy. Like this one nigga I use to fuck around with. I can't even remember his name… but this nigga was actin' like he ain't ever seen pretty, succulent pussy before. Talk about clingy; I couldn't take a shit without him wanting to wipe my ass. The only way I could get rid of the magnet muthafucka was to have Essence and Angie bring him by the house and act as if I had a surprise for him. I had one for his ass alright. As soon as he walked through the door, he was treated with the surprise of seeing my lips wrapped around another nigga's dick. The look on his face was priceless. Essence and Angie laughed for almost an hour behind that shit.

The worst part by far though was that the lame ass nigga didn't even have the self-respect to get mad. He just stood there cryin' like a bitch, askin' how could I do that to him. Now I know that I'm a bad bitch but damn, show some fuckin' dignity. If that situation taught me anything, it taught me that just because a nigga has a big dick doesn't mean that he can fuck.

Suddenly, I stopped thinkin' and rushed over to the window to look out into the darkness. I got annoyed because I still didn't see my girls, or any headlights comin' down the street. Not content with the view, I opened the door, walked on the porch and looked up and down the street. Still, nothing. Starting to get pissed, I flipped open my cell phone to call Angie.

"Yo', where the fuck y'all at, chick?"

"Keep yo' bra on hoe, we coming." Before I could spit out a comeback, Angie hung up on me.

"Bitch!" I shouted. I'ma get the last muthafuckin' laugh on her ass. That chick owes me ten dollars and as soon as she turns her head tonight, I'ma go through her purse and clip her trick ass. That was a promise. Friend or no friend, I never played when it came to money. I didn't have much, so what I had, I

6

needed..

Knowin' that there was nothing else that I could do be-sides wait, I went into the kitchen and grabbed a bottle of Mango Alizé that I had chillin' in the fridge. After gulpin' down a few swallows, I decided to call Angie's ass back and cuss her out for hangin' up on me. Just as I started to dial, the phone vi-brated in my hand. After checkin' the screen and seeing that it was my boss, Jason Sims, I let it go to voice mail.

As much as I loved havin' his white, eleven inch dick blowing my back out, tonight was girl's night out. Plus, I was sure to get a chance to test drive some fresh dick at the club. Dream needed variety. *Maybe I can catch him at work so we can sneak off somewhere. I really wanna suck him off*, I thought with a devious smirk.

I remembered the last time his pale-lookin' ass came over. Me and my girls were just chillin' out, smokin' a fat ass blunt and watchin' Martin re-runs. But as soon as he walked in with a duffle bag slung over his shoulder, I knew what time it was. Fifteen minutes later my girls were out the door and I was gettin' my ass waxed. Damn, just thinkin' about that night got me hot as fuck. As if it had a mind of its own, my right hand found its way to the top of my off the shoulder, metallic looking dress and dove inside. Ever so slowly, my hand slid over my left breast and caressed my size 34 Double D's.

"Oh shit," I inadvertently moaned as I pinched my now swollen nipple.

After bringin' my left hand up to squeeze my right nip-ple, I let my right hand drop toward the bottom of my dress. Be-fore I knew it, my finger was attacking my clit. Soon after, two fingers found their way inside my wet love hole. I finger fucked myself until both of my fingers were dripping with pre-cum. Wantin' to bust a nut in the worst way, I slid my fingers out of my pussy and guided them back up to my clit. I pinched, mes-saged, teased, and flicked my little man in the boat until I ex-ploded.

"Oooo, shit that felt good," I moaned to myself as hot

cum ran down my honey colored legs, slightly burning my inner thigh.

A voice sounded.

"Bitch, what the fuck you doing?"

Startled, I opened my eyes to see Essence and Angie standing in front of me with smirks on their faces. As usual, Angie's face was perfectly painted with tons of make-up; different color eye shadows, foundation, blush, and mascara that looked as if it would never come off. Her micro braids were pulled up into a tight ponytail.

"The fuck it look like I'm doin', Angie," I shot back, showin' them that I wasn't embarrassed in the least. "You hoes took so long; so I figured I'd get a nut off while I was waitin'."

"Damn, slut. Yo' nympho ass couldn't wait 'til you got back home?" Angie asked with her nose turned up.

"Nympho? Chick, you got a lotta nerve."

"Look, you two can argue in the car," Essence said in her overly proper voice. "Let's roll."

Essence led the way as me and Angie eye-balled each other, headed out the door in search of some hot action.

"And how come yo' ass don't never drive?" Angie had the nerve to ask me.

"Yes, how come you don't ever drive," Essence cosigned.

Jealous-ass hoes, I thought. Just as I was about to make up an excuse, I heard a deep, raspy voice call my name.

"Yo' Diamond, can I holla at chu fo' a minute?"

I turned my head to the right to see my neighbor, Paul, starin' at me with puppy dog eyes. Although this muthafucka was really starting to get on my fuckin' nerves, I smiled to myself at the thought of my pussy being so good that it kept on breakin' these weak-ass men down.

"Damn, girl, that nigga still sweating the fuck outta you?" whispered Angie.

Nodding my head and rollin' my eyes, I asked my friends to wait in Essence's whip. Like I knew those nosey bitches would, they let the windows down so they could eavesdrop. "Damn, you hoes nosey," I said, poppin' my lips. They gave me the finger as I turned around and walked toward Paul.

"What, nigga? Don't you see I'm 'bout to kick it with my girls?"

"Yeah...I mean...I just wanna holla at chu fo a second."

"What you want Paul?" I asked, rubbin' my temples like I was gettin' a headache.

"I'm jus' sayin' Diamond...I mean damn, what the fuck I do? I thought we had a good thing going and you just dropped a muthafucka!"

After lookin' at his screwed up face, I broke out into laughter. I know this sucka for love ass nigga don't call his self gettin' mad. Not when after I cut his ass off from the punanny, he cried like a bitch. After I finally stopped laughin', I put my hands on my shapely hips and went into check-a-nigga mode.

"First of all Paul, I told yo ass from the gate, I wasn't lookin' for no serious type shit. I ain't tryin' to be wifey to no muthafucka."

"I'm just sayin', Diamond, I ain't tryin' ta make you wifey, I just wanna keep havin' a good time wit chu."

I can't lie. I thought about goin' one more round in the sack with Paul, my El DeBarge look-alike. The nigga couldn't fuck worth shit, but his tongue game was on point like a mutha-fucka. I quickly dismissed that thought, knowin' that this nigga would get even more sprung if I gave him any more of my killer pussy. Dream was a beast.

"Look, Paul," I said preparin' him for the lie I was about to spit out. "I didn't wanna tell you this but apparently yo ass need to hear it. The reason I stopped fuckin' you is because me and my ex are gettin' back together. I didn't tell you at first be-cause I didn't wanna hurt your feelings, but you keep pressin' me about the shit." I paused to lick my thick lips 'cause I knew that shit turned him on. "Look, I gotta go. My girls gettin' impa-tient. Plus, I don't want my dude to do a ride by and catch me talkin' to you."

9

Without saying another word, I turned on my heels and headed for Essence's 2009 Nissan Pathfinder. By the time I jumped in and closed the door, my girls were already crackin' the fuck up.

"Damn, bitch. You got that fool's nose open wider than Essence's legs," cracked Angie.

As usual, Essence didn't get bent out of shape. She just frowned and gave Angie the finger. Her behavior seemed a lil' weird but I didn't say shit. That was her problem. I had my own issues to worry about.

"I keep tellin' you bitches that my pussy is the best thing since hair weave," I said, braggin' on my sweet sex. I took one last look at Paul's sad ass face as Essence pulled off.

Umph...pathetic ass nigga.

2

Angie

"Y'all ready to get yo' muthafuckin' party on," I yelled to my girls as Essence turned onto Grand street.

"Hell yeah. Let's do this shit, chick," Diamond hollered from the back seat like some seventeen year old on spring break.

She pulled on the blunt then blew smoke at the back of my neck. I wanted to jump in the back seat and whip her ass. But Essence gave me that "be mature" look. It pissed me off how Essence always wanted to do things the right way. Miss goody two-shoes.

"You know I'm just fuckin' with you, chick. Calm down," Diamond teased.

For some reason that even she couldn't explain, Diamond always called me and Essence, chick. It pissed me off but, hell, I didn't have any friends other than she and Essence. And no family in Cleveland other than the roaches that frequented my apartment. So, for now, I'd have to put up with Diamond's bullshit.

We all knew Diamond was sheisty, but overlooked most of her cattiness. She was a selfish broad that broke bridges wherever she traveled. I rolled my eyes just thinking about her. After watching Diamond baby sit the blunt for too long, I decided that it was time to get my smoke on.

"Damn, hurry up and pass the weed, jack off queen."

Diamond gave me the finger as Essence cracked up laughing. I was glad to see Essence get in a better mood. She'd been acting too quiet most of the night. "You okay?" I asked Essence.

She nodded.

Of course Diamond's selfish ass interjected. "Chick, you need to be askin' me if I'm okay, with all these niggas stalkin' me!"

"Whateva, bitch. You wish. Just pass the blunt."

"Just for that bitch, yo ass pullin' last." Diamond then passed the blunt to Essence who was driving so slow, in a daze, it seemed like we were standing still.

"Yo Ess, why the fuck you driving so slow?"

Because we're smoking weed in here, crazy. Besides, it took a lot for me to convince Ray to help me with the down payment on this baby."

I could never understand how Essence was the only one who could get dudes to pay for shit for her. It didn't matter whether it was clothes, the latest handbag, or just fabulous dinners at the hottest restaurants. She needed to teach us. "Ray got a friend?" I asked.

Essence's face formed about twenty crinkles in her forehead causing her perfect skin to look out of place. "Nah," she responded nonchalantly.

Something was bothering her big time. I could tell. Since she didn't cuss much, her facial expressions were the only thing we could go on to know when she was truly irritated. Essence took two pulls, then passed the blunt back to me.

"Nice dress, girl," I said to Diamond after inhaling a couple of times then passing the blunt to the back.

"So, let me get this straight. You talk shit about me, then tell me my dress is cute. Chick, you need help."

I simply rolled my eyes. But she did look good. I was jealous as hell of that asymmetrical look. Her silver dress was covered in huge rhinestones like she was on some star-shit, with one side hanging off her shoulder. And to top it off she wore the same damn electric blue pumps from Bakers that I had planned on getting next week when I got my check.

"I see you giving the men easy access tonight," I finally said.

"Nah. Just giving these niggas somethin' to look forward to. That's why I chose a dress from Forever 21. Cause I'm forever stealing somebody's man." Diamond paused to laugh at her own simple ass joke. Since we didn't, she kept talking. "Shit, I'on know about you bitches but I plan on ridin' a dick tonight."

This time we all laughed, even Essence, with Diamond's sounding a bit phony. I watched her touching up the few spikes on top of her head, thinking she was the shit. I had to admit, her short hair cut was sexy as hell. But my girl truly thought she was the Queen of England. For the rest of the ten minute ride, we rolled down Superior Avenue talking about who's fucking and sucking who. By the time we pulled into the parking lot of Club Odyssey, the blunt was gone and we had a nice buzz goin' on.

"Damn, this place is packed," I commented as we stepped out of the truck, and the October chill hit us in the face. After seeing how homely the broads standing in the line were looking, we felt like diamonds in a sea of coal.

Massive hate filled the air as me and my girls stepped to the front of the line looking like we belonged on a runway. I switched hard, rocking my hot pink, satin, strapless mini dress with a thin gold belt. Only because it was mid-October did I have the fitted, black blazer to go over top. But trust and believe it was coming off as soon as I got inside. Eyes rolled and lips popped as we strode up to the doorman with a smile on our face. After checking out my tight, short frame, the bouncer licked his lips and smiled back.

"Hey, baby. What's really good tonight?" I asked my fuck buddy, the love of my life, J-Bone. He was a small time crack dealer who was only working this job because of the provision in his probation that required him to have some kind, any kind of job.

"You tell me," he said looking at me like I was a late night snack.

"Damn, nigga, you can't speak," Diamond popped off.

"Oh shit, my bad. Sup Diamond, Essence?"

"Yeah, whateva," Diamond retorted. "When you see three top shelf bitches rollin' through, you speak to all of us. You got me?"

"Diamond, shut up!" I blasted then turned to J-Bone. "Listen baby, I got a deal for you," I said rubbing my hand up and down my thigh. I wanted to get his mind off Diamond's hostile attitude. "You let us in for free, and later on I'll let you in," I whispered seductively.

J-Bone snatched the rope back so fast it almost snapped in half.

Ignoring the grumbles and moans of the haters in line, we strutted in and headed straight for the bar. I ordered an Apple Martini while Diamond and Essence ordered Cosmopolitans. It didn't take long for Essence to jump on the dance floor and start shaking her hot, plump ass for every guy in the club to see, and for every girl to envy. The True Religion skinny jeans, and cropped shirt littered with sequins she wore showed off her tiny waistline and dream figure. No doubt, she had the prettiest face of the three of us, and definitely the fattest ass; a video chick type booty at its finest. Maybe that explained why she danced freakier than both me and Diamond combined. I often wondered if she was a closet freak. Unlike me and Diamond, she didn't tell much about her sex life, or her life at all. She was super private.

While Essence was on the floor getting her groove on, me and Diamond scoped out the crowd, bobbed our head to the music, and downed more drinks. Just as I was about to join Essence on the dance floor, J-Bone snuck up behind me and pressed his tall frame against my 5 foot 1 physique. He towered over me like a father behind his child.

"Hey, girl, come take a walk with me right quick."

I knew what that meant. J-Bone was ready to cash in his coochie coupon.

"What about my girl, Diamond?"

"Fuck her," he said playfully.

"You already did," Diamond smirked, reminding him of the time the three of us got pissy drunk, played truth or dare, and ended up having a threesome.

"Well, he ain't tonight," I said bursting her bubble before it even got blown up.

"Oh, by the way, Diamond, Darius is up in here somewhere," J-Bone announced abruptly. "He came in about an hour ago with a pack of chicks houndin'em."

"Oh yeah? Where he at?"

J-Bone hunched his shoulders, then made the worst joke he could make. "He probably gettin' some head by now. Check the bathroom."

Once again, Diamond showed her annoyance with J-Bone. But I could almost see her panties getting wet at the mention of her former lover's name. With J-Bone pulling on my hand, I waved goodbye to my girl and followed him to the back of the club where his Tahoe was parked. As soon as I jumped in the passenger's seat, I was lifting up my dress. I knew exactly how J-Bone liked to get down. He loved to get freaky in his truck, amongst other places too. I reached for my thongs but he was a step ahead of me, moaning, and salivating at the mouth. He ripped them off like he hadn't had pussy in two years.

Within seconds, I caught myself. "Aye, wait!" I told him, popping open his glove box, and searching for his stash of condoms.

He'd promised to always keep some in the car after our last episode where we fucked raw, and I cried thinking I was pregnant. I wasn't big on STD's, yeast infections, and all that other shit, so I preferred to strap up. While J-Bone did what was required, I quickly released the scrunchie that held my hair in place, and allowed my braids to dangle since I knew he liked long hair.

"Lean back against the door and spread yo' legs so I can look at that fat pussy."

I was all too happy to follow orders. J-Bone stroked his dick as I finger fucked myself waiting on him to stick it in. Then he slowly climbed his six foot two inch, slim but muscular frame on top of me. Putting one of my legs on his shoulder and letting the other hang on the floor, he stuck his nine and a half inch, rock hard meat into my soft, wet womb.

"Oh shit! That's what the fuck I'm talkin' 'bout! Hit that pussy, baby, just like that!"

That's all J-Bone needed to hear as he started smashing my pussy.

"Damn, girl, Yo pussy good as fuck!"

J-Bone's truck rocked from side to side as he continued to drill deep into my sexual core. My pussy grabbed his dick like a vice, pullin' him in deeper and deeper. His balls smacked up against my ass so hard, it sound like someone was slapping me in the face.

"Uh...Uhhh...Ooooooohhh, here- here- here- it comesssssssss!!" Cum squirted out of my sex hole and splashed on his leather seats.

"I'm bout to fuckin' cum, too!"

"No, baby wait," I said before he deposited his seeds inside me. "I wanna taste it!"

A large smile spread across J-Bone's face as he crawled up my body and inserted his dick inside my mouth. Within seconds, he erupted. Just seeing his eyes roll to the back of his head with satisfaction made my pussy wet all over again. With each satisfied gulp, my stomach was filled with sperm. And I was full. After shooting the last drops of his semen down my throat, J-Bone lay back on the driver's door and breathed heavily.

"Shit! That shit was the fuckin' bomb," I said panting. "I gotta get cleaned up, then get back to my girls though. If you ain't doin' nothin', come by later on for round two," I grinned wickedly.

"Bet, I'll be there. Shit, I betta get my ass back to work though. My fuckin' break was over ten minutes ago."

3

Essence

Even after dancing like a maniac for the last thirty minutes, I still had energy to burn. My leopard pumps, and five foot eight frame was ready for round two, especially since the Reggae was about to start. I couldn't say the same for my dance partner though. Maurice was ready to quit after about ten minutes of moving. He now stood about a yard from me, watching me like a hawk, while I stood in place, gyrating my body to the beats. We were both on the outskirts of the dance floor, I guess giving Maurice a break. A chance to revive himself.

All the time that we were dancing, I saw how he undressed me with his eyes. The way I was looking, I could understand why. My jeans were skin tight, and the expensive cropped top from Neiman's was tight enough to cut off the circulation in my tits. My perky breasts stood out as if they had kick stands, reeling Maurice in. And my long hair bounced up and down as if it had a life of its own.

Except for my mole, my light brown skin didn't have a blemish on it. Unlike Angie, I never wore make up because I didn't have to. My skin felt smooth like a baby's ass, and made most guys just want to touch it. I even caught Maurice's twin brother, Marcus, sneaking a peek at my body. As horny as I felt,

I would give both of them a run for their money tonight cause contrary to the agreement I'd made with myself, I wanted some dick. I took a few quick moments to think back to how I'd gotten to the place where I wanted revenge on the entire male species. My thoughts juggled from Eric to Kevin, to Kirk. Each had gotten what they deserved and none of them even knew yet. Once they found out, I was positive they'd want revenge too. I had become a master at my craft, and hadn't even told my girls yet. It troubled me to even think about what they'd say. Just then my thoughts were interrupted by Maurice, who told me he was going to check on something with his brother.

It sounded like game. But I didn't care. My goal was set. I walked back over to where Diamond was sitting, tossing back more drinks.

"Hey Diamond, found you a sucka to buy drinks, huh? And where's Angie?"

"That bitch left me here by myself while she snuck off with J-Bone to get some quick dick."

"You said that like it's a bad thing," I said to her.

"Nah." She laughed. "I'm just hatin' a little 'cause I ain't got none yet. At least not until I find Darius."

"Darius in here?" I asked quickly, not really believing her.

"Yep, I been lookin' for that nigga. And as soon as I see that sexy muthafucka, it's on! Now I know I'ma get some good dick tonight!"

"Girl, you know a paid dude like him, probably already got somebody on his arm."

"You must not recognize my charm. You know when he sees me, what it is," Diamond said with confidence.

I didn't believe that for one minute. Diamond was way too conceited. Darius played for the NBA, and although he warmed the bench, every available hooker in Club Odyssey would be after him tonight.

"Let's go to the other side of the club," Diamond suggested. "I wanna look for Darius again."

Just as she finished her sentence, Angie came back walking funny, stopping us from leaving.

"Damn, chick, straighten yo' muthafuckin' walk up," Diamond laughed.

"Don't hate, hoe."

Angie grimaced as she got up on the stool making it clear that J-Bone had indeed blew her back out.

"That nigga beat yo' pussy to pieces," Diamond said, as she stepped a few feet away from us. "I gotta go find my soul mate. I'll be right back."

While she was gone, Maurice and Marcus stopped by the bar and bought me and Angie two more drinks. "What you pretty ladies getting into later tonight," Maurice asked, making his move.

"Shit, hopefully into your bed," I said letting him know that I was down. Angie looked at me funny. She wasn't used to me being so open, but hell, I was horny, and had an agenda.

"What about you, sexy?" his brother asked Angie.

"I'm sorry, but I'm already booked for later tonight. Maybe next time."

"Oh, okay. That's cool," he said, sounding extremely disappointed.

"Don't worry about it, sexy," I said seductively. "We can have our own little party. No worries."

After tossing Angie the keys to the Pathfinder, I strutted past the two brothers switching my ass. When I was five feet away from them I looked back and motioned with my finger for them to follow me. They looked at each other, smiled, and followed behind me like little lost puppy dogs. *Got'em, I said to myself.*

I looked back at Angie, who just shook her head and mouthed the word *slut* as I left the club. She kept mouthing the word, *condom* to me my entire way out the door. I would've never done that in front of Diamond. She was way too judgmental to let her in my business too much. Angie and I had a much more open friendship. But on the real, I didn't have too much in common with either of them other than our sexual appetites. They spoke ghetto, I didn't. They were broke, I wasn't. They weren't educated beyond high school, I was, and they cussed like sailors, while I rarely said two curse words in the same week. But we damn sho' all loved to fuck.

I was so hot and horny that I gave Marcus a blowjob on the way back to their place. As I hurriedly walked through the lobby of their two story apartment building, I thought about the two dicks I was about to suck on. My mouth watered. After the door to the elevator closed, Maurice and Marcus were all over me. Maurice stood in front and snaked his tongue down my throat. He gently pinched my nipples while his brother stood behind me kissing my neck with his armed snaked around my leg, rubbing on my pussy. Marcus gently stuck his tongue in my ear and twirled it around. I was on fire as his saliva slid down my earlobe.

"We gonna fuck the shit outta yo' ass, bitch," Marcus whispered in my ear.

Just hearing him talk like that got me into fuck mode. "Oh yeah," I said, grabbing his dick harshly. "Hope your fuck game is right."

The elevator abruptly stopped one floor below theirs. When the doors opened, an old lady with a basket full of clothes looked at the three of us with wide eyes and her jaw hung low. Instantly, she dropped her laundry to the floor.

"Oh my," she screeched, covering her mouth.

I gave her a devilish smile then tongue kissed Maurice as she continued to stare until the doors closed. We got off on the next floor and all but ran to the apartment. As soon as we got inside, Marcus yanked off his clothes. We headed down the hallway to their bedroom at top speed. By the time we got within five feet of the bedroom door, I had littered the corridor with every stitch of my clothing, except my expensive, jeweled thongs. After Maurice flipped on the light, I laid back on their bed and spread my legs as wide as I could.

"Who wants to taste heaven first?" I asked as seductively

as I could. I watched them both look into my big brown eyes, the attribute that attracted all men, of every race.

With Maurice still taking his clothes off, Marcus dove headfirst into my sweet sex patch. He roughly pulled my thongs to the side and started lapping at my kitty cat.

"Yes! Eat this pussy! Eat it! Oohhhh yes!" I cried out.

While Marcus was busy licking at my clit, Maurice walked over to the side of the bed and let his half- hard dick hang over my face. My mouth began to water as I sized up his meat. By my calculations, it had to be around nine inches. I reached up, grabbed it, and hungrily stuffed it into my mouth, devouring it as if it were my last meal.

"Uhmmm…uhhmmm baby, this shit tastes good as fuck," I said, as I took it out of my mouth for just a second. Hearing me talk nasty like that must've turned Marcus on like a muthafucka 'cause he really started licking hard after that.

"Oooo...oooo…oh, shit nigga you gon' make me cum!" I tried to hold out as long as I could because I didn't wanna cum yet, but when Marcus started sucking on my clit, I lost it and drenched his chin with love juice.

"Oh fuck, I'm cumming!"

Marcus then pulled me up by my arms and lifted me off the bed. Maurice then laid on the bed, pulled a Trojan out of nowhere, and told me to come straddle him.

"Put that down. I need to feel the real you," I explained.

He took a few minutes to contemplate my request. "Aye, I can't take no chances of being a father right now."

"You're not going to be a father, silly."

I caressed my tits repeatedly, watching him slobber from the mouth. I gave him the puppy dog look, as I played my feelings, "Maurice, I want to feel skin not rubber...If I can't have the real dick, I don't want it. Let me feel you," I begged.

He paused for a second not saying anything, yet still slobbering. A few seconds later, Maurice had thrown the condom, proudly onto the floor. I quickly grinned and climbed on top of his now rock hard javelin. After a few enjoyable minutes of riding him like a rodeo star, I felt something wet and warm sliding down the crack of my ass. For a second, I thought it was Marcus getting ready to toss my salad, but when I felt something stiff and hard entering my asshole, I knew he was getting ready to bang my poopshoot out.

"Relax, that's just my finger. The big one comes in a second."

Damn, I sighed, letting it go in.

While I continued to ride Maurice, Marcus worked his finger in and out of my asshole, preparing it for the real deal.

"Stop teasin' me and stick the muthafucka in!" I yelled in anticipation.

Maurice momentarily stopped rocking so his brother could start fucking me in the ass.

"Oh shit!" I screamed as his thick pole went deep inside my back door. Inch by delicious inch Marcus eased it in. "Oh please do it now! Please fuck me in the ass," I begged. I hadn't been fucked in the ass for so long I had forgotten what it felt like.

Making sure that I didn't forget about him, Maurice thrust his hips up and jammed his nine inches into my stomach. I could tell that he wasn't trying to have his brother upstage him. They were trying to kill the pussy and the asshole but little did they know, they were fuckin with a professional dick taker.

As turned on as we were it didn't take long for all three of us to cum. Marcus came so hard in my asshole that instead of it going in my body, most of it ran down my leg and onto the mattress. Feeling extremely confident that we had satisfied each other, we all collapsed on the bed and drifted off to sleep. At around 2:30 in the morning, I woke up to strawberry whipped cream spread around my pussy and chocolate syrup dripping from my thighs. Slowly licking from side to side was Maurice.

"So, I see you wake up hungry."

Maurice just smiled and kept on doing his thing. By the time the syrup was gone and his tongue touched my dripping clit, I was ready to explode. I didn't know where his brother was but he was missing out on some tasty, revived pussy. Just before I came, Maurice told me to get on all fours. I happily obliged, knowing that I was about to get my pussy pounded again. But instead of giving me the third leg, Maurice surprised me by sticking his tongue in my asshole and tongue fucking it. It felt so good that I came in ten seconds flat.

After drifting back to sleep, I was awakened by a lot of noise in the next room. With my vagina still leaking and my bladder full, I got out of bed to look for the bathroom. When I was half-way out the bedroom door, I saw that Maurice had gotten fully dressed.

Seeing the puzzled look on my face, he offered up an explanation that was clearly a lie. "Hey, I was just about to wake you. Something came up…so me and my brother gotta make a run. Get dressed," he told me.

"It's 3 a.m., "I told him with frustration. "Can I just stay here 'til you come back?"

"Nah, I don't think so. You gotta go. We'll catch up some time next week."

The smug look on his face told me exactly what he was thinking. *Yeah, I got the ass so you can bounce now.* Little did he know, the joke was on him. I'd just given them both HIV. *Purposely.*

4

Diamond

The dick print in his jeans had me going. Then there was his smell. The smell I remembered all too well.

"So, what's up D, you rolling with me tonight or what?" Darius asked me in between the kisses he kept planting on the back of my neck.

We had been sitting in the V.I.P booth for what seemed like an hour, all along with him tryna get me to leave with him. I had to admit, seeing my high school boyfriend after all this time did excite me. My search had paid off. His high priced jewels glistened throughout the club, causing everyone to stop and stare. The blinged out Rolex with the diamond bezel, and the oversized chain with a diamond encrusted basketball made it clear that he had loot.

"D, you hear me?" he repeated. "You rolling with me?"

"So, what about the bitches that was all up on you before I came over here?"

"C'mon D, you know them broads don't mean nuffin to me. That's why I sent them from V.I.P as soon as I seen you."

"Ummmmm humph," I uttered, "save that game for somebody else, nigga. I know the real you, Darius."

"Nah, for real. I think you owe me that," he said through piercing eyes.

"Oh, I see you still tryna run the guilt game on me after all these years. It wasn't my fault, Darius," I told him with the most serious look I could muster. You gotta know that."

"C'mon D. I don't wanna go back there tonight. That's in our past. But you know I still got heavy feelings for you, right?"

He slid his hand in between the soft plush leather of the booth, and the satin material of my dress. I got wet instantly. I remembered having mad love for him in high school. I don't know if it was the fact that he was the first nigga to ever eat my pussy, or the fact that he was so damn fine. But the nigga still had some kinda spell on me. I mean, he wasn't the first nigga to hit this hole, but he was damn sure one of the best to hit it. The only reason that we broke up was because he was a year ahead of me and went off to college when I was in the twelfth grade. He had a b-ball scholarship to Ohio State, where he only went for two years, before he left for the pros. The Chicago Bulls drafted him in the second round and even though he ain't a big time star in the NBA, he plays on a regular basis, and is definitely a star in the hood. Now that he's in his fourth year in the league, he is definitely paid. I've only seen Darius four or five times after that but whenever I did, my legs seemed to part like the red sea. I couldn't get enough of his sweet dick.

Now, here he was, all six foot two, one hundred ninety five pounds of sexy milk chocolate staring me down and licking his luscious lips. I wanted this nigga bad, but I wasn't about to act desperate for his ass. Plus, I couldn't get over the fact that the two chicks he'd dismissed from VIP were staring at me like I was their worst enemy.

Looking to my left, I saw Angie rushing my way and grinning at me like a Cheshire cat. "What's up, Darius?" Angie greeted, letting herself through the red, velvet ropes.

"Nuffin much. Just tryna get your girl to go home wit' a nigga. She know she still love me." He smiled showing his pearly whites. "C'mon, let's leave, Diamond."

I remained silent. Intentionally. It was part of my game.

"Answer the man, Diamond," Angie blasted.

"Mind ya bidness chick," I said to her, givin' her the evil eye. "Let me get this straight." I had to play the hard roll. "I ain't seen yo' ass in six months and all of a sudden you show up at the club, and I'm just spose'ta to creep off with yo' ass? Yeah right! What about them groupie ass hoes I saw swingin' from ya nut sacks earlier, huh? What about them bitches?"

"Come on, D," he said ignoring my question. "Don't act like that. You know you want to roll with me girl."

I knew I would eventually go home with him. And I knew that tonight would be the night that I revealed to him a secret I'd been keeping for years. It was time he knew the truth. But for now, I had to play hard to get.

"Whateva nigga! What about that bitch over there that keep eye-balling me to death, huh? What about that hoe?" I pointed, then Angie's neck turned around like the chick from the exorcist.

"What about her? Fuck her!" Darius said loudly, causing the bad weave bandit to turn and walk away with an attitude.

That's what I wanted to hear. I didn't feel like being bothered with some tack head hoe tryna fight me over Darius. Just then the DJ announced the last call for alcohol and judgin' from the imprint in Darius' jeans, it was clear that he wanted me just as much as I wanted him. Just the thought of devourin' his delicious body had me bitin' my bottom lip. But as soon as we stepped into the general population, some light-skinned hoe stepped in between us.

"Excuse me, but can I have your autograph?"

I wanted to slap the shit outta this rude bitch. Instead, I crossed my hands over my chest and blew fire from my eyes. After Darius signed his name on the napkin, the bitch walked off on cloud nine. It wasn't long before she was gigglin' with some other bitch in the corner, and pointin' at Darius.

"That's Darius Jones, from the Chicago Bulls," I heard the tramp whisperin' to her girl.

Darius just looked at me and shrugged his shoulders, lettin' me know that this type of shit happened on a regular. Without saying a word, I grabbed his hand and pulled him toward the dance floor. The sound of Blackstreet's old school jam *Before I Let You Go* pulsated through the speakers as Darius sweetly hummed the lyrics in my ear. My pussy started simmerin' as Darius started licking on my neck and palming my ass. Then he grabbed my hand and guided it down to his crotch.

His dick felt hard, like steel. He had to have been related to Superman. It took every bit of restraint that I had to keep from dropping to my knees, unzippin' his pants, taking it out, and sticking it in my mouth. As we slow danced in a circle, I caught a glimpse of Angie giving me the thumbs up sign. Not wantin' to take my hands off of Darius, I simply winked at her. I was trying to remain cool and not show how horny I was...but when he slid his hand under my dress and up the crack of my ass, I lost it.

"Oh shit," I moaned as my whole body started to shiver. "Come on, baby," I whispered. "Let's get the fuck outta here."

"That's what I'm talkin' 'bout girl. Let's roll. The Benz is out front."

With my pussy smolderin', I grabbed his hand and headed toward the front door.

"Yo', hol' up a second. I think Angie trying to get yo attention."

I looked over and saw that Angie was motionin' for me to come over to the bar. "Damn, I forgot all about her." Quickly, Darius and I walked over to where she was standin'. "Yo, what's up chick? I'm leavin' with Darius."

"I figured that... wit' you out there grinding on the floor and shit. I guess I'm driving Essence's whip home alone, huh?" She paused to give me what I call the jealous look. "Come to the bathroom wit' me right quick before you leave. It'll only take a second."

After frowning and rolling my eyes at her, I followed Angie to the bathroom. As soon as we got inside, her nosey ass started talking shit, while playing with her braids in the mirror. "Damn, bitch, I thought you was gonna fuck dude right there on the dance floor, you freaky hoe. Y'all shoulda seen how mutha-fuckas was looking at y'all and shit."

"Shit, fuck them," I said, checkin' myself in the mirror to make sure my hair was still in place. Angie burst out laughin' as she reached into her purse and pulled out a Gold Wrapper.

"Here hoe. You know you gonna need this. We love sex, but let's do this shit safely so we don't end up in a coffin. That's why I wanted you to come in here. Take this damn condom."

"Nah chick, I'ma need these," I said, reaching into my purse and pullin' out a whole box of top notch condoms out of my purse. "I plan on fuckin' that nigga's brains out tonight so one pack ain't gonna do me no muthafuckin' good. That nigga might wanna marry me by the morning."

We both started laughin' as we walked out of the bath-room.

"You still got feelings for him, don't you?" Angie asked in a more serious tone.

I didn't answer. I wasn't looking for love; neither was Dream. Not payin' attention to where I was goin', I bumped right into a short, cocky looking dude with a drink in his hand and a huge, gold tooth in his mouth.

"Damn, bitch. Watch where the fuck you going," he screamed as his dark liquor splashed onto my shoes.

"Damn, nigga. My fault!" I added. "I'll buy you anotha fuckin' drink!"

He opened his mouth to say somethin' slick but after lookin' me up and down for a few seconds all he could say was, "Damn, you fine as fuck."

The nigga was Angie's height, too short for me. His slurred speech and glassy eyes told me that he was either drunk or high.

"You know what? Fuck the drink. Why don't you just let me get yo' number and we can call this shit even."

"Nah, I don't fuck midgets," I said as both me and Angie smirked a little, turning to walk away.

"Hol' up. What the fuck you say?" he asked with his face

scrunched into a knot.

"Just a little inside joke between me and my girl," I responded.

"Oh yeah? I see right now that y'all some stuck up ass saditty type bitches. You know what? Gimme my muthafuckin money fo' my drink, bitch!"

After staring at this fool for a few seconds, I showed my frustration, and motioned for Darius, who had been watching the whole thing. When he stood up and began walking toward us the dude looked at me and made an unexpected remark.

"The fuck you call that nigga over here fo? He ain't gonna do a fuckin' thing except miss a free throw."

Right then I knew he didn't have much respect for Darius.

"What's going on over here, D? Everything alright?"

"What's going on over here ain't got shit to do with you, weak-ass nigga. I don't give a fuck about you being a basketball player. And apparently nobody else in here cares either."

It was obvious that he was jealous and just hatin' cause bitches was definitely jockin' Darius.

"Hold up, my man. I'm just trying to make sure my home girl alright. I don't know who the fuck you think you talking to like that. Don't get fucked up in here!"

The drunk dude walked up to Darius and pointed his finger in his face.

"Nigga let me tell yo' bitch ass somethin'…"

A loud clapping sound echoed through my ear.

Before another syllable could be uttered, Darius punched him in the face. The drunk dude tried to retaliate but was too slow. He swung a wild right hand that Darius easily ducked and countered with a right-left combination that dropped him on his back. Without delay, Darius lifted his foot up to stomp this drunk ass nigga, but before he could do it, security was on top of him pinning him against the wall.

"Hey, wait a fuckin' minute!" I shouted. "That drunk ass muthafucka started the whole thing."

"We don't give a fuck who started it! All of y'all can get the fuck out," shouted the burley gentleman with the scraggly beard.

Judgin' from his authoritative tone and take charge attitude, he must have been the head of security. I looked around for J-Bone but didn't see him anywhere.

"Yo, man get the fuck off me," Darius screamed, as he pulled away from the other security guards.

A few seconds later, the manager of the club came out to see what was goin' on. "Hey, what's going on out...Oh, Mr. Jones! Are you okay, sir? What's going on?"

It was crazy how the manager sucked up to Darius which of course had security realizing they'd made a big mistake.

"Yeah, I'm cool. Some clown ass fool was disrespecting my lady friend here and I had to set him straight! Then your security people here tried to hem me up like I was some kind of common thug."

"I'm very sorry, Mr. Jones. Please have a bottle of our best Champagne, on us of course."

"I'm sorry, too," the burly security guard chimed in. "I didn't recognize you, Mr. Jones with all the chaos going on."

After looking at my voluptuous body and knowing that he was going to get him some tonight, Darius told the manager that he would take a rain check. He then assured the manager that he wasn't upset with him and promised him that he would be back. Darius then grabbed me by the hand and led me toward the front door.

With Angie walking beside me, we both shook our heads and laughed at all that had just happened. There was never a dull moment with our crew.

"Let's get the fuck out of here," Darius told me in that smooth tenor voice that almost caused my panties to moisten again.

Seeing Darius handle the situation like I think a real man should turned me on immensely. I couldn't wait to get his python in my mouth. By the time we got halfway to the door, I was making plans to suck the nigga dry.

"So, what's up baby, where we going? My place or yours?"

After thinking about it for a few minutes, I decided that it would be better for me to be able to wake up in my own bed, so I invited him to my place. We were about halfway to the door when…a piercing sound blasted!

"Oh my God!" I screamed as the unmistakable sound of gunshots ringin' out filled the air.

Quickly, I turned my head to the left to check on Angie and saw that she had already dropped to the floor and was crawlin' for the exit. Immediately, I stepped back slightly behind a thick pole in the center of the club, using it as my shield. My heart pounded while my chest heaved up and down. How the fuck would I escape the panicking crowd? People scattered. Shouts and screams filled the air.

Then more sounds. POW POW!

Two more shots echoed through the air as people were duckin' and divin' trying to avoid being hit. I too dropped on the floor. I raised my head and saw a young woman slumped over a table with blood pouring out of her head. She couldn't have been any older than twenty years old. Out of the blue, I began to cry fearing for my own life.

"Darius, we need to get the fuck up outta here! Some-body bustin' off in this bitch! Darius! Darius!" For the first time since the shootin' started, I realized that Darius wasn't beside me. I turned in a full circle lookin' for him when my heart dropped.

"Oh my God! Nooooooooooo!" I wailed.

Lookin' down on the floor, I saw Darius laid out, face down with a massive hole in his back, and blood spread all over him. Forgettin' about my own safety, I ran back over to where he laid, knelt over him, covering my hands in his blood. "Some-body, help me please!" Tears streamed down my face as Darius attempted to breathe. Looking around frantically, I saw Angie and J-Bone rushing over in a panic.

"Oh shit, oh shit, oh shit!" Angie kept repeating, trying to catch her breath.

Through my tear soaked eyes, I saw the dude that Darius had beat up running out of the club, but stopping briefly to look at me over his shoulder. I rationalized that he had to be the shooter. I had no idea how much time had passed, but before I knew it, I looked up and the paramedics were pushin' me out of the way. Angie wrapped her petite arms around me, trying to keep me calm while they worked hard tryin' to save Darius' life.

Once they got him into the ambulance, they sped through the Cleveland streets on the way to the hospital, with Angie and me right behind them; and me crying loudly all the way. Soon, Angie sped into the emergency parking lot on two wheels, and I jumped out of the truck before it even stopped.

I ran as fast as I could to the desk and told them who I was. I was told to wait in the waitin' room area and that the doctor would see us when they knew more. I tried to tell Angie that she could go ahead without me but she refused, sayin' there was no way that she was gonna leave me alone. I was her girl. Then she called Essence and told her what had happened and that she would call her back when we knew more.

After noddin' off for about twenty minutes, I felt Angie shaking me. Darius' mother and sister had just arrived, and things had suddenly become chaotic. Before I could speak to them, three doctors approached us, and one introduced himself as Dr. Rothford. After describing the type of injuries that Darius sustained, the doctor put his hand on Darius' mother's shoulder, whose wig was half-way off. Five seconds later, I collapsed into Angie's arms as the doctor informed us that Darius was dead.

5

Diamond

The sun had just come up as Angie turned off the exit closest to my house. Before leaving the hospital, I tried to talk to Darius' mother and sister to explain to them what happened, but the bitches didn't want to hear it. Somehow they blamed me. Didn't they see the dried up blood that covered my hands and arms? Wasn't that proof enough that I'd done all I could do? I leaned my head against the passenger's side window and thought back to how it all unfolded at the hospital.

After sitting me down in the chair, Angie had gone to get me a Ginger Ale. That's when his mother, Ms. Jones walked up to me and went off, getting all close up in my face. As crazy as it seemed, she reminded me of Keisha Cole's mom, Frankie, just a hundred pounds heavier.

"This is all your fucking fault you little tramp!" I remembered her saying, with her nubby finger pointing in my face. "Every time you come in contact with my son, it has a tragic ending! I guess it wasn't enough that you murdered my unborn grandchild! But now you've gotten my son killed, too! You shoulda pulled the trigger your damn self! I hate you Diamond! I hate your ass!"

The guilt poundin' away at my soul prevented me from having any kind of come back. Her tears made a puddle on the floor as her daughter, Kellie held on tightly to keep her from falling. "Oh God why!" she wailed.

My mind flipped back to the way she screamed as she looked up toward the ceiling. "Why did you take my son? Why did you put this woman in my son's life, God? Why?"

She slowly slumped down to the floor. Kellie, who wasn't a very big woman, must've had trouble holding her mother up as she slid to the ground with her. Then Ms. Jones' looked up at me with disgust in her eyes. "I guess getting him stabbed when you two were dating wasn't enough, huh? I guess you had to get him shot this time, huh?"

I couldn't take anymore. I jumped up and headed for the door almost knockin' the soda out of Angie's hand in the process. Although there were a few things that his mother needed to be set straight on, then was not the time.

"We here D," Angie said, bringing me back to the present.

"You sure you don't want me to stay with you girl," Angie asked after pullin' up in front of my house. "J-Bone's supposed to come over later, but I can tell him that we gonna have to do that shit another time. His ass will understand."

"Nah, that's okay," I said as tears still dripped from my face. "I'll be fine."

After huggin' Angie and sayin' goodbye, I slowly stepped out of the truck and staggered to the front door. Turnin' my head to the left, I saw that my neighbor, Paul's door was open as usual.

Why the fuck would anybody have their front door open at 8am, I thought to myself, hoping he wouldn't appear out of the blue at his screen door the way he normally did.

Not wantin' to be bothered with him in any kind of way, I hurriedly opened my door and walked inside. My arms flung to the side as I plopped down on the couch. For at least fifteen minutes without moving, I simply stared at the wall. Puddles of tears continued to sting my eyes as I couldn't get the sight of Darius lyin' on the floor bleedin' out of my mind. The bottle of

36

vodka on top of the refrigerator seemed to be calling my name so I kicked off my heels, and drug myself to the kitchen, filling the glass to the rim. The strong liquor burned as it went down my throat, past my chest. But it was nothin' compared to the pain of hearin' the doctor say that my old lover was dead.

"There was so much I should've shared with him," I whimpered. "I should've told him," I kept repeating.

Slammin' the glass down on the table, I screamed to the top of my lungs. Tellin' Angie that I wanted to be alone was a mistake. In hindsight, I wish I would've taken her up on her offer to stay with me.

"I gotta get the fuck outta here," I mumbled to myself. I grabbed my coat and headed for the door. I snatched it open and instantly jumped back when I saw J-Bone standing there with a bottle of Jack Daniels in his hand.

"Hey, D. Angie texted me after she dropped you off and told me about Darius. You okay?"

"Uh…yeah, I'm cool, I'm cool."

Saying that I was surprised to see J-Bone standing there was an understatement. I thought that Angie would be hopping up and down on his big dick by now.

"Can I come in?"

"Yeah, sure," I said welcoming the company.

After J-Bone poured us both a shot of Jack, we sat back on the couch. "Ain't you 'spose to be over Angie's blowing her back out," I asked trying to force out a smile.

"I'll hook up with her later. I was just riding through and thought that I would check on you. You gonna be alright?"

"I guess so, I mean…he was my first love," I said as tears invaded my eyes again.

"Damn, D. I'm so used to Angie saying you don't give a shit about nobody that I didn't know you had feelings for Darius like that."

"We got history. That's all," I said softly.

J-Bone scooted over and wrapped his muscular arm around me. Instinctively, my head fell to his shoulder.

"It's cool," he said, gently stroking my earlobe.

Heat surged through my body as his cologne invaded my nostrils, making me hot. Carnal thoughts entered my mind as my eyes fell to his crotch. The imprint of his dick caused my pussy to start tingling. J-Bone then grabbed my chin with his thumb and forefinger and tilted my head back. Leanin' forward, he softly pressed his lips to mine and stuck his tongue in my mouth. I never resisted; not for a minute.

His lips felt like silk pillows as he took my hand and guided it down to his zipper. That was all the proddin' I needed as I unzipped his pants, reached inside his boxers, and pulled out his soldier. J-Bone then grabbed the back of my head and lightly shoved it down into his lap. If I didn't know better I would think that this nigga planned this whole thing, just to take advantage of my vulnerability.

I thought about Angie briefly, feeling like shit as I wrapped my lips around J-Bone's dick and sucked the head slowly. *I really had to stop loving dick so much.* While I was busy givin' him a blowjob, J-Bone reached down under the back of my dress and stuck his middle finger inside my wet cum hole. Hungerin' for more of his meat, I let it slide deep down my throat until I came to his balls. Then, with his dick still entrenched, I stuck my tongue out and started licking his balls.

"Ahhhhhhhhhhhhh," he moaned as I continued to do what I did best. "Diamond, lem'me fuck the pussy," he begged through clinched teeth.

As if my legs had a mind of their own, I stood up, took him by the hand, and led J-Bone to my bedroom. Once inside, he walked me backwards toward my king-sized bed, and seductively pushed me forcefully onto it. Sittin' on the bed, I smiled and leaned back on my elbows.

"You know we wrong, right?"

He ignored me.

"I mean I should be mourning Darius' death right now. And you should be with Angie."

J-Bone ignored me again, then got down on his knees

and spread my legs apart. Just to turn him on even more, I reached down with my right hand and spread my pussy lips open with my middle and forefinger. Saliva escaped from the corner of his mouth as he leaned forward and started lickin' my clit. The feeling was just what I needed. I closed my eyes and grabbed the back of his head as he flicked his tongue back and forth on my love bump.

"Ooooo baby yeesss," I hissed as the heat from his breath warmed my insides. "Oh shit baby, eat that pussy! Eat it like you hungry, nigga."

Hearin' me talk nasty seemed to spur J-Bone on. He increased the speed in which he was eatin' my pussy, causin' my leg to shake. Just as I was about to explode, J-Bone abruptly got up, picked me up, and turned me over. "Uhhh…!" I screamed as he roughly entered me from behind. Being that I was already on the verge of coming when he turned me over, it only took a few long deep strokes for me to release a stream of cum onto his rock hard member. While my juices covered his dick, J-Bone couldn't hold back either.

"Ah…Ahh…Ahhhh…Diamond, I'ma about to bust!"

"C'mon, act like you want it! Gimme that shit," I said, beggin' for the cum.

With one long deep stroke, J-Bone nutted deep inside my sex core. He pumped so much nut inside me that my vagina couldn't hold it all. Hot cum burned my leg as it ran down my inner thigh. My whole body fell forward and my head collapsed onto the pillow. Thankfully, the window was up slightly, and allowed a breeze to come through, cooling the room. A part of me said to get up and least shut the curtains tightly, but I decided against it. I guess I shoulda felt bad about screwin' J-Bone, but fuck it. I needed the release. And we all make mistakes.

Two hours later my cell phone rang. Sleepily, I pressed the talk button and was snapped wide awake with the double shock of Angie being on the other end of the phone and J-Bone lying next to me snoring like a four hundred pound walrus. As fast as I could, I jumped up, and ran out of the room, ass-naked, and tits shaking. The last thing I needed Angie to hear was her man snoring in the background.

"Hello?"

"Hey, Diamond. How you doing? You okay?"

"Uh…yeah, I'm alright."

"I know it's only 10 a.m.., but I just wanted to call you and make sure that you were okay."

"Yeah, I'm okay. Angie, I'ma hook up with you and Essence later though. I just need a few hours alone."

"Cool. I love you, Diamond."

Damn, she'd never said no shit like that before in all the six years I'd known her.

"You hear me, Diamond?"

"Yeah, me too," I responded dryly.

"If you need anything, just call me. I'm here for you."

"Okay. Bye."

After hanging up from Angie, I walked back into the bedroom, like a zombie. I was sneaky, conniving, and most times a bitch. But this was foul. I woke J-Bone up and told him that he had to leave. I was just about to tell him about my conversation with Angie when a flash of light from the outside my window damn near blinded us.

"What the fuck," he roared, after seeing the reflection of a body fleeing the scene through the white, sheer drapes.

We both ran to the window at top speed. But when we got there whoever had been outside the window disappeared. I rushed toward my nightstand where I kept my .25. Ready to buss off, J-Bone gave me a look that said it was too late. Then his expression changed again.

He began looking at me crazily, while his meat swung back and forth. "Who the fuck was that?"

I shrugged my shoulders as worry filled my face. I still couldn't figure out why someone would've risked being outside my bedroom window.

"Did they snap a fuckin' picture of us?" J-Bone asked,

already knowing that they did. "And why the fuck didn't you think to close your curtains, stupid?"

"Kiss ass, J-Bone," I spat. "Kiss my entire ass."

⚡6

Angie

After talking to Diamond, I fell back onto the bed and tried to push Darius' bleeding body out of my mind. Lately, I had been feeling kind of sick but I pushed it to the side last night, wanting to kick it with my girls. My stomach seemed to be doing back flips and no matter which way I laid it didn't get any better. That was only half the reason that I was in a bad mood. The other half had to do with J-Bone's ass. I texted that nigga five times and he didn't call back once.

I don't know where the fuck that nigga at, but I better not find out that he somewhere laid up with some bitch, again. Unable to ignore my stomach any longer, I got out of the bed, went to the kitchen, and poured myself a glass of ginger ale. It was now 10:30 and I was still sleepy because I didn't get a full night's sleep.

After drowning the ginger ale in one gulp, I strutted into the living room, turned on the TV, and laid down on the couch still dressed in my pink and black laced one-piece, worn especially for J-Bone.

Shit, I figured that if the boring shit that came on that time of the morning couldn't put me to sleep then nothing could. It must've worked, 'cause the next thing that I heard was someone banging at my front door. I got up off the couch and walked across the floor half awake. After looking through the peephole, my temperature rose twenty degrees. Taking a couple of breaths to calm myself down, I slowly opened the door.

"What up, girl?" J-Bone asked, carrying a fuckin' bag from McDonalds in his hand and wearing the biggest smile I'd ever seen in my life.

"What up, girl? Nigga is that all you gotta say to me? Where the fuck you been? Yo' ass know what happened at the club last night! You know what happened! The least yo' ass coulda done was call and check on a bitch!"

"Aye yo', hol' up a second," he said throwing his hands up in surrender. "I just assumed that you would be over Diamond's house, you know with her being yo' girl and all."

"If you woulda answered yo text message, then you woulda knew that I was here waitin' on yo' ass."

"Baby, I'm sorry about that, but my battery was low as fuck. As a matter of fact it's still in the car charging."

He smiled causing me to chill a bit.

I brought you your favorite; a fish combo. And one of them strawberry banana smoothies you love so much."

I honestly didn't know whether to believe his ass or not. After all it was possible for me to have stayed the night at Diamond's house after what went down. I stood there with my hands on my hips staring into his eyes trying to find some semblance of a lie but I couldn't.

"You got some weed with you, nigga?"

With his freehand, J-bone dug into his pocket and pulled out a thick bag of kush.

"Come on in, nigga," I said as turned on my heels, popped my lips, and headed back toward the couch. I hope that this nigga wasn't in a fuckin' mood 'cause I had already made my mind up that I wasn't going to give up shit. After handing me the McDonalds bag he went into the bathroom to take a leak. I opened the bag and the strong smell of the fish attacked my nostrils. The smell reminded me that I hadn't eaten anything in the last fourteen hours and I was starving. When he came out of the bathroom he looked at me, then at the trash, then back at me. He frowned.

"Damn! You ate that shit up that quick?"

"Hell yeah! A bitch was hungry as fuck!"

J-Bone just laughed and dropped down in the recliner next to the couch. "Yo Ang, you really need to clean this place up."

"No, I really need to move out of this dump. I either need a job, or a good man." I emphasized the words *good man*, and stared him in the face with bulging eyes hoping he'd get my point. That nigga knew I didn't have a job, and no opportunities headed my way.

"So, how ya girl doin? You talked to her anymore since last night?"

For one brief second, jealousy invaded my mind. I was there too and this is my man. *Why he askin' how she doing*? "Yeah, I talked to her earlier this morning and she seemed to be doing ok. Me and Essence gonna swing by there later on and check on…Shit," I yelled as I grabbed my stomach and jetted for the bathroom, unable to finish my sentence.

"What the fuck wrong with you?" I heard J-Bone say as I knelt over the commode.

In one large hurl, I threw up everything in my system. After throwing up twice more, I stood up and rinsed my mouth out all the while wondering what the fuck was wrong with me. I turned around and J-Bone was standing there with a twisted up look on his face.

"Damn, girl, you a'ight?"

"Hell nah, I ain't alright, nigga! What McDonalds did you go to? That nasty ass one on 55th?"

 J-Bone cracked up laughing.

"What the fuck is so funny?"

Without saying a word, he threw his hands up and walked away. When I got back in the living room, I saw that he had rolled a blunt. At least he knew how to make me happy. I was a certified weed head. My attitude left instantly as I took the weed from him and blazed it. As we passed the blunt back and forth, I noticed that J-Bone still hadn't moved from the recliner to the couch.

"Nigga why you sitting all the way over there and shit," I asked suspiciously.

" 'Cause I don't want yo' sick ass to throw up all over me and shit," he laughed.

"Whateva."

I thought it was strange that this cock hound ass nigga hadn't asked for some pussy yet. Usually, he had his dick out as soon as he walked though the door. But no, he wanted to remain several feet away from me for some reason. Just as I was about to speak on it, my cell phone vibrated. After looking at the text message that popped up on it, I knew that I had to get rid of J-Bone quick. It took less than two minutes to sweep that nigga up off the recliner, telling him that my social worker called and would be there in less than fifteen minutes.

"Why I gotta go?" he asked, "is it against the law to have company…?"

"Bye nigga, bye," I told him pushing him out the door.

As soon as J-Bone left, I ran into the bathroom and jumped into the shower. With everything that was going on with Diamond, I completely forgot about my rent being due. J-Bone did hit me off with a few dollars here and there but not enough for me to really work with. And certainly nothing like he should have for the good pussy I was giving him. Besides, I needed my unemployment check for weed, alcohol, and food. That's where my landlord Mr. Shivers came in. I could tell by the look in his eyes the first time that I told him that I didn't have all of the rent money that he was a pervert. The way that he squeezed my big titties and creamy thighs, I knew that all I had to do was fuck and suck the old bastard and my rent problems were as good as solved.

The first time that I gave him a blowjob I had to hold my breath to keep from laughing when he took his four inch dick out. And although I really didn't feel much of anything when he entered me, I screamed like he was ripping my pussy to shreds. Blinded by his inflated ego, he couldn't write me out a rent paid receipt fast enough.

After showering, oiling my body down, and throwing on nothing but a thong, I splashed on the White Diamond perfume that he bought for me a few months ago. Then I took the Lil Wayne CD out of the CD player and replaced it with some old school, Marvin Gaye. Hell, up until three years ago, my twenty four year old ass didn't even know who Marvin Gaye was. Picking up my vibrating cell phone, I saw that Mr. Shivers had sent me another text message.

Leave da front door unlocked & da bedroom door closed. When I tap on da door, say come in with a sexy voice. Then lie back, spread yo legs, & close yo eyes. Be sure to wear the blindfold.

Damn, this muthafucka on some new shit today, but it's turning me on like a muthafucka. After lighting a few scented candles, I heard the front door open. Swiftly, I jumped in the bed, put the blindfold on he'd given me weeks ago, and laid back with my legs spread.

"Ooooooooohhhh, Mr. Shivers, please come in and get this pussy," I said after hearing the three light taps on the bedroom door.

As the door opened slightly, I continued to follow his instructions and closed my eyes tightly. I was trying to hear what he was doing, but all I heard were clothes dropping to the floor. My pussy started to pulsate as I felt the foot of the bed move a little.

"Oh, hell yeah," I moaned when I felt the wet slippery tongue travel down my inner thigh. After feeling a few flicks on my clit, I yelped in ecstasy as the pleasure & pain mix of gentle bites being inflicted on my clit drove me insane. Mr. Shivers had always been good at eating pussy but today he seemed to be going that extra mile.

"Do that shit, Mr. Shivers! Eat that muthafuckin' pussy, daddy!" He loved it when I talked nasty like that. He immedi-

47

ately started to lick faster. I was already on the verge of busting a serious nut, but when my clit stopped being licked and started getting sucked, I lost it.

"Aahhh shit! Yessssssss!"

I came so hard with repeat orgasms that I thought he was going to drown. After splashing a river of nut onto his chin, I was completely drained or at least, I thought I was. Instead of stopping, he continued to do a lap dance on my clit, forcing me to come two more times. The fact that he wouldn't let me open my eyes was even more of a turn on, but when I finally did take the blindfold off, I got the shock of my life.

7

Essence

Just after two o'clock, Marcus dropped me off at home. My sore pussy needed rest, so I decided to call off any original plans I'd made for the night. I decided to call Diamond to check up on her, but got no response. I hadn't heard from Angie since she called earlier to tell me about Darius, so naturally, when Diamond didn't answer either, I became worried. I knew I was being paranoid but hoped like hell, my girls didn't crash my truck, or no shit like that.

I was supposed to be at work by 3 o'clock, but figured the need to get my ride was important, so I called the hospital to call in sick. Besides, after all my drinking and sexcapades, I wasn't up for assisting any doctors on delivering babies today. Shaking my head, I smiled at the irony of that. One; a labor and delivery nurse calling in sick to work. And two; me monitoring couchies, after having mine monitored all night.

"Whatever. They can find someone else to cover for me today. I've smelled enough pussy in the last twelve hours," I mumbled to myself, and laughing at my own joke all at the same time.

My laughter soon turned into a violent coughing spell. The type I hated with a passion. It always reminded me of the seriousness of my situation. With all the drama that had been going on, I had been forgetting to take my medicine. When I was diagnosed they told me that missing or skipping dosages was a no-no. I quickly made my way to the bathroom, reached into the cabinet, and grabbed the almost empty bottle of pills. After scoffing them down, I got dressed and grabbed the extra set of truck keys off of the refrigerator just in case Angie wasn't home. She still hadn't brought my whip back so I figured that I would just pick it up on the way to Diamonds. My heart went out to my girl, but I had bigger problems than she did. And more deadly.

Before long, I was out the door, pissed that I had to catch a freakin' bus. I hadn't been on a bus in over eight years. It was beneath me, I told myself as I walked along the sidewalk attracting attention from several cars that passed me by. My four hundred dollar black, jump suit, and bolero jacket made me look like more than I was worth. It was crazy how my persona and attire just didn't fit into my neighborhood. Even the mere fact that I was headed to pay a fare with a $1500 dollar Gucci clutch under my arm appeared strange. *I should've switched bags, but there was no time.*

After walking a few blocks up to Central Avenue, and just before making it to the bus stop, I stepped into the corner store and picked up a paper. Everyone seemed to be talking about the tragic shooting of one of our local superstars. I didn't want to join the conversation, or act like I knew him personally, so, I paid for a copy of The Plain Dealer and left. When I got to the bus stop, I opened the newspaper to the metro section. Just as I thought, there was a picture of Darius next to the article about the shooting the night before.

"Damn, I can't believe that my boy is gone," a young looking, slim, dark skinned dude sitting next to me blurted.

"You knew him?" I asked in surprise.

"Yeah. We used to play basketball together at the Y two or three times a week. He lived the next street over from me so he used to come get me all the time when it was time to ball. I know that a lot of people saw him as this NBA basketball player, but he always acted like just one of the fellas around me.

"So, y'all were pretty close, huh," I pried, noticing that his eyes were getting moist.

"Yeah, he was kinda like my mentor. He taught me how to dribble with my left hand and go behind my back." The young kid stopped to smile. "And every single time that he came back home he would always stop by to make sure that I was staying on the straight and narrow. Even though he was in the NBA, he continued to look out for me. I loved that dude."

"I'm sorry for your loss. I only knew him slightly. You know just from him growing up around here."

"Thanks. His mother is really taking it hard though. As soon as I found out this morning, I jumped up out of my bed and went over to her house to see how she was doing."

"Has she planned the funeral services yet?" Now, I was fishing for information. From the way Angie told me that Darius' mother mean mugged Diamond at the hospital, it wasn't a stretch to think that she wouldn't want her at the services.

"She said that she wanted to just hurry up and get it over with, ya know?" He paused to run his hands over his young, blurry eyes. He was clearly upset as he continued in a softer tone, "Said that she was planning on having it this Friday at Morning Starr Baptist Church on Shaw."

By now tears were starting to roll down his cheeks. And I felt like shit for pressing him. With speed, I flipped open my Gucci and handed him a Kleenex.

"Yeah, I guess I can understand that," I said, standing, as the bus came to sight. When it finally arrived, I stepped on, surveying the driver, the riders, and the torn leather seats. Yuck!

I thought that Darius' friend was behind me until I heard the bus driver ask him if he was getting on. I looked back and saw that he was still sitting at the bus stop. He shook his head to the bus driver, then the door shut. I don't know if he didn't want to get on the bus because he didn't want people to see his tears, or if he just wanted to be alone. But he never even looked up as the bus pulled off.

****

Since the bus didn't stop directly in front of Angie's house, I had to walk about a block to get to her place. She also lived in East Cleveland, but where she laid her head was three times as rough as where I lived. And her place; not so nice like mine. She stayed on Orinoco, right across the street from Silverman's. I continuously looked behind me as I walked the mean streets that had been featured on the news nightly. My pussy was killing me as the friction from my raw lips rubbing against each other continued to irritate me. I took out my cell phone and tried to call Angie again, but didn't get an answer. I just sent her a text message telling her that I was taking my whip and going over to Diamond's. Then I called Diamond again, hoping that this time she would answer the phone.

"Hello?"

"Hey girl, how you doing?"

"I'm fine," she said taking a deep breath.

"I called you earlier but I guess you were asleep."

"Huh? Oh yeah, girl, I was knocked out up in this piece. I'm so fucked up about what happened to Darius. I need to put something on my stomach though. I'm hungry as fuck."

"Me too. I was on my way over there. I'll stop and pick us up some Kentucky Fried Chicken after I pick up my truck from Angie's spot."

"That's right, I almost forgot that she still had your truck."

"Yeah, I'm almost there now. You talked to her?" I asked, "'cause I been calling her and can't get her."

"This morning. She probably sleep."

"Yeah, you right. I'll see you in a bit after I get the food."

"Okay cool. Pick up a six pack of strawberry coolers, too."

"I got you," I told her, hanging up and waving off some

52

dude yelling at me from his car window. It was a Jetta. *Absolutely not!*

"Damn, red bone! You look gooder than a mufucka!"

I ignored him and kept moving swiftly toward Angie's house. My stomach kept growling big time and I couldn't wait to sink my teeth into some food. Finally, I saw my baby, sitting out front, left in the same condition from the night before. It was a little dirty like they'd been driving in the mud, but it was in tact at least. I walked up on Angie's porch and immediately got a funny feeling. I turned the knob, and to my surprise the door was unlocked.

"Angie," I called out to her hesitantly. "Where you at girl?"

I tiptoed up to her bedroom door and just shook my head after hearing moans and groans. This broad was in there getting her screw on. Whoever she had in the room must've really been putting it on her, cause her voice seemed to be a higher pitch than normal. I started to sling open the door and scare the hell out of her, but she would be mad at me for a while if I did that. So, I took out my phone, put it on camera mode, and slowly pushed the door open.

Raising the phone up, I got ready to take the picture and almost fainted at what I saw. Angie was down on all fours getting pounded by a man who looked old enough to be her uncle. Not only that, but while she was getting hammered from behind, she was licking some woman's pussy. In total shock, I slowly closed the door and walked back through the living room. Strangely, I was slightly turned on by seeing the threesome that was taking place.

By the time I got to my truck, my panties were dripping wet. Seeing Angie eating out another woman really turned me on and had me more curious than ever. For some reason, the visions wouldn't leave my mind. After stopping off to pick up the food, I rolled through Giant Eagles Supermarket to buy the coolers that Diamond had asked for. I love the fact that Giant Eagles had a liquor store inside of it. Since I was there, I figured I'd pick up a large bag of Sour Cream and Onion potato chips. I had been craving them all day. I was hoping to run in and out, but I guess all of Cleveland was low on food, because it was way too crowded. I had to wait in line for twenty minutes before I was finally able to get checked out. While coming out of the store, I accidentally bumped into a woman carrying a bottle of Absolute vodka. The impact caused her to drop the bottle, smashing it on the concrete.

"Damn. I'm sorry about that," I said, reaching into my purse to pay her for the bottle. I did feel really bad.

"Not a big deal," she said sniffling.

"You okay?"

"Not really, but I'll be fine. You know, this is a dangerous city we live in."

"Yes it is," I said being careful not to pry this time. I did want to know why she made a weird comment like that out of the blue.

"A friend of a friend of mine was recently killed and I'm still in shock a little."

"I'm sorry to hear that," I said for the second time in less than an hour. "I had a friend of mine pass away recently, too. Well, actually it was a friend of a friend, but I did know him well."

"You know any good bars? I'm tired of going to the same ones, but I need a fuckin' drink," she said.

My expression showed that I was surprised to hear her curse. Her stylish way of dressing made me think otherwise. I could tell she had money from the Monogram Louis Vuitton on her arm, and the diamond bracelet on her wrist. It was funny how we obviously liked the same style. She reminded me of my myself...just slighter older; my guess, her early thirties.

"Ahhhhh, let's see. I know all the hot spots, but there is one cozy spot that I go to from time to time when I just wanna chill with regular people."

The woman laughed. "So, give up the info since you made me drop my vodka." She smiled slightly letting me know she was cool with what happened.

"It's a place on Mayfield Road called Malloy's. They serve food, too."

"Cool. I wanna try a different place tonight," she said, perking up a little.

"You'll like it. And it'll make you feel better. You sure you don't want me to pay for the Vodka?" I asked going into my purse.

"Nah. But I'll take the purse. I like that, girl."

We both laughed and talked a little more while going back inside to get her another bottle. She didn't give any information on the death of her friend's friend, or her name. By the time we got out of the store, she must've been feeling a little better because she was smiling, and talking to me like we'd known each other for years.

"So, what's your name?"

"Essence. And yours?"

"I'm Gwen."

"Alright Gwen. Have fun at Malloy's tonight."

"Girl, you need to come too, so we can hang out. Have a little fun," she added while grabbing her cell. "What's your number? I'll call you from my phone now so my number will pop up on yours."

Within seconds we'd exchanged numbers, and I'd found a new friend. Apparently a rich one, I told myself watching her hit the chirp to her white, CLK Benz from her car key.

"Well, I have to get going," she said, smiling. "Hopefully, I'll see you tonight. Be prepared to drink hard, and have a good time," she laughed.

"Okay," I replied back to her, glad that I was able to change her entire mood. No sooner than I pulled out of the Giant Eagles parking lot, Diamond called.

"Damn, chick, what's taking you so long? A bitch starving like hell ova here."

I see she's getting back to herself pretty quickly, I thought.

"I'm on my way. I should be there in a few minutes." It took me less than five minutes to get to Diamond's house. The moment I walked in, I could smell the sex permeating from the bedroom.

"What?" she asked when she saw me shaking my head.

"Nothing girl," I said, paying close attention to the booty shorts she wore, and white T that allowed her nipples to be seen clearly.

Diamond must've really been hungry 'cause she tore into that chicken like she hadn't had a meal in a week. I didn't plan on staying too long, once I saw that Diamond was doing okay, so I got down to business and told her what I learned about Darius' funeral. I also told her that I wouldn't be able to go with her because I had to work. I had already taken off for the day and couldn't afford to do that again so soon. My job was serious; with benefits, a good salary, and consequences.

"That's cool. Angie will probably go with me so I'll be straight. What you doin' for the rest of the day?" she asked.

Up until she said it, I really hadn't thought about it. I had planned on spending the day with her and Angie, but Angie was tied up. Literally. I laughed at the thought. And the vibe I got from Diamond made me feel like she didn't want to be bothered today anyway.

"I don't know. I might just lie around and watch some TV for the rest of the day. I gotta go though, girl. I just came by to check on you."

"Yeah, I'm cool chick. I'm just gonna lay around here and chill for the rest of the day. I don't feel like going no damn where. I gotta work tomorrow though."

"Yeah, me too," I said getting up to leave. "If you need me just give me a call. And when are you going to leave Progressive? You know there's more to life than working in that claims division, and making ten dollars an hour," I told her.

"I know. I'll work on that," she said, opening the door for me to leave. "Thanks."

After leaving her house, and more than fifteen minutes

later; I realized that I never took the coolers out of the back seat. Even though I didn't feel like it, I turned around and headed back to Diamond's house; only because I knew she was mourning and needed the drinks. As soon as I pulled back onto her street, I just shook my head and kept on going. Although it didn't shock me, I was disappointed to see J-Bone's ride parked in front of her house. But it didn't shock me to see Paul out front looking like a jealous boyfriend on stake-out.

To make matters worse, my cell rang showcasing the number to my doctor's office on the screen. Each and every time they called me it was to deliver more bad news. I was done with the pity party, and all the extra office visits. *What could they possibly want now? I wondered.*

I answered with attitude. "How can I help you?"

"Essence, this is Shenetta, from Dr. Caldwell's office. The doctor really needs to speak with you soon. She wants you to come in tomorrow. Can you?"

"I might."

Shenetta paused. She was probably thinking about all the problems I'd caused her over the years; like the time when she asked me to provide them with a list of all my sexual partners, so she could contact them to be tested for HIV. I remembered telling her they didn't deserve to be contacted. Let them find out on their own.

"But the person who gave it to you was honorable enough to let you know," she'd told me.

I remembered telling her to fuck off just as I was contemplating now.

"Anything else?" I asked sassily.

"This is really serious, Ms. Carter," she warned. "Are you coming in?"

"I said, I might." I pressed end before she could say anything else.

My mood had just turned sour again. *Why couldn't they just let me take my meds, infect every nigga possible, and live as long as I could without any other instructions?*

8

Essence

I drove straight home and poured myself a glass of wine. I knew beyond a shadow of a doubt that the Diamond and Angie situation would get much worse before it got better. After the funeral, I was going to make sure that I talked to Diamond about J-Bone. I wasn't naïve by any means, and I didn't have to see the dick going in and out to know when someone was fucking somebody. The last thing that I wanted to do was choose between the two of them just because Diamond's trifling ass couldn't keep her legs closed. I quickly downed that glass and poured myself another one.

That shit that Diamond was doing was low down as fuck. She'd done many shady things since I'd known her, but this was real foul. She needed a lesson on friendship. I used to think that shit she pulled in our senior year was at the top of the list. I still get pissed when I think about it. She'd invited me and Angie to a sleepover one Friday night. At the last minute Angie got sick and had to cancel on her, but I went anyway. Now, I wish that I hadn't. While I was in the shower, this bitch had the nerve to take a picture of me while I was in the shower. At first I laughed right along with her…until she took it to school and showed the entire class. It took me a long time to forgive her ass for that so called practical joke. I'd had enough of thinking about Diamond. I had problems of my own. I needed to figure out how to live as long as I could.

What I really needed was some of that top dollar medicine Magic Johnson had gotten his hands on. The stuff that made you live forever.

I sprawled out on the couch, ready to get some rest, so I'd be ready to hang out later, when my cell rang. I looked at my buzzing phone and saw that it was Maurice. I contemplated taking the call but decided that I was done with him and his lies. I'd catch up with him in Heaven or Hell. I hadn't made any official plans for the night, but couldn't decide between hanging out with Gwen, my new buddy, or calling up Jerome who I'd been trying to smash off for a while.

I needed to get to him before my time was up; before being buried under the dirt. I'd been wanting to infect him for a while. He'd been claiming for weeks that he wanted to remain faithful to his girl, who was pregnant with his baby. Jerome claimed he just wanted to kick it with me, no sex involved, no strings attached. He seemed to be a challenge. I guess that's what made me want him even more. I made myself stop thinking, and was about to fall asleep, until another call came in.

"Ugghhhh," I mouthed in frustration. I needed sleep, but it was my girl, so I answered.

"What's up girl?" Angie greeted. "Did you go by and check on our friend today?"

"Yeah."

I got quiet for a few seconds.

"Well, is she okay?" Angie asked.

"Yeah, she's cool."

More silence.

"Essence? What the hell is wrong with you? Why the hell you being so damn quiet? You been acting weird for the last few days anyways."

"Oh, my bad, Angie. I was falling asleep. I'm so tired, girl. So, where the hell were you when I came by and picked up my ride earlier," I asked, determined to see if she would lie.

"I'on know. I mighta ran to the store or something."

Yeah right, I thought to myself. *We all had secrets.* Some just more severe than others. Just hearing her voice had me thinking about what I saw earlier. My whole pussy started to tingle as the picture of Angie eating that other woman out flashed in my mind.

"Essence! Essence! Girl what hell you doing? I know yo ass ain't fall asleep on me! You hear me?"

"Huh? Oh, I told you I'm really tired."

"That's because you been fucking all night! You did use a condom, right?"

"You know it, Miss Safe Sex."

"Well, take yo' sleepy ass to bed. I'll talk to you tomorrow."

"Alright."

As soon as I got off the phone with Angie, I fell into a deep sleep. For some reason, I had about four different dreams, some more pleasant than the others. The first one had crazy images of me and my family at some sort of gathering. It seemed so surreal. My mother and my uncles were there along with my older sister, Tierra, who I hated with a passion. The dream seemed to imitate my life as my father wasn't around in the dream either. But of course not. After all, he was still in jail after being convicted of raping a fifteen year old white girl.

I'd always tried to keep my distance from them, *the family from hell*, simply stopping by the house when I found the time. Yet they hated me for some reason. A deep hatred. In the dream, Tierra kept taunting me in front of everyone, pulling on my expensive clothes, saying I thought I was better than them. Rushing to escape her grasp, reminded me of my teenage days when I'd run from her on a regular. I always did my best to avoid Tierra, especially after what she did to me when I was ten. That one night changed my life forever. It made me who I am today.

The secrets that I have from those years will go to the grave with me. Tierra was twice my age and took advantage of me looking up to her. My mother didn't say one word during those years, never ever protecting me, yet in the dream she stared me down like I'd stolen something from her.

An hour later, luckily I'd made it to dream number two, three, and four. They were all filled with sex and made me happier than a faggot with a dick in his mouth. I finally woke up hot and bothered, ready for action.

"Whew," I mumbled to myself. I felt a need to get out of the house. I checked my phone realizing I had six text messages. Five were booty requests and one from Gwen saying, "Thanks for makin me laugh earlier. Hope u come out tonight. I'll be there by 9 @ the bar."

I contemplated on which nigga to call first, then quickly decided to forgo men for the night. I thought about Gwen, remembering her smile, and fun attitude. *She seemed real cool earlier...somebody more my style. Besides, I needed a few new friends who were educated.*

Fuck it, I thought. I didn't have shit else to do. I jumped in the shower. As soon as the hot water hit my pussy it started tingling. Off and on, the scene of Angie eating that woman out kept running through my mind. I'd been wondering what another woman's pussy tasted like. Apparently it must taste pretty good the way my older sister ate the hell out of mine when I was younger.

After cleaning my body, I jumped out of the shower and rubbed myself down with coconut scented lotion. I parted my hair slightly down the middle to let my hair hang on both sides of my head. Deciding on my outfit was the difficult part. My girls knew I loved to dress, and bought all high-dollar items, but I wanted to go light on Gwen. I didn't want her thinking I was stuck-up so I decided on some black leggings, an off the shoulder sweater straight off the racks at Saks, and my new Christian Louboutin platform pumps that made me look taller than I really was. Even though the plan was to have a girls night out with Gwen, who knew what would happen so I had to at least look fuckable. Besides, my new road dog might be a sex addict like me, and we'd both find ten inch dicks to ride on later in the night. Before I left, I looked in the mirror to check my appearance one last time. I didn't wear much make-up , but decided to add some mascara to accent my eyes.

When I was satisfied with my beauty, I strutted out the door, grabbing my soft leather jacket, and quilted Chanel bag.

I thought about calling Angie to join us, but decided against it until I found out more about Gwen. The two of them may not have been a good match. Gwen didn't appear to be the weed smoking type. She seemed more laid back.

Not wanting to push a dirty ride, I rolled through Al Paul's car wash on Warrensville Center Road. Apparently everyone else was thinking the same thing because the car wash line was long as hell. After tipping the cute guy that put the finishing touches on my Pathfinder, I cruised down the street feeling better just knowing that my truck was cleaner.

The parking lot at Malloy's was almost filled to capacity when I got there. I hurriedly pulled in, and grabbed a parking space before they were all gone. I checked myself in the mirror one last time before, hopping out of my truck and walking toward the entrance.

"Is there a cover charge?" I asked the guy standing at the door.

"Nah, not for you pretty lady. It's ladies night."

I hit him with a wide grin thinking, keep on flirting, and you might be my next victim.

After strolling in, I started looking around for Gwen near the bar. The atmosphere in Malloy's was warm and cozy. The lights were dim and created a sexy ambiance. R Kelly's, *Marry Me*, pulsated from the juke box that sat in the corner. After a few seconds of looking around, I saw Gwen sitting at a table by herself sipping on some kind of mixed drink. Seeing her dressed up a little made me realize just how pretty and classy she was. Gwen had a dark honey complexion and very light hazel eyes reminding me of Terri from Soul Food. Her short hair cut resembled a honey color with streaks throughout. And her body appeared firm, proving she was no stranger to the gym.

"Hey girl," I said as I walked over and slid into the booth, taking a seat near her.

"Hey! What's up? I was wondering if you were going to make it." she said that like she already knew I was coming.

"Girl, I had a good nap. So this was perfect."

"I feel you girl. I got a table instead of a seat at the bar because I remember that you told me they served food in here and I'm hungry as hell."

"That's cool. I'm pretty hungry myself. The wings here are slamming."

"Oooo girl, I love me some wings," Gwen said, applying more gloss to her already shiny lips.

"What you sipping on?" I asked.

"A strawberry martini."

"That's sounds good." I attempted to catch the bubbly waiter rushing by. I assumed he was gay from checking his bizarre mannerisms.

"May I help you, Miss?"

"Yes, let me have a Strawberry Martini and I'd also like to order a dozen barbeque wings. Could you please rush the martini? I've got problems."

"You got it," said the smiling waiter. "And we all got problems." He hit me with a finger snap. But five minutes later, he was back with a glass, filled to the rim. I smiled and rubbed my hands together anticipating the smooth but biting liquor that was getting ready to wash the days stress away.

"Here ya go, Miss. Would you like to pay now or would you like to run up a tab?"

Knowing that I wasn't going to leave any time soon I told him to run a tab. I slowly raised the glass up my lips and sipped my drink. The burning sensation seemed to somehow burn away the troubles of my life.

"Now, that's what I'm talking about," I said as I suddenly started to feel hot. I don't know what kind of perfume Gwen had on but it was intoxicating as hell. At the risk of her thinking that I was gay, I decided to ask her.

"Gwen, I'm not trying to be funny and I hope you don't take this the wrong way, but what kind of perfume is that you have on?"

"Oh, you like it girl? It's Faubourgh by Hermes…$1,500 dollars a bottle. People say I'm crazy for buying it, but I love it! And what do you mean don't take this the wrong way?"

"I'm just saying, I didn't want you to think that I was a dyke."

"Hey, to each his own, right?" Her hand went up in the air gracefully. "Who am I to judge?"

I smiled then took another long sip from my drink. When I sat the glass down, it looked like Gwen had fallen into a daze.

"Yo Gwen, you okay?"

"Huh? Oh yeah, I'm fine. I was just thinking about my friend's friend that got killed."

"Do you want to talk about it?" I asked sensing that she had something to get off her chest. After debating for about five seconds, she shook her head.

"Nah, I'm going to have a tough enough time at the funeral. Tonight I wanna just relax."

"No problem," I said shrugging my shoulders.

The wings came and we devoured them in record time. I didn't realize how hungry I was until I took that first bite. After we got done devouring all the food on the table, Gwen surprised the hell outta me with her next question.

"Are you homophobic?"

"Huh?"

"Are you homophobic? Do you have something against lesbians?"

The question caught me off guard. "Uh, no why you ask me that?"

"I was just asking," she said as she rubbed my thigh, "Because you made the dyke comment earlier, and…well….well… I'm a lesbian."

I froze for at least thirty seconds.

The minute she caressed my leg more sensually, heat radiated throughout my inner sanctum. From the tips of my toes to the top of my head, my body tingled. Gwen had that special touch. The minute she compressed my upper thigh bone, I almost came on myself. But still couldn't speak.

"Do you have anything against lesbians?" she asked me again.

"Nooo," I purred, loving the way her hand felt on my leg.

"Are you a lesbian?"

She had me hypnotized. I could barely respond. "Nooooo," I finally said slowly, and softly.

"Are you sure," she whispered. "Cause you seem to be really enjoying my little massage."

"I like dick." My voice grew louder. "Long, thick, dicks."

"You can like pussy, too."

I smiled inwardly, figuring that now would be the perfect opportunity to taste another woman's pussy besides my own. Licking her lips, Gwen reached into her purse and pulled out a magazine, opening it to the center. Was she about to make me read about lesbians? This was all so different. At first I didn't know what she was doing, but then realized that she was using it as a cover for why she really scooted closer to me.

Opening the magazine with her left hand, Gwen sneakily and seductively ran her right hand up my thigh and landed on my pussy, all the while pretending to show me pictures of clothes. Her perfume had me wanting to explode. I sat frozen, not sure what to do next. All I could do was throw my hair behind my right ear and relish in the moment.

"Damn, baby, you wet as fuck," she said after caressing my hot spot for minutes. She then leaned over and whispered in my ear.

"Let's get outta here and go have some real fun."

Feeling her hot breath combined with the saliva from her tongue caused me to slightly cum on myself. Gwen grabbed my hand and led me out of the bar like a toddler. I couldn't wait to taste her. My first thought was what would my girls think if they found out? We all loved dick. But then I looked at Gwen's glistening skin, and moist lips, and said, "Fuck it."

****

Once we got downtown to the Westin, Gwen didn't waste any time. She all but dragged me into the bedroom and ripped my clothes off. I had to admit, it turned me on the way she took control. It's how I handled my men. When I was completely naked, Gwen looked at me and smiled.

"Get down on all fours," she commanded. I did as I was told and let my knees slide apart so my pussy would open. "Fuck, you dripping already." I dripped even more when I felt her hot tongue slide up my calf and make its way to my ass.

"Ooh shit baby yesss," I moaned as Gwen gently bit my ass cheeks.

"You like that?" she asked just before sticking her tongue into my pussy.

"Shit baby, you gonna make me cum already," I purred. "Oh shit….oh shit," I cried out as I released a river of cum all over her face. "Oh shit…Oh shit! I've never had my pussy ate like that!"

"Oh, we're not done Miss Essence," she said, turning me over. Looking in her right hand, I saw the silver dildo.

"Grab that pillow and put it under your ass," she ordered.

After complying with her wishes, I got excited all over again wondering what she was about to do next.

"You want this? You want this chrome dick bitch," she said sticking the dildo into her mouth.

Gwen was completely turning me on. "Oooo stop teasing me," I begged. "Let me have it."

Gwen smiled and then inserted the dildo into my awaiting womb. After slowly easing it in and out a few times, she thrust all eight inches up inside it.

67

"Oh shit!"

The fake dick traveled deep inside my core, touching my sweet spot. As Gwen worked the dildo in and out of me, her tongue snaked its way inside my asshole. "Ooooooooh, it feels sooooooo good!"

For the second time in less the twenty minutes, I exploded. The feeling of getting my salad tossed along with Gwen fucking me with the dildo was so sensational that I passed out.

At about eleven thirty, I woke up to Gwen licking my pussy and finger fucking herself at the same time. I was in heaven as she licked every inch of my pussy. "Oh God…Oh my God," I screamed as my leg began to shake violently. "UUHH!!" I yelled. Falling back on the bed, I could barely move as I rained a shower of cum all over Gwen's face.

"Did you like being with a woman?"

"Oh…hell…yeah! I loved every…bit of it!"

"I thought you would," she said grinning widely. "So, when is our next date?"

9

Diamond

I woke up the day of the funeral in a rut. For the past three days I'd found myself numb. I just couldn't believe that Darius was dead. I got up out of the bed and picked out a very sexy but respectful black dress to attend the services in. After getting showered and dressed, my body got a good dose of baby oil, then a splash of some off-brand perfume on my neck, before sitting on the edge of the bed.

Silence echoed through the air as I reminisced on the first time me and Darius got our fuck on. It was right after one of his Junior High school games and Essence dared me to grab his ass when he walked back to the locker room. Of course I did it, and by the time I made it home, his dick had been shoved down my throat, and my pussy had been severely pounded. I had been experimenting with dildos since the age of twelve, but to have real live meat inside me was something totally different. I smiled at the thought of Darius taking my virginity.

Our next few years went pretty good, except for when him and his family vowed to hate me for life. It all happened so quick. One day I told them I was pregnant and that I'd gotten an abortion the day before; all in the same breath. Somehow, Darius and me got through it, but his mother and sister never did. After he went away to college we promised to stay together but he was too far away for me to trust him. Plus, my pussy was always in need-a-dick in it mode.

I still regret the day that he came home and busted my ass with another dude, ending in bloodshed. It was a Saturday and my mom had gone grocery shopping. From prior experience, I knew that she was going to be gone for a minimum of an hour and a half. As soon as she left, I called up the dude from down the block. Leave it to my mother to pick this day of all days to leave the door unlocked. I guess knocking on the door and not getting an answer didn't sit well with Darius so he just walked right in. I know he was hurt when he walked up the stairs and saw dude on top of me, working it like we was making a porno movie. He got so mad that he attacked the dude. They scrambled to the floor, but the guy had a blade. He ended up stabbing Darius, landing him in the hospital. Just another reason for his mother to hate my guts.

Over the next few months, even Darius cursed me out every time he saw me. He even had the nerve to start calling me a nympho.

Things got worse when I found out I was pregnant again. Of course he said it wasn't his, and I damn sho didn't know who the father was. My mom kept pushing for an abortion, and soon Darius was gone off to college leaving me alone.

The sound of the doorbell snapped me back from my trip down memory lane. I walked through the living room, opened the door, and plopped back down on the couch. Angie walked in wearing a ton of make-up, and sat down beside me. Her braids hung in an attempt to dress her black khaki pants up. I gazed at her carefully, wanting to comment on her shabby look.

"You alright, home girl?"

That surprised me 'cause the bitch hadn't called me in two days. She must've been busy with J-Bone. "Yeah, I guess so," I answered. "I just can't believe he's gone though, chick."

Angie put her hand on my shoulder and rubbed it gently. "We better get going," she said. "It's going to be crowded as hell at the church. They've been talking about his funeral all over

70

Cleveland."

"You driving?"

I looked at Angie like she was crazy. "Girl, you know I don't have no gas. Besides, I'm in mourning. Drive, bitch."

Angie just shook her head.

We got up, left for the church, and prepared to say goodbye to my first, and only, true love.

****

Finding somewhere to park was a bitch. There were cars lined up everywhere. It was clear that Darius was a superstar, the Biggie Smalls of Cleveland, but he was also well liked in the community. After driving around for the better part of ten minutes, we gave up and parked in front of a fire hydrant. I lied and told Angie if she got a ticket, I'd pay half.

The morning chill bit at my ankles as we walked fast to get to the Greater Cleveland Church of God. By the time we made our way inside the sanctuary, it was standing room only. As we ambled slowly down the aisle, my knees buckled. Angie grabbed me, making sure that I didn't collapse. The closer we got to the casket, the more I felt like throwing up as the organ playing in the background kept stirring up more emotions.

I hadn't been to a funeral since my father's and although Angie was with me, I felt like I was all by myself. Since I thought being in love was for suckers, I'd never admitted to anyone that I did, at one time, love Darius. But while he was getting used to the famous life, my pussy stayed hotter than fish grease and wetter than Lake Erie; there was no way that I was gonna stay faithful to a man that I couldn't fuck on a regular basis. Now, I wish I'd done things differently.

Finally, after seemingly an hour, we reached the casket. Darius looked so peaceful. It was almost as if he was sleeping. I looked down at him, and if I didn't know better I would've sworn he was smiling at me. Not wanting to hold up the people behind me, I turned to my right and saw his mother and sister glaring at me. *Okay now what the fuck is this shit all about,* I thought to myself. I calmly walked over to them and extended my hand toward Ms. Jones.

"Hi Ms. Jones. I just wanna say that I'm really sorry about what happened to Darius. I would do anything to change what happened that night."

When Darius' mother didn't say anything, I mistakenly took that as a sign to keep talkin'. "Ms Jones, I really want to put the thing that happened at the hospital behind us. And everything else from our past. Let's exchange numbers and…"

Before I could even blink, Darius' mother stood up and spat in my face. I was in complete shock as spit driveled down my cheek and landed on the floor.

"No the fuck she didn't," Angie mumbled.

"Bitch, you done lost yo' muthafuckin' mind!" I yelled out.

"You are the bitch," she said as she pointed her finger in my face. "If it wasn't for your slutty ass my son would still be alive today!"

The reverend looked like he wanted to strangle all four of us. All eyes were on us as Darius' mother continued to throw verbal insults at me while her daughter, Kellie, twisted her face and balled up her fists. I couldn't believe she looked so hard, and dykish, wearing a man's pant suit to her brother's funeral. Although she had a cute, soft looking face, her sexuality had always bothered me. But now with the boyish fade, I had to wonder no more. The bitch was clearly a dyke.

Angie saw me starin' Kellie down and immediately stuck her hand in her plastic looking, purse. I should've known her ghetto ass would have her razor at a funeral. I gave her a quick shake of my head, begging her not to do it. Slowly, she took her hand back out. Hell, the last thing I needed was to become an accessory to a stabbing. Especially at a funeral.

"I told my son that a bitch like you couldn't be trusted," his mother carried on, "but I guess he always had a thing for tramps."

As the shock of her spittin' in my face started to subside,

my temperature rose. By the time Darius' mother ended her tirade with a "Now get the fuck out," I was ready to snap. Ms. Jones punctuated her point by jabbing her crooked, finger in my face. I hated when she did that.

Before she knew what hit her, I had grabbed her finger and bent it back as far as it would go. She screamed in pain as Kellie reached for my neck. She didn't have it long though as Angie hit Kellie with a two piece and knocked her back into the first pew. Out of the corner of my eye, I saw the reverend dialing numbers on his cell phone.

"Diamond, we have to get out of here! The preacher is about to call the police," Angie whispered to me.

I pushed Darius' mother down on the floor, as people began to rush toward the front of the church. It felt like an ambush was coming, but I was ready for whateva. It didn't take long for us to push our way through the crowds, and out the front door. When the air hit my face, I was thankful we were able to roll out before the police showed up.

"What the fuck was that about!" I yelled once we got inside Angie's whip. My breathing had settled a bit.

"That's what the fuck I wanna know," Angie said, rubbing her knuckles.

"You a'ight, Angie?" I asked, seeing her with her head down.

"Hell yeah, I'm straight! Bitches underestimate me 'cause I'm short. You see the way I two-pieced that dyke-looking bitch?" She sounded excited.

"I saw you, girl. I need a fuckin' drink," I told her.

"Well then let's go get a fuckin' drink, bitch."

Panic surged through my body as I looked behind us and saw a police car comin' up fast from behind with the lights blaring. Angie scrambled for her purse; my guess to figure out what to do with the razor and the weed. But at the last minute, the cops yanked around us and sped off down the street. We looked at each other and sighed.

"Damn, I thought they was comin' to get our asses," I

said.

Angie let out a nervous laugh and gripped the wheel a little tighter. My cell phone went off and after looking at the number on the screen, my mood got even worse.

"Yeah, Ma," I answered, without even saying hello.

"Hi, Diamond," she said dryly. There was no love lost between me and my mother. We never got along. "Look, I called you for a couple of reasons. The first one is that I was wondering if you've seen someone yet about your problem."

"I don't have one," I said keeping my answers short and sweet. I had no intention of letting Angie into my business.

"Hmmph, yeah alright," my mother spat.

"Is there anything else, Ma?"

"Actually there is. Hold on." After a brief pause, a voice came on the other end and caused my heart to drop.

"Hey, Mama," Candice said in her sweet, soprano voice.

"He...Hey," I said, caught completely off guard. I cut my eyes at Angie and noticed that she was doin' her best to eavesdrop on my conversation.

"Mama, when are you coming to pick me up? I thought we were supposed to hang out this past weekend."

"Oh, I'm sorry. They called me in to work," I lied. "We can do it this weekend."

"For real?" Candice asked excitedly. After that I heard mumblin' in the background.

"Mama, I was just wondering if I could come and stay with you this summer."

I shoulda known that was comin.' There was no doubt in mind that my mother had put her up to askin' that shit. I know I was wrong for not wantin' my own child to come and stay with me, but the summer months were the months when I liked to get loose. I loved my child and I did miss her but havin' my space was important to me.

"We'll talk about it," I said, not able to think of a lie fast enough.

"Oh, okay," she said, in a disappointed manner. My heart

74

wrenched at the way she sounded. The last thing I wanted to do was hurt her.

"Grandma wants to speak back to you."

"Okay."

"What did you tell this child?" she asked, ready to tear me a new asshole. It was obvious that she had seen the look on Candice's face.

"I'll think about it," I said carefully. I was determined not to let Angie's nosey ass catch on to anything that I was talkin' about.

"Look Diamond. You need to spend some time with this girl. I'm starting to think that she may have the same problem that you have."

"And that would be what?" I replied smartly.

"You know damn well what! This girl has gone boy crazy. She's too young to be starting that. And you know she started her period about three months ago. You need to…"

"Look Ma, I gotta go," I said, cuttin' her off. I wasn't about to sit there and let my mother yell at me like I was some kinda fuckin' kid. I pressed end, closed my phone shut, and threw it into my purse.

"Damn girl, what the fuck was that about," Angie's prying ass asked.

"Nothin' chick. Just mother daughter stuff," I said, makin' it clear that I wasn't about to discuss it with her ass.

"Tell me girl. You know we tell each other everything."

I looked at Angie crazily, wondering if she really believed that shit. I had many skeletons in my closet; one I would take to my grave. If they ever found out they'd be devastated.

"Listen, I'ma have to cancel on havin' that drink Angie," I told her. I was hopin' that she would think it was because of my mother but truth be told, after hearin' my daughter's voice, I wanted to just go home and be alone.

"Are you sure?"

"Yeah, I'm sure, chick."

"No problem."

Heaviness fell on my heart as I thought about my twelve year old daughter. The fact that I'd never allowed her to live with me was no good. She'd asked me over and over again, why she couldn't live with me, and why she didn't have a father. As Angie continued to drive, I turned my head toward the window so she couldn't see the tears that were beginning to form in the corners of my eyes. I needed some dick immediately to cure my broken heart.

10

Diamond

Ten minutes after droppin' me off at home, Angie called. I didn't answer. Five minutes after that, Essence called. I didn't feel like talkin' to either one of them so I ignored her too. I knew that my girls were tryin' to look out for me but after the fiasco at Darius' funeral, all I wanted to do was kick back, have a couple of stiff drinks, and be left alone. I still couldn't believe that Ms. Jones had the nerve to put her fuckin' finger in my face like that. If it wasn't for Angie telling me that the reverend was callin' the police, I woulda stomped her drunk looking ass up in there. Church or no church that bitch almost got dealt with. Feelin' tense and tight, I ran into the bathroom and ran myself a nice hot bubble bath. When the water was ready, I climbed into the tub and let the soothin' H2O massage my body. The longer I sat in the water, the more I started to relax.

Throwin' my head back, thoughts of J-Bone's sweet love stick tunnelin' through my sex cave the other day started to dominate my thoughts. I know it was shady to fuck my friend's man behind her back, but at that particular moment, I needed someone and he happened to be at the right place at the right time. I hadn't called any of the niggas on my line-up lately, so J-Bone worked for the moment.

Hell, she knew I had already fucked the nigga, anyway. I

still remember that hot threesome that we had. This bitch just dared me to suck her man's dick in front of her and although I knew it was the alcohol talkin' that night, there was no way I was gonna let a chance like that get away. I'd been wanting to taste J-Bone anyway, ever since Angie's dumb ass told me and Essence how big his dick was.

We all cut from the same cloth, so this broad shoulda known not to tell another freaky bitch how sweet her man's loving is. Thinkin' about that night was turnin' me on more and more by the second. Reachin' down into the water, I gently started to massage my clit. Slow, circular motions had me biting my bottom lip. Then I used my middle finger to enter myself.

Damn, could I use some dick right now, I thought to myself. Pullin' my finger out of my love nest, I started to rub my clit again. I needed to release in the worst way. But for some reason, my pussy didn't want to cooperate. I rubbed harder and harder but still couldn't make myself have an orgasm.

"Fuck," I screamed as I slammed my hand down into the water causin' it to splash onto the floor. Mad as fuck, I jumped out of the water, stomped into my bedroom, and yanked open my closet door.

Then I reached down into my "fuck" box and grabbed the biggest dildo that I had in my collection. I laid back on the bed, spread my legs, and inserted it into my wet hole. I pushed faster and harder and still nothing. "Shit, what the fuck is wrong with me?" I screamed. This had never happened to me before. I had always been able to get my rocks off. "Fuck this shit," I said as I stuck it back in. I shoved it inside as hard and fast as I could for the next five minutes. "Aaahhh!" I screamed, becomin' more and more frustrated.

It wasn't like I didn't know what I needed. I needed some real meat but I didn't feel like leaving the house. Smilin' to myself I knew just how I would fix this dilemma. Pickin' up my cell phone, I dialed the seven digits that I knew would get me laid. *I shoulda done this in the first fuckin' place,* I thought to myself.

As soon as Paul answered the phone, I went into my act. "Hi Paul," I said snifflin' like I was cryin'.

"Diamond? What's wrong?" he asked, concern filling his voice.

"Can you come over please? I really need someone to talk to. My girls are mad at me so they ain't answerin' they phones. I really need some company right now."

"Okay baby, don't cry. I'll be right over."

I wanted some dick but I wanted some clean dick. "I mean, it's ok if you have to get ready first. I need to take a shower anyways. Give me about thirty minutes, ok?"

"That's cool baby. I was about to take a shower myself."

Lyin' ass nigga.

After endin' the call, I went into the kitchen to pour me a glass of Chardonnay. I smiled at the thought of his tongue swirlin' around in my clit. If there was one thing that I could count on was Paul making me cum. His tongue was pure gold. Too bad his dick didn't have the same magic. The more I sipped the wine, the hornier I became. To pass a little bit of time, I threw in a porno movie. An idea suddenly popped into my head. Why watch a porno movie when I can fuckin' make one. I thought about how Kim Kardashian and the Video Vixen chick all made their mark from a sex tape. So, why couldn't I be living in Hollywood by next month. Trying to hurry before Paul got there; I jumped up, ran into the bedroom, and got my video recorder out of the closet.

Quickly, I set up the tripod and attached the camera to the top. After checkin' to make sure that I had enough recordin' time on my disc, I moved the tripod to the corner of the room and pressed record. No sooner than I'd finished setting it up, my doorbell rang. I walked up to the front door and stopped. I almost forget that I pretended to be crying when I talked to Paul. I quickly ran to the kitchen sink, turned the water on, stuck my fingers up under the faucet, and dabbed my eyes with water to give the appearance that I had been crying. Then I ran back to the door, straightened up my posture and then opened the door

79

in a frenzy. I was quickly taken aback as Paul rushed in the door and embraced me in his arms.

"You a'ight, Diamond? Tell daddy what's wrong."

Playing this game to the utmost, I took Paul by the hand and pulled him to the couch. Then, after my dramatic pause, I let my head fall onto his shoulder, covered with tons of tatoos.

"Oh Paul," I said, turning on the water works. While it was true that I could've just called him up and told him to come over and give me some dick, I didn't want his clingy ass to get the idea that we were a couple or some dumb ass shit like that.

"Diamond, what's wrong?"

"He's gone. I can't believe he's gone."

"Who's gone?"

"A friend of mine who I went to high school with. He got killed a few days ago. I went to the funeral today and it was harder than I thought it would be. I...I just needed someone to talk to Paul, you know? Someone that could help me get my mind off of things for a little while."

"It's okay, Diamond. You can talk to me," he said, rubbing my back.

I had this nigga right where I wanted him. In a few short minutes, he would be between my legs pleasin' the fuck outta me. I wiggled the upper half of my body just enough to make my right tit pop halfway out. Knowing that he had seen it, I looked down at the front of his crotch and saw his rock hard dick attemptin' to bust through his pants. Lookin' up into his eyes, I smoothly let my right hand down and squeezed his dick. Then I looked directly into his eyes and reeled him in.

"Can you do that for me Paul? Can you do somethin' for me to help me get my mind off of things?"

All the while I was talkin' to him, I was unzippin' his pants. Paul tried to suppress a smile but I knew that he was enjoying it. His pecker couldn't wait to jump out of his boxers. Funny thing is, I could never remember it being this hard or big. Although I called him over to eat my pussy, my mouth actually started to water at the sight of his rock hard rod. Lowerin' my head down on it, I opened my mouth wide and engulfed all of his man meat. I bobbed up and down on his dick like I was dunkin' for apples.

"Oh, shit baby, that feels good. Suck it, Diamond, suck it."

After suckin' his dick for about five minutes, I couldn't take it anymore. I wanted it inside my pussy, no matter how bad of a fuck he was. I got up, stood in front of him, and let my robe fall to the floor, showing off my firm, fit body. After he pushed his pants down to the floor, I mounted him and eased down on his thunder. "Oooooooooooh," I moaned as it went deep inside my womb.

To my surprise, his dick felt good going in and out. I leaned forward and wrapped my arms around his neck as his love tool throbbed inside. Seizing the moment, Paul hooked my shoulders and thrust his dick so deep up in me it felt like he was hitting my sternum. It wasn't the best piece of dick that I'd ever had but it was pretty damn good. Now, I was ready for him to eat my pussy. As if he could read my mind, Paul stood up with his dick still inside me. Then he laid me on the couch and spread my legs wide. Easing down on one knee, he threw my right leg over his shoulder and stuck his magic tongue inside my womb. Spit mixed with pre cum ran down my leg.

"Oh shit! Please….please don't stop eatin' me!" I slurred. I was on the verge of explodin' when Paul spread my pussy lips and started flickin' his tongue back and forth across my clit. "Ooooo….Ooooo fuck, right there baby, right there! Oh shit! I'm almost there!" My whole body started to convulse as Paul licked faster and faster. "I'm almost there! Ooohh shit Paul, here it comes…here it comes! AAHH SHIT!" I screamed at the top of my lungs as I released a gallon of cum all over Paul's face.

"Damn, Diamond, I hope I helped you feel better."

"Sorta," I responded nonchalantly.

"What?" His expression seemed perplexed as I clearly showed that I didn't want to be bothered anymore.

Paul reached to touch my face, and I moved quickly like he had a disease. He simply laid back pondering what the hell was wrong with me. After a five minute rest, I was ready for him to leave. He had fulfilled his purpose.

"It's gettin' late Paul. I think I'm about to go to bed. You're gonna have to leave now."

Lookin' as confused as he always does, Paul twisted up his face pale-looking face. *The nigga needed hours of sun.*

"Huh? Leave? Why?"

"I just told you, it's gettin' late."

"But why can't I spend the night?"

"Spend the night? Are you fuckin' crazy? Are you tryin' to get us both killed?"

"By who," he asked getting angry. "That punk ass nigga that you had over here last week?"

"What? Nigga how the fuck did you know that I had somebody over here? You been spying on me?"

His expression said…guilty.

Then it hit me. Paul was the muthafucka who had taken me and J-Bones picture through the window last week. I had to think quick, try to understand his motive. I walked over to my loveseat and sat down with my legs spread wide open. "So what's the point of taking pictures of me with someone else?"

"You never know if I'll need it," he admitted.

"Paul, get the fuck out! I was trying to be nice to yo' ass, but you served yo' purpose! Now, get the fuck out!"

"What about us?" his weak ass asked with tears in his eyes.

"Us?" I laughed so hard I got a headache. "Muthafucka, ain't no us! Get that through your fuckin' head! I just needed some dick! And yes, you have been used. Get the fuck out!"

"Diamond, believe me…you got some shit coming your way," he said leaving with his shirt in his hand.

I thought about telling him that I'd recorded our fuck fest, but then decided against it. He had dirt on me, and now I had something on him, too.

11

Angie

"Are you fucking serious?" I was furious. "No! Tell me you're lying!"

I hung up on the caller before they could even finish the sentence. I couldn't believe she'd fucked J-Bone. I was gonna kill somebody; preferably Diamond. I threw on a pair of jogging pants and a T shirt, and bolted out the door, ready for war. After jumping into my car, I peeled out of the driveway with mayhem on my mind. I knew that I was risking getting a ticket but I didn't give a fuck. All I could think about was getting to Diamond's ass. When I reached her house, I yanked into her driveway like a woman possessed. Jumping out of the car, I ran up the steps and started beating on her door like the police.

"Open this door! Open this muthafuckin' door, you low down, no good slut!" I went back to my car and started blowing the horn repeatedly. "I know yo' ass in there," I yelled.

Her neighbor Paul, showed his face, and shot me a suspicious grin, but I kept blowing. Suddenly, Diamond opened the door and stormed onto the porch.

"Bitch, what the fuck is wrong wit' yo' ass, comin' over to my crib makin' all this fuckin' noise? Are you fuckin' crazy or somethin'," she screamed.

"Crazy? Crazy? Bitch, I'll show yo' ass crazy!" I rushed back up on the porch and pushed inside of her house and slammed the door.

"Angie, what the fuck is wrong with you? You high or somethin'?"

"Hell nah, I ain't high! I wanna know why you been fuckin' my man behind my back!"

"What? Ain't nobody fuckin' yo' damn man! Get the fuck outta my house with that bullshit!"

"I ain't goin' no muthafuckin' where until you tell me what the fuck is going on!"

Tears started to fill my eyes as visions of J-Bone and Diamond fucking entered my mind. My fists started trembling by my side all the while Diamond just stood there acting like she didn't know what I was talking about.

"Say something," I said to her in a low demonic tone that scared the shit out us both.

"Angie, I don't know where the fuck you're gettin' your information from, but you need to either calm down or get the fuck up out of here until you can calm down."

"Calm down? Fuck you!"

Not being able to control my anger anymore, I rushed at Diamond and grabbed her by the throat. Diamond responded by clutching at my braids. She tried to break my grip by slinging me to the floor but I held on and we both ended up taking a fall. Somehow I ended up on top of her and started punching my longtime friend in the face. Diamond swung back wildly in an attempt to get me off of her. In a rage by now, my strength seemed to double. The blows she was landing had little or no effect. I reached down and wrapped my hands around her neck and began squeezing for all I was worth. Slowly but surely the fight started to leave Diamond as she grew weaker by the second.

"Why Diamond? Why the fuck would you do some shit like this to me," I cried. "We were supposed to be friends!"

"Get the fuck off of her," I heard a voice say just before I

84

went tumbling across the floor.

I looked up and couldn't believe my eyes as J-Bone stood there with nothing on but a pair of boxers. The head of his dick was sticking out and that made me even madder seeing the meat that I enjoyed swinging so freely in this bitches' house. Then, to add insult to injury, this dirty muthafucka leaned down and helped *her* up.

"I'm sorry you had to find out like this, Angie. But it is what it is," he smirked.

After Diamond regained her strength, she looked at me like I never meant anything to her.

"Now, get the fuck outta my house, you dry pussy having hoe!"

I jumped up and ran toward her ass again. But this time J-Bone blocked my path to her.

"Nigga, get the fuck outta my way! I'ma kill that bitch!"

Then I remembered that Diamond sometimes kept her gun in the night stand in her bed room. I stopped trying to get to her and bolted for her bedroom door. Knowing what I was thinking, Diamond was right behind me. Right after I got inside her bed room, she caught up with me and tackled me to the floor. As we struggled on the floor, somehow one of us kicked the door shut. Diamond had told me and Essence before that her bedroom door locks automatically when it shuts. So with J-Bone on the outside of the door beating on it like crazy, it was me and Diamond in there fighting like bitter enemies.

We fought all the way over to the night stand. With both of us reaching for the drawer, Diamond kneed me in the stomach. I went down like a ton of bricks. The few seconds that it took me to recuperate was all she needed to reach her hand into the drawer and pull out her gun. I looked up just in time to see Diamond pointing it directly at my head. My heart sank. Was I really about to die over a man that probably didn't give a fuck about either one of us? Then I stopped being scared. Deep in my heart I knew that Diamond would not pull the trigger. We had been through too much together as friends for her to kill me over some nigga.

"Diamond look, let's just talk about…"

POW!

****

After waking up in a cold sweat, I ran to the bathroom, once again, to throw up. I had been doing that a lot lately but this was the first time that I had done it at night. I was freaked out by having a dream where one of my best friends blew my brains out. Maybe it was my subconscious trying to tell me something. My stomach started swimming again and I threw up a second time. Looking into the mirror, I noticed that I had started to gain weight. Then I realized that my period hadn't come last month. I was always told that a woman could skip one period but after missing two, it was time to worry. I looked at the clock and saw that it was a little after ten 'o clock. I really didn't feel like driving, so I called J-Bone and told him that I needed him to come run me to the store.

"What? How come you can't drive yourself?"

"Cause I don't feel like it."

"If I come all the way back over there to take yo' ass to the store, I want something out the deal."

"That fuckin' figures."

"Hey I'm just sayin', gas is high now-a-days."

"So is pussy."

"Oh, so now you charging me for it?" Getting aggravated with his antics, I got ready to hang up.

"You know what, never mind," I said.

"Alright, alright, I'm on my way. Can I at least get my dick sucked?"

"I'll think about it."

It took J-Bone exactly ten minutes to get to my house after I ended the call. All the way to the store he kept pressing me about giving him a blowjob.

"Nigga, will you quit bugging the shit outta me about that shit? I told yo' ass that I would think about it."

86

"Whateva. What the fuck you going to the store to get anyway," he asked. I didn't want to say anything to J-Bone until I was sure if I was pregnant or not so I lied and told him that I was picking up a test for Diamond.

"Diamond," he said like he was surprised.

"Yeah, Diamond. Why the fuck you acting all surprised? Her ass is single and probably fuckin' more than I am. And why you worried about her anyway?" I asked with attitude before hopping out of the Tahoe. I ran into the store, and bought the test, the cheapest they had. On the way back, J-Bone stopped at the convenient store to pick grab a pack of Newport's. Feeling a little thirsty, I asked him to get a four pack of coolers. After he got inside the store, I decided that to keep his ass from saying that he forgot, I walked in with him. On the way out, we ran into Diamond's neighbor, Paul.

"Hey Paul, what's good," I said speaking to him. A strange look crossed his face as he looked at me and then at J-Bone.

"Hey, uh, Angie right?"

"Yep. This is my boyfriend J-Bone," I said, introducing him.

"Sup cuz," J-Bone said.

Once again Paul looked back and forth between me and J-Bone.

"Nice to meet you, man."

After the two men gave each other a pound, me and J-Bone hopped back in the truck and rolled out. Right before we pulled out of the parking lot, I looked back and Paul was watching us leave, examining our every move. He was rubbing his hands together and had the weirdest smile on his face. Shrugging it off, I turned back around and thought, *damn, that dude is weird.*

♪12

Essence

Gwen had sucked so much love juice out of me the night before that I drove to work with my legs feeling like jelly. The sexual tongue lashing she put on me left no doubt in my mind that women ate pussy better than any man alive. But although I more than enjoyed our back to back sexual encounters, and her chrome dick, I surely wasn't ready to give up *good, real* dick.

I thought back to the best meat I'd ever had. The one that gave me HIV. It was Trevon's, six years ago on a Friday night. I remember it like it was yesterday. We were sitting at his dinner table sipping cheap alcohol and eating steaks. It was his birthday and I wanted to do something special; something no other girls were doing at my age, so I cooked for him. But like most men, his idea of the perfect birthday gift rested between my legs.

He'd been trying to smash for weeks, but I had been resisting him. It hadn't been easy though. His dark, chocolate skin and muscular 6'3 frame made my mouth water regularly. Every time I rubbed his shiny bald head, I got weak in the knees. But I really liked Trevon, so there was no way that I was going to allow him to think that I was some kind of jump off by giving up the booty right off the bat. All through dinner, we laughed and joked with each other, making me feel like we had a future.

After we got finished eating, we made our way to his

oversized couch. He popped a movie in, but I could tell by the way he scoped my legs that he wasn't interested in watching anything but me. Five seconds into the first scene, my theory proved correct as he started running his heavy hand across my legs. The touch of Trevon's fingers on my bare skin made me want to rip off my skirt right there on the couch. By the time his hand had traveled up to my sweet spot and he discovered that I didn't have any panties on, his dick was rock hard. He then leaned in close to me and our lips met in a lustful touch. Opening my mouth, I welcomed his slick tongue inside. By that time I was on fire and couldn't stand another minute of not having his meat fill me up. We both started tearing off our clothes, throwing them across the floor as the anticipation of supreme satisfaction overtook us. Before I knew it, he was on top of me, with his dick just inches away from my love hole.

"Hold on a second," I remembered saying to him. "You got a condom?"

"Baby, I wanna feel you, not some fuckin' piece of rubber."

I looked at him strangely thinking back to all I'd learned in school about protecting yourself during sex. He had learned the same thing…I was sure. "But I…"

"Shhhhh," he said, placing a finger over my mouth. "Essence, this is what big girls and boys do," he said grinding, making me wetter. "That shit is for underclassmen. Not seniors. Fuck a rubber."

"Ah- AH- AH- ," I moaned as Trevon shoved all eight inches of his meat inside of me without any further hesitation. I never even had time to resist again as Trevon drilled in and out of my hole with aggression.

Yelling rape was out of the question. And it felt so good that I couldn't tell him to stop. My mouth wouldn't allow it. I wanted him, bareback and all. I thought he was going to take it easy since he kept telling me how much he loved me, and wanted to be with me, but instead he pounded my guts into submission. By the time Trevon finished, I was certain my pussy had sores, but I was completely satisfied. The moment was bittersweet because that was the one and only time that Trevon and I made love. Right after that he started ignoring my calls and making excuses not to talk to me. Eventually, I got the message and stopped calling him.

Over time, I forgot about him, thankful that I didn't get pregnant. I quickly went back to using condoms until five years later when I developed a fever that wouldn't break. After going to the doctor, I was told that my lymph nodes had swollen. They did blood work and when it came back, my worst fears were realized. I had contracted the deadliest virus known to man, HIV.

As soon as the words left the doctors mouth, my whole body went numb. Rage immediately filled me as I thought to how I had given my body to a low down man only to be burned in the end. Strangely, three days later, I'd received a call from Trevon's doctor saying that I was on his list of women he'd slept with. They wanted me to get tested. I told them no need. It was confirmed. The bastard had given me a death sentence. I swore from that day on that I would dish this poison out to every man that I could. In my mind, men were pieces of shit, liars, crooks, and totally no good. And they were all going to pay.

Now, my mind was all messed up. I pulled into the underground parking lot of University Hospital just in time to see the mobile vending truck getting ready to close up shop for the morning. Quickly I parked, jumped out of my whip and sprinted for the truck. My lunch break wasn't until 11:30 and I didn't eat breakfast at home. If I didn't get something to eat now, then I would be starving to death the whole morning. I knew one of the ways to live longer without my HIV turning into AIDS was to eat healthier, but I needed to eat. So the slop from the vending truck would have to do.

"Wait! Hold up," I yelled, sprinting across the spacious lot. The short pot bellied man twisted up his face when he saw me running to catch him before he closed up. Out of breath, I leaned on the truck's counter and placed my order. "Let me get…a sausage and egg croissant with cheese and a bottle of orange juice."

The fat man sighed heavily and I got an instant attitude.

"Is there a problem?" I asked.

"No ma'am, no problem."

"Are you sure? 'Cause if it is, I can take my money somewhere else."

"I'm sure ma'am. There is no problem."

After getting my change, I snatched my food off of the counter and stormed away. The smell of the croissant instantly made me hungry. I ate the whole thing on the elevator ride up to the floor where I worked. I hopped off the elevator and noticed that everyone was smiling at me. Before I could ask what was going on, my cell phone vibrated. When I looked at it, I saw that it was a text from Jerome, asking if he could take me to lunch around twelve o'clock. I responded, yes, then glared up at my co-workers who were still giving me these goofy ass smiles.

"What the hell is everybody smiling about?" I asked.

Dawn, the girl that I was going to be relieving, grabbed a bouquet of flowers off the nurses' station and handed them to me.

"Who are these from?" I looked at her suspiciously. I was still pissed at her because she wouldn't trade shifts with me so I could go to Darius' funeral and support my girl.

"I'on know, girl. Read the damn card."

All eyes were on me as I took the card out of the basket. I looked up at my nosy co-workers as they acted like they were waiting for me to read it aloud. Why bother? I was positive they'd already read the card.

"Well, what does it say?" the new girl, Sally asked.

Damn, I thought. *This bitch ain't been here but a minute and already she in my business.* Shaking my head I looked down at the card. *Hey E, I hope you had as good a time as I did last night. Let me now if you wanna get together tonight, G.* I smiled and appreciated the fact that Gwen didn't use her full name. The last thing I needed was for these nosey bitches to get wind of me swinging both ways.

"What does it say," the prying rookie asked again.

"Why you all up in mine, newbie?"

"Shit girl, whoever sent them damn flowers must be laying some long ass pipe, cause you blushing like a muthafucka," Teri said. She was an old ghetto ass heifer who had been talking about retiring for the last three years. I wish she would take her ass on.

"Look, I'm not about to play kiss and tell with you broads, I got things to do. I came to work. Let me do my job."

Before they could dig any deeper, I walked away from them. All morning long, they bugged the shit out of me trying to get details out of me about what happened the night before. My lunch break couldn't have come fast enough. As soon as it did, I flew out the door. I got outside and saw Jerome waiting for me in his Lincoln Navigator. Little did he know his sexy ass would be a victim soon. As soon as I hopped in the car and smelled his cologne, my pussy started to sweat.

"Hey, beautiful. Long time no see," he said teasingly.

"Has it been that long?"

"Long enough," he said as he rubbed my leg. "Where you wanna grab something to eat at?"

"It's a deli right up the street. The corn beef sandwiches are big as hell. Let's go there."

After picking up the food from the deli, we sat in his ride, ate, and ran off at the mouth for a while.

Checking my watch, I knew I'd have to get back to work soon. So I cut to the point. "So, can I see you tonight?"

"I can't tonight. I gotta go with my girl to Lamaze class."

"Are you serious?"

He had a stupid expression on his face. "I promised her," he told me buntly then shrugged his shoulders.

"What about us? I had something real special in mind." Quickly, I unclipped my bra, allowing my big tits to hang freely. With a speedily move, I moved closer to Jerome, grabbed his hand, and forced him to carress my right breast.

Within seconds, his demeanor changed. I could tell he

93

was tempted. I looked down toward his thighs and decided that before I went back to work that I would up the ante.

"Jerome, let me give you something to think about for the rest of the day."

I leaned over and kissed him on the neck. While my tongue tasted his flesh, my hand snuck over to his crotch. My mouth started to water as I felt his steel rod poking through his jeans. I slowly and sensually pulled down the zipper and reached inside.

"Damn, Essence." He seethed through his teeth as I pulled out his thick penis. The head of it was throbbing and pre cum oozed from the tip. After getting some of it on my finger, I leaned my head down, stuck out my tongue, and licked it off.

"Ummmmmmmmmmm. You taste so goooood, Jerome."

"You like that, huh, girl? You like tasting my cum?" he asked, eyes rolling to the back of his head.

"You know I do."

I cupped his nuts in my hand and gently guided them into my mouth. They were so tight, I thought they would burst. I gave him five seconds of pleasure then stopped.

"Yo-yo-yo-yo-yo… pleaseeeeeeee put it back in yo' mouth. Pleaseeee, Essence," he kept begging.

"We going out tonight?" I taunted.

"I…I can't."

I stopped abruptly.

Jerome quickly sang another tune. "I mean yes, yes. Yes we are. Now, put it back in your mouth, girl. Don't stop."

I was all too happy to oblige him. I grabbed the base of his shaft and guided it back into my mouth. Knowing that I didn't have much time before I had to get back to work, I started sucking his dick like I was trying to win the dick sucking championship of the world. I massaged his nuts as I pulled his pipe trying to get him to come faster. I knew that I was succeeding when I felt his body jerk. I rose up and licked my lips making sure that I didn't spill a drop. I loved to swallow cum, and I squeezed the shaft of his dick just to make sure that all of it came out.

"Aweeee," he sighed, breathing like he'd done some work. "Where'd you learn to do that shit?" He was serious.

"That's just the appetizer, Jerome. The rest comes tonight. Be at my spot by seven."

"I'll be there," he told me with a wild, satisfied look in his eyes.

"And bring the seven hundred for that new bag I told you about."

"I got you."

I smiled, jumped out of his car, and made my way back to my work station. When I got there the nosey ass new girl was there waiting for me. Thinking that she was getting ready to ask me some more questions about my private life, I prepared myself to blast her first.

"Girl, I been looking all over for you. Yo' friend Angie been calling ever since you went on break."

Because Angie and Diamond routinely called me at work, I didn't think anything out of the ordinary. "Did she leave a message?"

"Nah, she just said to call her. Told me to tell you that it's important."

Now I was curious, and to be honest, a little concerned. Without saying another word, I flipped open my cell phone and dialed Angie's number.

"Hello?"

"Yeah, girl, what's up? Everything okay?"

"Girl, I don't even know where to fuckin' start! I'm so fuckin' distraught; I can't even think straight right now."

My mind played ping pong with all sorts of crazy thoughts. I wondered if she'd found out about J-Bone and Diamond.

"Just spit it out Angie. I'm at work so I don't have a lot of time to talk."

"You ready for this?"

"I been ready."

"I'm fuckin' pregnant!"

"Pregnant? Damn girl! What's J-Bone saying about it?" I looked around to see who was listening.

"He don't know yet."

"Huh? You didn't tell the man that he was gonna be a father Angie?"

"Hell nah! I didn't say shit to him 'cause I wanted to be sure first."

"When did you take the test?"

"Last night after J-Bone left."

"Damn girl!" I shook my head. You keep preaching to me about condoms and you're the one pregnant. Crazy," I ended.

"I know, right? That one time that I didn't make him strap up, and now this. I almost slipped up when he took me to the store to get the test."

"Wait. He took you to the store to get the test? If that's the case then you know you're going to have to tell him sooner or later."

"I got time girl. I told him that I was buying the test for Diamond."

Uh oh. Now, J-Bone is going to be wondering if Diamond is pregnant by him. *Trouble,* I thought.

"You keeping it?"

"Probably. I do love J-Bone," she admitted.

Damn, I thought to myself, feeling terrible for Angie.

"Uh…hey girl I got to get back to work. I'll call you later, okay?"

"That's cool. I'll holla."

I hung up and shook my head. I knew right then and there I was right. The situation would definitely get worse before getting better. The next thing I knew, my cell was ringing again. I smiled widely after glancing at the screen. It was Gwen.

13

Diamond

Two weeks had passed since Darius' funeral, and I'd decided to rejoin society. The second my eyes popped open and I saw the numbers on my alarm clock flashing, I shoulda known it was gonna be a fucked up day. I thought back to how I'd grabbed my watch off the night stand, after realizing I'd be late for work. I had already been written up twice; once for not showing up for work, and the other for being late yesterday. My boss quickly informed that if I was late one more time, I would be suspended.

Yeah, right. Like I was worried about that. I had a full proof way of warding that off. After rushing out of the house, trying to hurry up, I ran through my yard and stepped right into a pile of dog shit that took the forty KFC napkins in my glove box to get the shit off. If that wasn't bad enough, I got a fucking speeding ticket just two blocks away from the job.

Now, I found myself sitting at this fuckin' cubicle, listening to these whining ass people complain' about their deductibles. Just when I thought things had settled down for the morning, they took a turn for the worse.

"Diamond! I'd like to see you in my office, now!"

Damn. I thought I had managed to sneak in without being seen but apparently that wasn't the case. Not liking the way my boss, Jason Sims talked to me, I walked as slow as I could to his office, switching arrogantly along the way.

"Close the door and have a seat," he said to me once I walked inside.

While I was sitting down, Mr. Sims reached into his file cabinet and pulled out the time cards. My heart dropped as he slid mine to me across his desk. I tried to stall, thinking up a lie to tell him about why I didn't clock in, but before I could he started questioning me.

"You want to explain to me, Miss Robinson, why everyone clocked in besides you?"

"Oh, yeah. I had a lot on my mind this morning and I guess I just forgot."

I ended with a quick, hunch of the shoulders. This muthafucka wasn't fooling me. His white-ass just wanted to get me in his office and ask me why I hadn't called him, or answered his calls. I could tell by the way he examined me that he missed Dream, and just wanted to get inside of her again.

"Oh, is that right," he said.

He reached into his file cabinet again and this time took out a suspension slip. I almost laughed in his face when he started to fill it out. He wasn't going to suspend me and he knew it. He just wanted me to tell him that I would do anything if he would just give me another chance. My boss loved to do this type of shit. And and to be honest, it did turn me on.

"What are you doing, Mr. Sims? I mean…Jason," I added with a little more sex appeal in my voice.

"What does it looks like I'm doing? I'm writing out a suspension slip." His voice suddenly sounded even more proper than before.

"But why, Sir?"

"Diamond, don't play dumb with me," he said as he stood up and walked around the desk to approach me. Leaning over to whisper in my ear, he lowered his voice. "First, you don't return my phone calls and now you want to try and steal time from the company? Am I supposed to just let you slide because your pussy is good? I don't think so, Miss lady," he said, slipping his hands into the pockets of his expensive looking pant suit.

"When did you call me, Sir? I don't remember seein' a missed call in my phone," I said, still playin' the game with him.

He walked back around to his desk and began looking out the window, all along keeping his back toward me.

"Check your phone again. It should be there." He turned to look me dead in the eye.

"It's in my purse at my desk."

"Well, go get it then."

Hesitantly, I got up and walked out of his office, teasin' him by switchin' along the way. After gettin' my phone from my purse, I made my way back toward his office. I was about ten feet away from it when his secretary came running down the hall like she was being chased by the police.

"Diamond, can you do me a favor and tell Mr. Sims that his wife called about five minutes ago and said that she'll be here at 12:30? She says that she tried to call his office, but didn't get an answer."

I looked at my watch and saw that it was 12:20. "Sure, I'll let him know," I said, smilin' on the inside. I got hot as hell thinkin' about the excitin' risk that I was about to take.

When I walked back into the office, Mr. Sims was still standin' at the window. Something seemed to be troubling him. That's odd, I didn't think white people had any problems. Finally, he walked back to his desk to sit back down. I could see the rock hard imprint that his massive dick put in his pants. My legs quivered, and I bit the bottom of my lip as I visualized it goin' down my throat or knockin' the bottom out of my pussy. I walked slowly back to the chair and plopped down.

"Oh, you know what, Mr. Sims? Here it is," I said lookin' at my phone. "I didn't see it at first," I said, with a seductive smile, "but I see you did call. My bad."

"Ummm hmm. I think you are lying Ms. Robinson."

"Maybe I should be punished then," I said, lickin' my

lips.

"Yes, Miss Robinson, you should be."

"Sir, there has to be some other way I can be punished besides suspendin' me," I said soundin' like a little girl.

His smile grew wider. "Lock the door Diamond."

I got up, walked over to the door, and grabbed the latch. Little did he know he was in for a surprise. My sexual battery was charged up as I thought about what was about to go down.

"Is it locked?" he asked, loosening his colorful tie.

"Um hmm," I said seductively, laughing on the inside.

Because he had a strict 'no eatin' at your station' rule, he knew everyone was now gone to the hour long lunch, which was the main reason that he chose to call me into his office at this particular time. I watched him throw his jacket across his chair, along with his tie. Within seconds, he walked halfway to my chair, unzipped his pants, and stopped.

"Come and get this dick, bitch," he told me.

I didn't want to disobey authority on the job, so I got out of the chair, dropped to my knees, and started crawlin' toward his man meat. Once I reached him, I stuck my hand inside the crotch of his slacks, and wrapped my hand around his already throbbin' penis. It seemed to spring out of his pants and point itself toward my mouth. My eyes got big as I looked up at my smirkin' boss. The last time we got together, he beat the shit out of my womb. I opened my mouth as wide as I could to fill my mouth with the sweet white meat.

"Uuhhmm," I moaned as I let his boa constrictor enter my jaws.

"Yes, Diamond, suck my dick like you really want it."

Jason grabbed the back of my head and tried to force me to deep throat every inch of his white anaconda. I was more than up for the challenge. Inch by delicious inch, I devoured the succulent treat that stood before me. The more it slid down my throat, the more my pussy started to tingle. Then, out of the blue, he reached down and squeezed one of my hard nipples through my blouse. By now, I was off of my knees, squattin' and finger fuckin' myself. As soon as I got the whole thing in my mouth, he started fuckin' my mouth like it was a pussy.

He grabbed the sides of my jaws and slowly pumped in and out. When he looked down at me, I winked at him and it seemed to drive him crazy. Before I knew it, Jason started pumpin' my mouth faster as I increased the suction on his dick. A Hoover Vacuum didn't have shit on me as I sucked for all I was worth.

"Ah shit!!" he screamed as he erupted like a volcano inside my mouth.

Feelin' the sensitive sensation, he jerked back, causin' his dick to come out of my mouth and squirt the rest of his cum onto my lips. Wantin' to taste more, I crawled toward him, grabbed the shaft of his meat, and licked the rest of the cum off the head of his dick. Again, turned on by my nasty ways, his dick sprung back to life.

"You like that, Jason?" I asked him, loving that I could always call him by his first name when having sex with him.

He didn't answer. He simply reached down and helped me up. After that he guided me over to the edge of the desk and bent me over. Next, he placed his left hand on my back and with his right hand pulled my panties down to my ankles. My pussy instantly got wet as I anticipated his rawness rammin' into my backside. I reached down between my legs and started fingerin' myself again and tensed up my ass cheeks as I awaited the pleasurable pain that came with the sodomy that he was about to perform. He loved to fuck me in the ass and listen to me scream in passion. Even though I knew he would take it easy on my asshole, I still tensed up expectin' his monster.

After lubricatin' his dick with KY jelly, he eased the tip of it inside my backdoor, causing me to bite down on my bottom lip. Carefully, he continued to insert his white thunder into my tightness.

"Oh…oh…oh…my …oooooohhhhh," I moaned as he increased the pressure.

"That's it, that's it, yeah!"

The more I moaned, the faster he pumped.

"Oooo...Ohhh shit...Ooo fuck!! Fuck me harder," I screamed.

My boss was more than happy to oblige me. He started slammin' into my asshole like a mad man.

"Uhh...Uhhh...Uuuhhh!! Ahhh shiieett baaaabyyy!!!"

Just when I thought I couldn't take any more, the door slung open. After looking up and seeing his wife standin' there givin' us a death stare, Mr. Sims looked at me like he wanted to choke me for not lockin' the door. Backin' away from me, Mr. Sims scrambled to get his pants up. "Ahhh...ahhh..." he stuttered.

"Ooopsie," I said, hunching my shoulders with an innocent look. I covered my mouth, smilin'. "My bad, Mr. Sims." The smirk on my face all but told him that I had left the door unlocked on purpose.

"What the fuck!" screamed the slightly overweight brunette, ready to attack me.

"Wait, honey. This is not what it looks like."

"What the fuck do you mean it's not what it looks like? It looks like I've just bust your cheating ass in here fucking some niglet bitch!"

"Niglet? Fuck you, you white bitch!" I spat.

In the wrong or not, I wasn't about to stand there and let this bitch insult me. With Mr. Sims standin' there lookin' as guilty as OJ, his wife kicked off her shoes and made a beeline toward me. I reached for my purse and stuck my hand inside. If this big boned bitch got within two feet of me, I was gonna slice her ass up like cheese. Mr. Sims jumped in front of her and tried to stop her but ended up getting assaulted in the process.

"You mean to tell me that I've been faithful to your ass since the day we got married and you've been fucking around on me all this time?" She swung wildly with lefts and rights that Mr. Sims tried to ward off. Takin' this as my cue to leave, I headed for the door. She tried to get at me again but once again, her husband blocked her path.

"Honey, calm down. Please, we can talk about this, let me explain."

"Fuck that!"

Seein' that she couldn't get past her husband, Mrs. Sims picked up a vase that was sittin' on the desk and threw it at my head. I ducked just in time as the vase crashed into the door. With the speed of lightening, she knocked everything that was on his desk onto the floor, screaming like a raging animal in the process. By this time, tears drenched her face. Mr. Sims was trying to hold her and calm her down but she wasn't tryin' to hear it.

"Get off of me, Jason! Get the fuck off of me!" she cried out.

Realizin' that I was leaving my shoes, I made way back over to the desk to get them. By this time she had broken loose from her husband again. She stared at me with hatred in her eyes, stormin' toward the door. She opened the door slowly, and stopped abruptly. Turnin' back around, she looked at her husband and gave him a sinister smile.

"Let's see how you like it when I take half of your shit in the divorce, asshole! And as for you, you black bitch, this isn't over by a long shot!"

"Fuck you cracker," I yelled refusin' to be upstaged. Mrs. Sims then stomped out of the door, past the small crowd that had formed. They all had smiles on their faces; ones I wouldn't be able to live down. Everything seemed to be fucked up. And I had now made an enemy for life.

****

After the drama that happened at work, I hobbled my well-fucked ass to my car and got inside. Mr. Sims was so worried about his wife's divorce threat that he sent everyone home early so that he could go home and try to fix things with her. Sadly, his punk ass fired me on my way out, then had security lock the doors so I couldn't get back in to get my shit. *Punk-ass, white muthufucka.* All I wanted to do was go home, take a long hot shower, and have a drink. I knew that I wasn't going to cook anything once I got home, so I decided to stop at Popeye's. I guess I wasn't the only one thinkin' along those lines because the drive-thru line was seven cars long and the inside line was just as bad.

Even though I didn't want to, I waltzed inside, and waited in line to order. I couldn't shake the feeling that someone was watchin' me. Thinkin' that I was just being paranoid, I shook it off, waited for the ugly man to put my spicy, three-piece into a bag. I got out of there as quickly as I could. I was halfway to my Taurus when I felt someone shove me in the back so hard that I stumbled to the ground.

"What the fuck!"

My food went scatterin' across the ground as I hit the concrete. I turned to see Darius' sister, Kellie, and the other woman that I'd seen at the funeral.

"I told you! I told you it was that bitch," Kellie yelled. "I'ma kick this hoe's ass!"

"You fucked with the wrong one, bitch," the other woman said as they moved toward me.

But while they were busy runnin' their mouths, I was busy diggin' in my purse for my blade. As soon as the woman that was with Kellie got close enough, I sliced her across the arm with my box cutter. Seein' that I wasn't fuckin' around, the two of them quickly retreated. The woman with Darius' sister had now dropped down to one knee and was holdin' her badly bleedin' arm.

"Yeah, you bitches betta back the fuck up," I bragged, backing away. And looking to see if any of my food had been saved. Fuck! It wasn't.

Before anyone could figure out what had happened, I jumped into my ride and sped toward the street. With the window down, I could hear Darius' sister issuin' threats as I looked out the side mirror.

"I'ma get you bitch," she yelled. "I'ma send you to be

with my brother if it's the last thing I do!"

"Fuck you bitch! The next time I'ma slice your face up!"

I stuck up my middle finger and sped off down the street at top speed, mad as hell about my chicken.

14

Essence

After finishing another twelve hour shift, I couldn't wait to get home and relax, but knew that would have to wait because I had a hair appointment scheduled right after work. I made my way down the street and into the parking lot of Proper Kreations hair salon.

I checked my watch and saw that I was fifteen minutes early. Experience told me that if I didn't get there at least ten minutes ahead of the time, my beautician wouldn't start doing my hair until an hour later. She was petty like that. That thought alone made me hurry up and scoff down the honey bun and cookies that I been waiting to devour. I had no intentions on being at the salon for eight hours. After I finished eating, I hopped out of my ride and quickly made my way toward the entrance. Judging from all the cars that were in the parking lot, I couldn't afford to walk slow. As soon as I walked inside, my hairdresser Patrice, glared at me and then looked at her watch. It was clear that she was getting ready to put someone else in the chair.

"Don't even think about it," I said smiling at her.

"You must've read my mind," she said. "You was about to be ass out, girl."

"Now, I know you wasn't about to play me like that," I

said, even though I knew better.

"Play you like what? Like you didn't wanna get your hair done? Girl, you oughta know how I get down by now. Time is money and I don't have either one of them to waste, girlfriend. Sit ya ass down in this chair," she said laughing.

Patrice was as ghetto as they came, but the woman could definitely do some hair. She had been styling since she was fifteen. Rumor has it that after her ex-boyfriend, Mack, sent her to cosmetology school, and bought the shop, she snitched on him to the Feds. Mack was a medium level dope dealer in Cleveland and her snitching was payback for him getting two women pregnant while in a relationship with her.

"Girl, you know how Patrice is when it comes to her paper," Cookie said, one of the beauticians that worked there.

"It's just you two today? Where's Sheila?" I asked wondering about the third stylist.

"The bitch is about to be out of a fuckin' job," growled Patrice. "This the second time this week her ass done called off sick. She do that again and she gon' be unemployed."

Since I only got my hair done one way; flat ironed, bone straight, there was no need in telling her how I wanted it. Patrice was ghetto fabulous. She kept her weave tight and her nails done. The mole on her upper lip made her look like a black Marilyn Monroe. And although she kept her nails done, her hands were a little rough. I had heard that she used to get into a lot of fights when she was younger and from the look and feel of her hands, I could believe it.

"So, what's been up with you E?"

"Not much. Just kicking back and hanging with my girls from time to time."

"Hanging with yo' girls, huh?"

Here it comes, I thought to myself.

"Well, when you see yo' girl Diamond, tell her that if she think I done forgot, her ass is sadly mistaken."

About a year ago, Patrice accused Diamond of messing around with her man. Her man gave her an STD and swore up and down that the only person that he had messed around with was Diamond. Although Diamond denies it to this day, I knew for a fact that it was true.

Although she never revealed this to me or Angie, I saw a bottle of Penicillin in her bathroom one night that confirmed it. But knowing that Diamond was guilty was one thing. Snitching her out to Patrice was something all together different.

"Come on, Trice. My girl told you that she wasn't messing around with your dude," I said covering for Diamond.

"Essence, if you believe that shit, you need your fuckin' head examined. Her ass is lucky that it was something that a shot could get rid of. Because if it wasn't, then I woulda had to shoot the bitch."

"Well," one of the ladies said who waited to get her hair done.

"You know they say it takes a few years for that package to show up in the tests," Carla announced.

Immediately, a lump formed in my throat.

Carla was the one who turned me on to Proper Kreations. I met her one night when she brought her pregnant sister to the hospital. Patrice shot her a look of death. I could tell that she didn't even want to think of anything like that.

"What you need to do is mind yo' muthafuckin' business, Carla," Patrice spat. "Anyway," she said, turning her attention back to me, "tell yo' slutty ass friend that if I ever see her again, I'ma stomp her ass."

Not wanting to aggravate the woman who was about to do my hair, I quickly closed my mouth and left that subject alone. "You got it, Patrice."

"Oh shit. Hol'on a second E. I gotta go to the bathroom."

I checked my watch to see what time it was because I did not want to be up in Proper Kreations all night. Apparently Patrice saw me cause she rolled her eyes and kept on walking. Figuring that she wouldn't be long, I grabbed one of the Black Hair magazines that was on the counter and started flipping through it. While Patrice was gone, a short, charcoal black looking woman walked in with a young, snotty-nosed kid hanging around her leg.

"Reesie, you know good and damn well that Patrice don't allow kids up in her spot," Carla said.

"First of all, you ain't Patrice so you need to mind ya bidnesss. Second of all, if she want this damn money she'll let him stay in here." Then she eye-balled me from head to toe.

"What the fuck is going on in here?" Patrice yelled as she made her way back to the front of the salon. "A bitch can't even go to the bathroom to change her fuckin' pad without you bitches actin' a muthafuckin' fool in here! Reesie, why the fuck you all up in my spot causin' problems?"

"I ain't causin' no problem, Patrice! It's that bitch," she said, pointing her finger at me.

"What! I don't even know you."

"Oh, don't be trying to look all innocent, bitch! You hang out with that bitch, Diamond."

"Reesie, I don't need yo' fuckin' money!" Patrice blasted, while I sat with my mouth still hung open. "Now, get yo' broke ass outta here and take that little snotty nosed crumb snatcha with you! You know I don't allow no kids in here."

I kept checking her appearance, wondering where she'd seen me before. Each scene played in my mind, but kept coming up with zero. I'd never seen that girl in my life.

Reesie grabbed her son by the hand and started toward the door. "Diamond, really got some shit comin' her way. You tell her, Kenneth died last month."

Wrinkles appeared in my forehead. Who the fuck was Kenneth? And what did Diamond have to do with his death? A part of me said I would ask Diamond later, then I quickly decided against it, knowing she would lie.

"Go Reesie. Leave now," Patrice pressed.

"You know what? Fuck you, Patrice!" Reesie ended as the door slammed.

We all made comments, mumbling under our breath.

"Sit yo' ass back down in this chair, Essence… so I can

hook yo' shit up right quick. I threw Reesie's ass out because she started that shit. But you do need to stop hanging with Diamond's trifflin' ass. I see I ain't the only one who wanna fuck her up."

After getting back into the chair, I started thinking about what Patrice said. Then I thought about what Reesie said about Diamond. While she was doing my hair, it dawned on me that this wasn't the first time that I had gotten into it with another woman over Diamond's trifling ways. Plus the guilt of knowing that she was fooling around with J-Bone was weighing down on me like a lead balloon. If she would do this to Angie, then she would damn sure do this to me. My thoughts were interrupted by someone calling my name and a light tap on my arm.

"E! Girl where the hell y' mind float off to? I'm tryin' to get yo to vouch for my skills and you in la la land!"

"Huh? Oh my bad 'Trice. What's up?"

"I was tellin' this potential customer here that I'm the best hair stylist on the East Side! And I was trying to get you to vouch for me but your head was in the clouds somewhere!"

Looking at the stranger, I cocked my head slightly to the side. There was something vaguely familiar about her. "Yes, I can vouch for Patrice," I said. "She does immaculate work."

"Okay," the woman replied. "I'll give you a shot. I'm Charmaine," she said, extending her hand toward Patrice. After the introduction, Charmaine took a seat at the shampoo bowl, while one of the other girls shampooed her. When I got up to get under the dryer, Patrice motioned for Charmaine to get in the chair.

Carla held her hands up as if to say "Hey, I was next." Patrice looked at her as if to say, 'Aren't you getting your hair done for half price? Sit down and shut up." Carla then dropped her arms and sat back, pouting.

I hurried under the dryer, hoping that I could get done in time to set something up with Gwen later on. After getting comfortable under the dryer, I started to doze off like I usually do. Feeling the presence of someone sitting next to me, I opened my

111

eyes and saw Charmaine resting in the next chair over.

"That was quick," I said.

"Yeah, I'm only getting a wash and wrap for today. Next week, I'll get something else."

"Oh cool. Where do you usually go to get your hair done?" I asked.

"Actually, I just moved back to Cleveland. I've been living in Akron the last few years," she said.

It was a good thing that we were the only two people sitting under the dryer at that particular time because we had to talk louder than normal to hear each other. I was trying not to stare at her but something about her looked very familiar to me. Before we could get any deeper into the conversation, she reached into her pocket and pulled out her vibrating cell phone. Call it curious or just plain nosey but I scooted down in the chair so that my ears were below the dryer. This way I could hear what was being said. With each word that was being passed between Charmaine and who ever she was talking to, it became apparent why this woman looked so familiar.

"I didn't put Mama up to doing shit," she yelled into the phone.

"If you were a better mother instead of acting like you don't even have a fuckin' child…" Charmaine was cut off by the barrage of words that came from the other end of the phone.

"You know what Diamond, Fuck you! Instead of getting pregnant with you, Mama shoulda had your ass vacuumed and sucked out when she had the chance!"

After that vile comment, Charmaine clamped her phone shut and left me blown away. It was now obvious why she looked so familiar. Charmaine was Diamond's sister that I'd only seen in pictures. To find out that my girl had a child that I knew nothing about was crazy. My trip to the hair salon had now taken it's toll on me. I didn't need to hear, or find out anything else about Diamond.

Apparently her conversation with Diamond put Charmaine in a bad mood because she didn't say another word after getting off the phone. She just leaned back and closed her eyes. For the rest of my time in the shop I was in a daze. Once I was done I went to my truck, got in, and just sat there, stunned. It turned out that the woman who I thought was my friend had been keeping secrets from me and Angie all this time; especially Angie.

The more I thought about how foul Diamond was being by sleeping with J-Bone, the more ticked off I became. Shaking my head in disgust, I took my phone out and started to dial.

⚡15

Diamond

The dick pulsated in the palm of my hand as I gently squeezed. Its throbbing head expanded and the eye seemed to wink at me as I watched it drool. The way I was combining sperm today, you woulda thought I was tryin' to make mixed drinks in my throat. My old flame, Greg, had just left thirty minutes ago after leaving his ice cream melting inside my mouth. And now, here I was again.

Just as I leaned down to kiss the head, my cell phone vibrated. I looked at the scream and frowned.

"Damn! What the fuck does she want?" I asked myself as I looked at the number that popped up on my cell phone screen. I hadn't talked to my mother in days. That was just like her to call when I had my hands full. It was bad enough that I couldn't get in touch with my girls today after I had to put my blade to work. But now I had to hear whatever dumb shit she was about to say. I thought about ignoring the call and continue doing what the fuck I was doing. But if I didn't answer, she would keep calling back.

"Yeah, Ma," I answered.

"Is that anyway to greet your mother?"

"Ma, I'm kinda busy right now. I'ma have to call you back later."

"Diamond Renee Robinson, either you talk to me right now, or I'll come over there and see you face to face!"

That was something I damn sure didn't want. I had no intentions on letting her fuck up my groove.

"Okay, what is it, Ma?

"I hear you talked to your sister."

"Yeah, the bitch is back in town, and?"

"Well, she said that you asked her if she put me up to having your daughter call you, is this true?"

"Yep, only because I know how she likes to mind other people's business!"

My mother ignored my comment and asked me the question that I had gotten tired of long ago.

"Have you gotten any help for your problem?"

I shoulda known her ass was gonna bring that shit up. Why can't she just leave me the hell alone and let me get my fuck on. Hell, if I wanted to fuck four, five, or six times a day that was my business. *I'm a grown ass woman.*

"Diamond!" my mother yelled, snapping me out my mental tirade.

"Huh? Oh, what did you say?"

"I asked you if you been gettin' some help for your problem."

"What problem? I don't have a problem," I snapped. I moved a few inches away from the dick. She'd blown all my horny feelings.

"Yes, you do child. You're a damn sex fiend. I believe the technical term is nymphomaniac. You even tried to sleep with my boyfriend, remember that?"

"Why would you bring that up?" I asked as tears filled my eyes.

"Because I want you to recognize that you have a problem and get some help."

I paused for a few seconds to think about what my mother said. Deep in my heart, I knew she was right. But I also knew that it was too late to get any help. I loved sex more than I

116

loved anything else in life; more than my friends, my family, or even my own life. If I couldn't fuck, there would be, in my opinion no reason to live.

"Look child. I didn't call to upset you. I just called you because you said that you were going to call Candice back and you haven't. As a matter of fact, why haven't you called this child back yet?"

" 'Cause I been busy, that's why."

"Busy? What the hell do you mean busy," my mother exploded. "Too busy for your own damn child?"

"That ain't what the hell I said," I spat back matching her tone.

"Well, that's what the hell it sounded like to me! Diamond, you're the devil in disguise!"

"Look, I ain't got time for this bullshit right now. I gotta go!" Before my mother could badger me any further, I hung up on her ass.

"You okay, Diamond," J. Bone asked.

"Yeah, I'm straight."

"Then what the hell you crying for?"

I reached up to my right cheek and felt the wet spot. I was so lost in my thoughts, that I didn't even realize I was crying until J-Bone mentioned it.

"Look, maybe we should do this another..."

"No!" I yelled, gripping his now limp dick in my hand. I leaned down, kissed the head of it, and then looked back up at him. "I don't wanna wait until later. I wanna suck this dick right now."

I smiled devilishly as I lowered my head down onto his rod.

"Uhm hmm," I moaned, taking half of it into my throat, abruptly.

It only took J- Bone a few seconds to get rock hard again. After sucking it for about five minutes, I stopped, got up off the couch, and walked into the kitchen.

"Hey, where you going girl? You gonna just leave a

nigga hanging like this?"

Ignoring his pleas, I continued walking to the kitchen. Opening up the freezer, I grabbed two ice cubes and made my way back to the couch. Then, right before straddling him, I pushed it up into my hot vagina. J-Bone smile as I climbed on top of his dick. I eased down on it slowly and awaited the reaction that I knew was sure to come. As soon as the cold ice touched the tip of his dick, J- Bone's groin area shook and twisted from the chilly sensation.

"Yeeesss, that's my spot," I screamed. Sticky cum and cold water mixed together in my womb and slid down the shaft of his dick.

"Damn Diamond, I can't hold it, I'm 'bout to cum," J-Bone screeched.

"Don't even try to," I replied. "Let me feel that shit nigga! Fill me up!"

I didn't have to tell him twice as J-Bone sprayed my walls with semen. Content, but not completely satisfied, I hopped off of his Johnson and got between his legs.

"Oohhh Godddddddd!" he yelled once I started licking the remaining cum from his penis. After swallowing a combination of his cum and mine, I got up, went into the kitchen and grabbed my bottle of vodka off the counter.

The combination of my mother bringing up the incident with my sister again and the fact that I was fucking one of my best friend's boyfriend behind her back had me feeling disgusted with myself. After snatching the top off the bottle, I walked back into the living room, turning the bottle up along the way. When I pushed the bottle toward J-Bone, offering him a sip, he twisted up in face and shook his head.

Bitch ass nigga. "Oh, so now you want to act like I'm too nasty, after I just licked your ass and balls?"

"Ain't nobody acting like nothing girl. Quit tripping."

"Then how come your ass ain't drinkin' then?"

"Because I don't feel like it, Diamond."

All of a sudden I had a sincere desire to be alone.

"You know what? You gotta roll out."

"What the fuck is your problem, Diamond?"

"My problem is that I'm fucking my best friend's man behind her back and I'm starting to feel like shit about it!"

"What? You joking right? You been giving me that pussy for the past two months and now yo' ass wanna have a conscious? Girl go 'head on with that bullshit."

"You know what nigga, just get the fuck out!"

"Yeah, whatever," he said, putting his clothes back on. Once he got fully dressed, he walked over to me and got in my face. "So, what you saying is that you don't want no more of this dick?"

To keep him from seeing the expression on my face, I turned my back to him. "Yeah, that's what the fuck I thought," he said slapping me on my ass before walking out the door.

Just before he left, he turned to me and said," By the way, is your ass pregnant?"

"What? Hell nah, I ain't pregnant! Where the fuck did you hear that shit?"

"Just checking," he said, then walked through the door. As soon as the door closed, I ran to it, and locked it. Then, I darted to the couch, fell face first, and cried myself to sleep.

****

Still feeling like shit, I woke up to loud banging on the door. It seemed like not even an hour had gone by. I stumbled off the couch, and made my way to the front door. Whoever it was on the other side continued to pound on my door.

"Alright, dammit, I'm coming!"

As soon as I got to the door, I snatched it open ready to lay somebody the fuck out. My mouth fell open as I looked dead into the face of my mother. Standing beside her was Candice, with a bag slung over her shoulder and an old looking flowery, suit case in her hand.

"Hey Mama," Candice bellowed, as she ran over to me

119

and threw her arms around my neck.

"What the hell is this?" I mouthed to my mother.

Without answerin' me, my mother said to Candice, "Take your stuff back in the spare room, if you can remember where it is."

When Candice was out of ear shot, I turned to my mother, who was standing there with her hands on her hips. "Ma, what are you doin'?"

"What does it look like I'm doing? I'm bringing you your daughter."

"What? What the hell am I 'spose to do with her?"

My mother looked at me like I had just asked the stupidest question in the world. "Raise her Diamond. She is *your* daughter."

"But what am I 'spose to do about work?" I asked, trying to get out of it. I hadn't told her that I no longer had a job.

"Oh, don't worry about that. With me being retired now, I have no problem with watching her while you're at work, Diamond. But this is *YOUR* daughter and you need to start raising her as such."

A few seconds later Candice came back into the room.

"Come here baby," my mother said. She then embraced Candice in an extra long hug and kissed her on the cheek, treating her like a baby. *For God's sake. The girl's twelve*, I thought, pissed off.

"Grandma is always just a call away if you need to talk. Have fun you two," she said, just before getting up, and walking out the door.

With my mother now gone, all of my attention shifted to Candice. For the first time in a long time, I took a really good look at my daughter. She was the spitting image of her father. She had a peanut butter complexion with light brown eyes. And when she smiled, her dimples were easily seen. Her shiny black hair was pulled back in a pony tail as she stood in the middle of the floor trying to figure out which one of us would say the first word.

"Mama, can I have something to eat?" she finally asked in her Toni Braxton sounding voice. "I haven't had anything since Grandma cooked this morning."

My heart broke as I heard her ask for food. *Hell, we'd have to run up to the Popeye's again.* Standing next to her, it had just occurred to me how tall she was for her age. But I guess that was to be expected, seeing how tall her daddy was. As I stood there and admired her beauty, I couldn't help but feel guilty that years ago I had screwed my own uncle and gotten pregnant with his child.

16

Angie

I threw my cordless, house phone up against the wall and smashed it into five different pieces. "Okay bitch," I screamed. "If you don't wanna answer the phone, the I'ma come see yo' ass!"

I threw on the pair of gray sweatpants and the Ohio State t-shirt that I had on earlier. Crazily, I reached up under the bed and pulled out a pair of Nike Air Max tennis shoes. I could barely see through my tears as I grabbed a blue nylon scarf off of the dresser and wrapped it around my head. To say I was ready for war would have been an understatement. I'd been calling Diamond repeatedly, yet my calls had gone unanswered. Purposely, I was sure.

If Diamond admitted to fuckin' J-Bone, then I was gonna stomp that bitch in her own house. If she said that she wasn't messing with him and I didn't believe her then I was going to kick her ass anyway. I shoulda known that fuckin' dream I had was a sign. I can't believe that all the time I been kickin' it with this hoe, she was stabbing me in the back the whole time. Rotten, dirty, low down, bitch!

I snatched my keys and my cell phone off the dresser and

stormed out the door with a purpose. I know I told Essence that I would wait until all three of us were together to talk about this shit, but fuck that! I figured she would want to make peace between the three of us but as far as I was concerned, we were done!

From the time I hopped in my car and started over to Diamond's house, Essence called my cell three times. I let all three go to voice mail. If I woulda answered the phone, she woulda just tried to talk me outta what I was going to do. I wasn't having it. A sudden thought occurred to me as I got closer to her house. Grabbing my cell phone off the seat, I dialed J-Bone's number. I had no idea what I was going to say if he answered the phone but when he didn't, I got even madder.

"This muthafucka bet' not have his ass ova here!" I pulled up into Diamond's driveway, looking around for J-Bone's truck. "Yeah, you lucky muthafucka," I mumbled.

I jumped out of my car and sprinted up onto her porch. As soon as I got to her door, I started beating on it as hard as I could. Fuck ringing the door bell. That was for people who were trying to be polite. I had come to kick ass.

"Open this door! Open this muthafuckin' door, you scandalous ass hoe!"

I stood there for five minutes banging on the door like a wild woman. Diamond still didn't come out. My anger peaked as I looked around in her yard for a rock to throw through her window. If she was in there trying to get her some dick, I was about to fuck her whole mission up. I smiled as I saw a crusty red brick laying on the ground. After bending down to pick it up, I ran back up on the porch and cocked my arm back. Just as I was about to shatter her window with it, the door flew open.

"Angie, don't throw that brick through my fuckin' window, chick! Have you lost your damn mind?"

It took every bit of strength in me not to crack her skull in half. "No bitch, you done lost yo' damn mind!"

"Chick, what the hell is you talking about?"

"You know good and damn well what I'm talking

about!"

She just stood there with a stupid look on her face, looking back and forth over her shoulder like she was hiding something from me. "Diamond, I'm gonna ask your ass something and I want you to tell me the truth!" I seethed with anger while my chest heaved up and down. "Are you fuckin' my man? 'Cause a reliable source told me that you been fuckin' the shit out of him!"

After a slight pause, she said, "Who told you that bullshit?"

"Is it true?"

"I don't know what the fuck you talkin' about, chick," she said as she leaned on her door and folded her arms. It was a dead give a way.

Immediately, I tried to get past Diamond, making my way into the house. She acted like she didn't want me inside, but I didn't want any witnesses when I beat that ass. "You know what, bitch, I shoulda known! I shoulda fuckin' known that your low down ass was up to no good!"

"Angie, I don't know where you gettin' yo' info from, but I ain't fuckin' wit' yo' man!"

Her mouth said one thing but her face and attitude said something all together different. Diamond closed her front door, then began pacing the floor.

"I don't believe you, bitch! Yo' ass is lying," I said as tears started cascading down my face. I couldn't be completely sure but I almost thought I saw a smirk on her face when she saw me crying. "Why Diamond? Why J-Bone? Almost every man in the neighborhood wants you! Why you have to fuck with my man?" All of a sudden my feelings erupted and I cried like a teething toddler. "I can't believe you, Diamond! You were supposed to be my friend, and this is how the fuck you treat me! Why are you so fuckin' selfish? Why do you have to hurt everybody you come in contact with?"

"Look you silly, bitch! I already told you that I ain't fuckin' around wit' yo' man. But if you chose not to believe it

125

then that's on you," she said. "Now, close the damn door on your way out! I got shit to do!"

Diamond turned around to walk toward her kitchen as my anger transformed to rage.

"Bitch, don't turn your back on me," I yelled. I charged her ass and tackled her from behind. We both fell onto the couch and then tumbled on the floor.

"Get the fuck off me, hoe!" she yelled.

"Bitch, I'm about to beat yo' muthafuckin' ass," I said, grabbing her hair, while trying to bang her head against the floor. Trying to get me off of her, Diamond dug her finger nails into my neck.

"Bitch, let go of me," she yelled. I couldn't believe that me and my girl were going for blood like this. But Diamond's actions with J-Bone had cut me to the bone. Before long, we were standing up again, swinging away at each other. During the fight, I managed to rip Diamond's ear ring out of her ear.

"Oww, shit Angie," she said pushing me back.

Blood dripped from her ear to the floor. I wanted to go after her ass again but I was too tired. All of a sudden, I started feeling light headed. I tried to shake my head to see if I could see clearly, but it was no use. Before I knew it I was stumbling back against the door.

"Angie!" Diamond called out, worriedly. Despite the fact that we had just had a fight, Diamond rushed to my aid. "Angie, are you alright?"

"Get off me, Diamond," I said still pissed at her. Respecting my wishes, she stepped back but continued to stare at me. Even though I did see concern in her eyes, that didn't stop me from being pissed.

"Angie, somethin' ain't right. Maybe you should go sit down. You look like you about to faint."

"Don't fuckin' worry about me, Diamond! I'm fine! Ain't shit wrong with me that some prenatal vitamins won't cure!"

"What? Prenatal vitamins?" Seeing the look on Diamond's face when I said this was priceless.

"That's right Diamond; I'm pregnant with J-Bone's baby!"

"Damn, Angie I didn't know."

I looked at her ass like she was crazy. I know damn well that she didn't think that was going to change shit. Then outta the blue, a young girl appeared behind Diamond. She resembled Diamond to a tee. My mind started doing flips wondering if she'd finally gotten right with her family, and had her sister over, until the next set of words threw me for a loop.

"Mama..." I heard the girl say. "Can I go outside and wait on Theresa?"

I shot Diamond a look of disbelief. "Did she say mommy?"

After giving Candice a look that said, *girl you talk too fuckin' much,* Diamond asked her, "What are you talking about, Candice? I told you to wait in the back." Diamond massaged her temples.

"You said that I could go over my friend's house for a little while, remember. You called grandma and asked her if it was okay for Theresa's sister to come pick me up?"

"You have a child, Diamond?" I interrupted. I couldn't believe my ears.

"No, I don't," she lied straight in my face. "Oh yeah, go ahead, Candice." She turned to the teenaged looking girl.

"Hello, sweetie." I took her hand and shook it. "You're pretty. What's your name?"

"Candice."

"That's a pretty name, Candice. So, where have you been hiding," I asked, prying.

Diamond stepped in between us.

"Candice, go outside and wait on your friend's sister." It was clear that she didn't want me talking to her.

"Okay...oh there she is now, Mama," she said when she heard a car horn.

After Candice walked out of the house, I just stared at

127

Diamond. This bitch didn't even have the common sense to go and see what the person who was driving away with her daughter looked like. I pushed that thought to the side as I still couldn't believe that this hoe was boning my man.

"You know Diamond," I said as the tears began to fall again, "Stay the fuck away from me, you hear? Just stay the fuck outta my life! You got a fuckin daughter that you never told me about and you fuckin my man?"

I bolted out of the door like a running back for the Cleveland Browns. Diamond was right behind me calling my name. I ignored her because as far as I was concerned, our friendship was over. Everything about her was a lie. After hopping back into my car, I peeled away from the curb, and zipped off down the street, doing about eighty miles per hour. I hoped on the freeway on the way to an unknown destination. I had no idea where I was going. I just wanted to get away. With tears slowly blinding me, I grabbed my cell phone and tried to call J-Bone. When it went straight to his voice mail again, I went off.

"J-Bone, you a dirty muthafucka! I can't believe yo' low down ass was fuckin' my girl behind my back! Well you know what, you fuckin' slimy ass nigga? The son that you always talked about wantin' is growing in my stomach!"

Horns from other cars blew loudly as I swerved from lane to lane. I was six inches from side swiping a man on a Harley Davidson motorcycle but my thoughts were not on anybody's safety including my own. All I wanted to do was give J-Bone a piece of my mind. "That's right muthafucka, I'm pregnant but you know what? It'll be a cold day in hell before you see your son! Since you think Diamond's pussy is so good to you, you can continue to fuck that bitch!"

I was coming up fast on the back of a U-Haul truck as my emotions exploded even more. I put the pedal to the metal, increasing my speed even more. My heart was broken and my eyes were so watery; I could barely see in front of me. All of a sudden the U-haul in front of me swerved, revealing an eighteen wheeler in my path.

At the last minute, I yanked to the right hoping to avoid the collision. Unfortunately, there was a stalled car with its hazard lights on, parked on the shoulder. I slammed on the brakes as fast as I could but there was nothing I could do to avoid the massive crash. I closed my eyes and gripped the steering wheel tight as my car slammed forcefully into the back of the broke down vehicle. The last thing I remember doing was quickly praying to the Lord to spare my unborn child. Shortly after that, my world went black.

$17

Essence

The next day rolled around with me realizing I'd have to live life to the fullest. Things had just gotten bad. I hopped in the Pathfinder, slamming the door, considering driving off a bridge. I'd just come from the doctor's office where I'd been told that if I didn't straighten up and start taking care of myself then the rest of my life was going to be a whole lot shorter. The doctor told me that she'd noticed that I seemed to have lost weight since my last appointment. She scolded me about not taking my medication properly, which she was sure that I wasn't doing. But the biggest scare of all came when she blurted that my CD4 cells had fallen to dangerously low levels. I got hit with a frown when she explained that they had fallen to 210 and that once they go under 200, I would officially have AIDS. With my mind fully occupied by the conversation with my doctor, I made a right onto Eastway Street on 105th and St. Clair, which would've been fine if it wasn't a one way street. People were blowing and acting all crazy. "It was a simple mistake," I screamed.

After turning around and headed back in the right direction, tears started to fall down my face as I began thinking about what the doctor told me that I could expect; lack of energy, weight loss, and frequent yeast infections headed the list. Then, after writing me a prescription for Viread, Zerit, and Epivir, she jammed the pad into my hand. She was obviously upset that I hadn't been acting right as far as my health was concerned. The doctor then walked over to me, placed a hand on my shoulder, and told me to live life to the fullest.

"Don't let this thing hold you hostage," she'd told me.

I walked into my house and slammed the door behind me. Walking straight to the refrigerator, I took out a bottle of Moscato and poured me a glass. Right then I decided that's just what I was going to do. For the rest of my time on earth, I was going to live my life care free and have as much fun as possible. With tears still streaming down my face, I smiled slightly as I thought about Jerome. I'd finally gotten that nigga to give it to me raw. And once I threw my legs around him and pulled that raw meat inside me, I had his ass. I put this pussy on his ass so good, that nigga even bought me the Chanel bag that I had been clamoring for. Stupid nigga.

I smiled even more as I hopped on the couch, and thought about Gwen. I was really starting to feel her. We'd only been together four times since we met, but I was sure...I wanted to be with her more and more. Every time I thought about her sweet sex, I almost creamed on myself. Gwen had used every available sex toy ever made, and it was turning me out.

Now, almost an hour later, I was on my fourth glass of Moscato. I was still shaking my head and laughing in stunned disbelief thinking about what I had learned about Diamond the day before. Now that I thought about it, it may have been a blessing in disguise. I still couldn't understand why Diamond chose to keep her past a secret from us, nor why she chose to screw J-Bone. Hell, we all liked sex, but it seemed like Diamond messed around with everybody's man. Now that I sat thinking about it, there were times when we went out and Diamond disappeared on us and we didn't know where she went. Every time that we would ask about her whereabouts, she would just shrug and change the subject. I believe the correct term for that is Nympho.

132

Speak of the devil, I told myself as the phone rang, and Diamond's number popped up. I answered like I really didn't want to talk. "Hello."

"What's up chick?" Something about the sound of her voice was off. I started to wonder if Angie had talked to her about J-Bone.

"You okay?" I asked her.

"Hell nah, chick, I feel like I'm about ready to go off the deep end."

"Damn, girl, what's wrong?" I prayed that Angie didn't go there and blast off after I called and snitched.

"Girl, it's just that a lotta bullshit been happenin' to me lately."

"Like what?" *Spending time with your daughter, I wanted to say.*

"Just a lotta dumb shit, you know? I'll tell you the details later. I'm so stressed the fuck out I don't know what to do! My fuckin' boss been trippin' and shit, his wife actin' a bitch, my mother been getting' on my fuckin' nerves and shit! I tell you chick, fuck a mixed drink, I'm about to take the whole bottle of Absolute to the head!"

"Come on girl, don't let them people stress you out like that," I told her.

"Oh, wait though, chick! That ain't even the worst of it all! Can you believe I had to cut a bitch yesterday? Darius' bitch ass sister and her friend tried to jump my ass."

"What? When the hell was this and how come you didn't call me and Angie?"

"Shit, it happened so fast, I didn't have time to call no-body! Them hoes stepped to me at Popeye's yesterday after I got off of work. Kellie's friend rushed me and I opened her ass up! Both of them hoes lucky that we was in a public place or I woulda really fucked them bitches up!"

"Wait. Don't tell me that Kellie still blame's you for Dar-ius' death."

"Hell yeah! And everything else she can think of from

me and Darius' path. She even had the nerve to tell me that she was gonna send me to be with her brother if it's the last thing she does! I'm telling you, the next time that bitch steps to me, I'ma put her ass in the hospital!"

"I know that's right, girl!"

Right then and there, I decided that since Angie hadn't said anything to Diamond yet about J-Bone, neither would I. Besides, it was better for us to talk face to face. Before we could continue our conversation, my other line clicked. I smiled from ear to ear when I saw that it was, Gwen.

"Hold on Diamond," I said, never giving her a chance to say another word. I clicked over quickly and answered like the love of my life was on the line.

"Hey, baby," she said, causing me to smile from ear to ear.

"Hey ya self, beautiful. What's up?"

"Just chilling. What's good with you?"

"Let me come over tonight and I'll show you exactly what's good with me," she said seductively. My pussy instantly got wet. After giving her my address, I clicked back over and rushed Diamond off the phone.

"Hey D, let me call you back later on. Something came up that I gotta take care of."

"That's cool, chick. I was about to go to bed anyway."

I hung up from Diamond and started straightening up my place. I was never a junky person, so I didn't have that much to do. After that, I jumped in the shower and gave myself a quick washing. The last thing I wanted to be was funky when Gwen showed up. It was crazy how I felt about her. I never imagined my feelings getting so deep, but Gwen was someone I could see myself with. Once I got out of the shower and dried myself off, I rubbed my entire body down with two different types of oils I picked up from some guy at the hair salon.

After slipping into my red satin negligee, I lit a few vanilla scented candles and placed them on my bedroom dresser. Looking at the light blue satin sheets on my king sized bed, I smiled like a kid at Christmas. The way I saw it, those sheets were going to be drenched with cum in about an hour or so. I couldn't wait to taste her sweet love. With my French manicure and matching pedicure shining, I walked into the kitchen and poured yet another glass of wine. As much drinking as I was doing, I knew that I would pay for it in the morning but I didn't care.

I poured Gwen a glass and put it in the fridge until she got there. As I sat down and leaned back on the couch, I started thinking about all the nasty things that I wanted to do to Gwen. With the wine kicking in, I started feeling drowsy. Luckily for me the doorbell rang when it did. Otherwise, I may have fallen asleep before she got there. I got up and strutted to the door, eager to let my new lover in. I opened the door and almost melted at the sight of my gorgeous lover.

Her skin glistened and the sweet smell of whatever perfume she had on nearly caused me to rape her right on the spot. After flashing a sinister smile, Gwen sexily sauntered through the front door. Her sex appeal was mesmerizing. She intentionally brushed up against me as she passed by causing my nipples to harden.

"Hey, baby. You missed me," she said sensually.

"You know I did." My mouth salivated at the sight of Gwen standing in front of me, looking super luscious. Her skin was smooth and shiny and her hair had been trimmed even shorter, appearing even more chic. I was a few inches taller than her, but the heels that she was wearing made our height even. She had on a black leather mini skirt that rose just above the middle of her thigh, I assumed in an attempt to entice me. I noticed that she had a band aid on her arm, but for fear of killing the mood, I didn't ask her about it.

I knew I should've told her about my condition but I honestly didn't feel like there was a need for her to know. It's not like we were penetrating each other so what sense did it make to tell, and risk losing her just because she might've thought there was a possibility of her getting infected? I wasn't worried though. Since there was no penetration, I couldn't see her contracting the disease from me. Plus, there were only four ways to get HIV; mother to child, where the innocent really suffers, sharing needles, sharing fresh blood, and unprotected sex.

"Well, are you just gonna stand there or are you gonna come over here and greet me properly," she said sassily. Before the last syllable left her mouth, I was up in her face.

"Gwen, you smell…" I didn't get a chance to finish my statement as Gwen grabbed the back of my head, pulled my head in close and stuck her tongue down my throat.

"Mhhmm," I moaned after tasting her sweetness. "Come on," I said, pulling her by her hand into my dimly lit bedroom.

"Slow down, beautiful. I ain't going nowhere," she told me. "I'm kinda thirsty. You got something for me to drink?"

"Yeah, I got a little something for you, sexy."

Quickly, I ran to the kitchen and retrieved the glass of wine that I'd set inside for her. Naturally, I didn't want her to drink alone, so I poured myself another one. I was going to have a nice headache in the morning but fuck it. I didn't have to work tomorrow. After walking back into the bedroom, I got hotter than I already was. Gwen had taken off her shirt and was reared back on the bed exposing her flat stomach. My legs almost stalled as I walked over and handed her the glass.

"You know Essence," she started, "I was thinking that maybe we could do a little something different tonight."

"Like what?" I asked suspiciously.

"Well…" Before she could finish her sentence, her cell phone rang. I watched as her smile slowly turned into a frown. "Yeah a'ight," she said as she clamped it shut.

"What's wrong?"

"Well, I wanted to surprise you tonight. I had a couple of male friends of mine lined up to swing by and give us some dick action, if it was ok with you."

"An orgy? I thought you were into girls."

"Baby, I'm into whatever makes my pussy tingle."

"Okay…uh…so what happened?"

"Apparently, their wives got suspicious when they got dressed up and told them that wherever they were going they would have to take them. Needless to say, that killed that planned. I don't suppose you know any big dick niggas that can come by and dick us down."

"What? I'm not enough for you?" I asked, only half joking.

"Oh, baby, you know it's not that. I was just hoping that we could do a little something special tonight."

I didn't want to disappoint Gwen. Right away, my mind shot to Maurice and Marcus even though I vowed to never call them again. I went back to the living room, picked up my cell phone and dialed Maurice's number. I could almost see the smile on their faces when I invited them over for a little adult fun. I didn't tell them about Gwen. I wanted that to be a surprise.

****

A little over an hour later, me and Gwen were bent over side by side as the brothers rammed inside of us. I looked over at Gwen's facial expressions and immediately got jealous. I honestly didn't know why I did, I just did. Crazy thoughts sped through my mind. I started wondering if she enjoyed them more than she enjoyed being with me. Gwen made me feel a little better when she leaned her head over and kissed me in the mouth. Maurice then asked us to get in the sixty nine position. I was more than ready to taste her juicy goods so I jumped up as quickly as I could and climbed on top. I had no idea why they wanted us this way and I really didn't care. All I knew was that I was about to get a slice of heaven.

"Oh shit," I screamed when I felt the reason why they wanted us this way.

Maurice was plunging his thick, black, pole into my ass hole. Looking up I saw that Marcus had propped Gwen's ass up with two pillows, so that while I was eating her out he had easy access to her anal area. Gwen took it like a pro and I even think that it turned her on more as she lapped at my pussy like a starved dog. As if they planned it, Marcus and Maurice came at the same time, covering our faces with sperm. The taste of nut in my mouth combined with Gwen eating my pussy made me cum harder than I had in the past month. Gwen came too so we both were satisfied.

After getting washed up, the guys said that they had to leave. "Something came up," Marcus chimed. I didn't believe for one minute that something had come up in the middle of the night again, but who cared. To be honest, I was ready for them to go. I enjoyed our little foursome. But I wanted Gwen all to myself for the rest of the night. To my disappointment, she told me that she had to go too.

"I'm sorry, boo," she said, as she headed toward the door. "I gotta get home before my girlfriend starts blowing my phone up."

"Girlfriend?" I mumbled to myself as she gently closed the door. "She never told me that she had a fuckin' girlfriend."

♀18

Diamond

I peeled out of my mother's driveway as fast as I could. Although by my calculations, she wouldn't get back for another thirty minutes, I didn't want to take the chance of her coming home and finding out what I was up to. In order to keep from hurting Candice, I had to make up a lie about why I was dropping her back off at her grandmother's house. My mother was gonna hit the roof when she came home and found Candice there, but I would cross that bridge when I got to it.

Shit, I realized Candice was my daughter and all, but I just wasn't cut out for this motherhood shit. I was put on this earth to fuck, suck, and cum as much as possible, and I didn't want to take the chance of my mother coming over and ruining my good time.

I needed some dick and I needed it bad. I looked at the clock on the dashboard and saw that I had another couple of hours before I had to be at the doctor for my pap smear. I'd called Chris and J.T both who'd probably had enough of my games. They sent me straight to voicemail. I thought about calling J-Bone, but Angie probably had his ass on lock. Starting to feel bad, I quickly put my friend out of my mind. I thought about calling her, but then thought, hell, the bitch hadn't called me, so fuck her.

As soon as I got in the house, I jumped in the shower and took a quick one, all the while thinking about who I was gong to get to put out the fire that had begun to spread between my legs. I called a couple of my other boy toys and they were either at work or couldn't get away from their girlfriends. So as a last resort, I picked up the phone and called Paul. I knew he would be mad at me for the way I treated him the other day but I also knew that he couldn't resist this good pussy. The phone rang about three times and went to voice mail. I knew his ass was still at home because his car was out front.

Apparently, he was still pissed off and wasn't feeling me. I hung up and called again. And again. If I could get him on the phone, then I could get him to give up the dick. I really didn't want to be bothered with his clingy ass but I didn't have a choice. Seeing that he didn't want to answer the phone, he left me no choice but to go over to his house and bang on the door. He was gonna give up the dick whether he wanted to or not. I cut across his grass, ran up the steps, and started to bang on the door. That's when I noticed that his door was slightly ajar. I softly pushed on the door and it opened right up. Then I peaked inside to see if I saw Paul anywhere. I didn't see him so I got a little bolder and walked in.

"Paul," I said softly as I looked around.

The house was dark and quiet. Having been inside many times before, I made my way down to his bedroom door.

"Oh shit," I heard him moan.

If this muthafucka got company, her ass is either gonna have to get up or move the fuck over. I was gonna get some dick and wasn't no other bitch gonna stop me. I eased open the door and was only slightly surprised when I saw Paul lying in his bed butt naked with the picture that he took of me a few days ago through the window clutched in his left hand. With his right hand, he was slowly stroking his steel hard dick. I glanced to the right. On his dresser sat a bottle of Viagra and a bottle of Prozac.

Damn, I thought. *No wonder his shit was so hard and big the last time we fucked. This nigga been taking the blue Gods.*

Then I thought about the Prozac. *Damn, this muthafucka crazy.*

Seeing that his eyes were closed, I crept inside of the room and over to the side of the bed. He was so engrossed in jacking off to my picture that he never even heard me come in. After standing there and watching him for a few seconds, I unbuttoned my shirt until my bra and stomach were exposed. I decided to stand there another ten seconds and give him a chance to open his eyes. If he didn't open them by then, I was just gonna have to surprise him by sliding my tongue across his dick. As if he heard me thinking, Paul opened his eyes and jumped at the sight of me staring at him.

"Diamond, what the fuck are you doing in my house?"

"You left the door open so I figured that you wanted me to come in," I joked. After looking down at his naked body and the picture that he held in his hand of me and J-Bone, Paul knew that he was busted. Closing his eyes in embarrassment, he said, "Diamond, you need to leave."

I took advantage of the fact that his eyes were closed and quickly took off my shirt and bra. When he opened his eyes, my titties were staring him in the face.

"You sure you want me to leave?"

Paul opened his mouth but no sound came out. That told me all I needed to know. I slowly took off the stretch pants that I had thrown on and threw them to the side. Then I grabbed Paul by the back of the head and pulled his face up into chest. Like a starved child, Paul's mouth latched onto my right breast and sucked away. My nipples grew to the size of nickels as Paul fed like a newborn. While he was quenching his hunger, I was finger fucking myself with my right hand and rubbing his dick with my left. With my pussy wet and throbbing, I backed away from him and took off my panties. His dick was at full attention as I climbed on top of Paul and took the rodeo ride.

"Oh, hell yeah, nigga! Awwwwwwweeeee shit!"

I put both of my hands onto Paul's chest for support and started jumping up and down on his rod like a wild woman. After two minutes of riding, my body started to tremble. The mini orgasm that I had just had left me less than satisfied. I was aiming for the big one. I continued to buck like I was riding a bronco when all of a sudden, Paul flipped me over. He grabbed my right leg and threw it over his left shoulder and started pounding my guts. It felt good but I wanted more. I kicked my left leg up and motioned for him to grab it and throw it onto his other shoulder. He was more than happy to oblige me. I was pleasantly surprised. Paul had never laid dick to me like that. I guess that Viagra worked.

"Oh shit! That's it baby! Oh, shit baby, please, please make me cum! Fuck me, baby! Fuck the shit outta me! Uhh…Uhhh… Uuhhh…Oohh fuck nigga, you gon' make a bitch cum!!"

That was it. I couldn't take it any longer. I had to bust.

And so did Paul as he squirted up in my love patch. "Oooooooohhhh, bitch," he screamed while coming. Then he collapsed back onto the bed. I was right behind him as I fell onto his chest.

"Damn, that shit was good," he said. "I gotta go the bathroom, but I wanna talk to you when I get back."

Right then I knew that it was time to get the fuck outta there. By the tone of his voice I knew exactly what he wanted to talk about. He wanted to start that relationship talk again. As soon as he went into the bathroom and closed the door, I jumped up and put my clothes on as fast as I could, grabbing my picture in the process. I don't know why in the fuck this nigga insisted on trying to lock a bitch like me down. It couldn't be done. I was almost to the door when I heard his booming voice rumbling through my ears.

"Diamond, where the fuck you going? I told you that I wanted to talk to you."

"And I told yo' ass that I had somewhere to go so stop sweatin' the fuck outta me."

Paul just stood there and looked at me like I had lost my mind by talkin' to him like that. "Bye nigga," I said, before poppin' my lips and turning toward the door.

Apparently Paul had had enough of my mistreatment. Forcefully, he wrapped his strong arms around my neck when I reached for the door. Surprisingly, he yanked me backwards causing my feet to lift from the floor.

"Paul, what the fuck!"

"Bitch who the fuck you think you disrespectin' like that? I'll beat yo muthafuckin' ass!"

Damn, I thought to myself, *this nigga done snapped.*

"Nigga, get the fuck offa me!"

I tried to scratch his hands like an angry cat so that he would release me, but all that seemed to do was piss him off even more. Paul picked me up as if I was as light as a feather and slammed me to the floor. The jolt from hittin' the hardwood temporarily knocked the wind out of me. Teary-eyed, I watched the photo fly from my hand.

"Aweeeee!" I screamed as I felt the tip of his foot kick me in the stomach. That moment told me things had gotten serious. Paul was more than angry, I told myself feeling another hard kick to the ribs. Instantly, I felt like I was gonna throw up.

"Come here, bitch," he shouted, yanking me off the floor. "I'm tired of your games." Paul grabbed me by my neck and slammed me into the wall, followed by a vicious slap to my face that knocked my equilibrium off, causing me to fall to the floor again.

Oh my God, I thought, this nigga is actually trying to kill my ass. I panicked!

On my hands and knees, I tried my best to crawl for the door. My neck felt like it was about to snap as Paul picked me up in a full nelson wrestling move and pushed my head forward. My life flashed before my eyes. Strangely enough it was Candice's face that I saw the most. I don't know what that meant, but if I didn't do something soon, I would never see her again.

"You won't do this shit to nobody else bitch!" Paul yelled, continuing to punish my face.

Cuttin' my eyes from side to side, I noticed that Paul's legs were spread apart. Using a move that I'd once seen on an old movie, I swung my leg backwards with all my might and kicked him squarely in the nuts. Paul instantly released me and fell to the floor. I thought about getting him while he was down, but if he recovered enough to grab me, then he would have really fucked me up. Barely able to catch my breath, I grabbed the knob, turned it, and ran out the door as fast as I could, not even bothering to look back.

Although I know I was wrong for leading him on, that nigga still didn't have no business putting his hands on me. And because he did, I was going to make him pay dearly.

19

Diamond

I woke up the followin' mornin' hopin' that it would be better than the day before. My face was all bruised the fuck up from Paul beatin' my ass. After fixin' myself some scrambled eggs, I sat down and ate, debatin' on whether or not I would keep my appointment. I had already cancelled yesterday and rescheduled for today. I didn't want anybody to see me lookin' like I had gone twelve rounds with Mike Tyson. Puttin' somethin' on my stomach made me feel better so I said fuck it. Even bruised up, I looked better than most of these tired ass hoes anyway. Besides, I was long overdue for a pap smear, so I figured I would go ahead and get it over with.

After throwin' on a blue, Juicy Sweatsuit, I grabbed my pair of extra large knockoff Gucci sunglasses, threw them on, and walked out the door, feeling like my face was going to explode. It took me less than fifteen minutes to get to Cleveland Clinic from my house. Although the sunglasses covered my eyes, the bruise on the right side of my cheek was still visible and my jaw was slightly swollen. The receptionist tried to pretend she didn't notice but she woulda had to be Ray Charles not to. Thinkin' about what Paul had done to me, I walked over to one of the couches simmerin'. I still couldn't believe that this bitch ass nigga had the nerve to put his fuckin' hands on me. He done lost his muthafuckin' mind fo' real.

I must've been lookin' some kind of mad because the teen-aged girl sittin' across from me kept starin' at me. I guess she was wonderin' why my face was so fucked up. After givin' her a nasty look, I picked up a Sister to Sister magazine and started browsin' through it. Then, while flippin' through the pages, I happened to look up and see the girl whisperin' into an older woman's ear who was sittin' next to her.

"*Here we go*," I said through gritted teeth. I sat my magazine down for a second.

The woman abruptly sat her magazine down too and stared at me for a good ten seconds. I guess she wanted me to look up but I refused to give the bitch the satisfaction. Once she saw that I wasn't about to engage her in bullshit, she made the first move.

"Excuse me Miss thang, but do you have a problem with my daughter?" I looked to the side as if there was somebody else that she could have been talkin' to.

"You talkin' to me?"

"Yeah, I'm talkin' to you. My daughter said that you mean mugged her. Now, like I asked the first time, do you have a problem?" I threw the magazine to the floor and sat up in my chair. Out of the corner of my eye, I could see the receptionist dialin' numbers on the phone. I guess she saw somethin' about to jump off and called security.

"No sweetie, I don't have a problem with your daughter, but what I do have a problem with is people starin' me all in the fuckin' mouth and not mindin' they damn business."

"My daughter can look wherever the fuck she wanna look. And that includes at yo' ass."

"Well, if she gon' be all in grown people's mouths, then she's gonna get whatever the fuck she got comin' to her ass."

"Oh, is that right?" she asked standing up.

"Hell yeah, that's right," I said standin' right up with her ass.

"Bitch, you better sit yo' ass down before you get yo' ass

whupped…again," she said smirkin'.

"Well, what the fuck you wanna do then hoe," I yelled, getting' more pissed off by the minute.

By this time the security guard had made his way over to the drama.

"Ladies, what's goin' on over here?" asked the thin, white man. Before anyone could say anything else, a nurse appeared from the back and called my name.

"You lucky, bitch," she mumbled.

"No, you lucky, slut," I shot right back.

The guard got in between us makin' sure that we didn't touch each other as I passed by. That was a good thing too cause if that bitch woulda so much as grazed me, I was gonna mop the floor with her and her skinny ass daughter. I walked back to the back as slowly as I could. I wasn't about to let them bitches think that I was scared of they asses by speedin' back there. I walked into one of the rooms and could tell right away that somethin' was wrong. The nurse closed the door and began apologizin' before I could even say one word. I wanted to say, 'bitch what the fuck are you apologizin' for?'

"Miss Robinson, we've been tryin' to get in touch with you all day. Your regular doctor had a family emergency that she had to take care of and we could only find one other doctor to fill in. His name is Dr. Eugene Curry."

This bitch had to be joking. All this damn apologizin' because they had to find another doctor? The shit seemed stupid as hell to me.

"If you want, we can reschedule for another date.

Reschedule? Nah, fuck that. I wanna get this bullshit over with right now. "No, that's fine. I can see the fill in doctor."

"Okay great. He'll be with you shortly."

I sat there for about ten minutes before the doctor walked in, blowing me away. He was handsome as hell, about six-feet two, and from what I could tell, a solid two hundred pounds. His teeth were as white as could be and his smile lit up the room.

Right away, I was attracted to his deep, dark skin and his shiny bald head. I slyly scoped out his ring finger to see if he was married. I don't why I did that. I'd never cared if a man was married or not, and I sure as hell wasn't about to start now. My pussy started to do a dance as he walked over to me and introduced himself.

"Hi. My name is Dr. Eugene Curry and I'll be filling in for your regular doctor today."

His deep baritone voice caused my nipples to get hard.

"I hope you don't mind," he said smiling.

Mind? Hell nah, I didn't mind. I threw my sweet, innocent voice on'em. "No it's okay doctor."

"What happened to your face? You're a beautiful girl," he added without giving me a chance to answer, "So make sure you surround yourself with real men."

I guess that was his way of telling me to stop lettin' niggas beat my ass. I appreciated the advice. Just hearing him talk got me so excited. As my pussy got hotter and my imagination ran wild, I laid back and put my legs in the stirrups. I could feel the pre cum ooz down my leg. I wanted to fuck this doctor in the worst way. I know it's sad, but I just couldn't help it. I can't explain it but the more I thought about fuckin' the more I want to do it. Every time I saw a good lookin' man, I just want to get down on my knees and suck his dick. When the doctor turned around to put gloves on, I looked at his tight ass and lost it. I quickly eased my hand down the middle of my stomach until I came to my clit. Visualizin' the doc fuckin' me caused me to moan softly.

"Oh God," I said as I pinched my clit.

Apparently the doc thought I was talking about the procedure because he said, "It's okay, Miss Robinson. I've done this procedure hundreds if not thousands of times."

I smiled to myself as I imagined the look on his face when he turned around and saw me playin' with my punanny. Stickin' two fingers into my vagina, I slowly started finger fuckin' myself.

148

"Okay Miss Robinson, shall we…"

His words caught in his throat like a mouse in a mouse trap. For at least ten seconds, Dr. Curry stood there with a blank look on his face. I could have sworn that I saw a dribble of spit form in the corner of his mouth. Dr. Curry looked like a mannequin as he stood there and stared at me playing with my pussy.

"Dr., are you gonna stand there and drool, or are you gonna help me put this fire out?"

Dr. Curry looked at the door and then back at me. A lustful smile crept across his face as he walked toward me. I smiled back as the doctor leaned his head forward and buried his face in my love patch. I moaned heavily as the doctor hungrily lapped at my pussy causin' me to lay my head back in ecstasy. The indescribable feelin' of a tongue touchin' my clit was the greatest feelin' in the world to me. Dr. Curry then reached his arms over my thighs and spread my pussy lips as wide as they would stretch. Without hesitation, he then stuck his tongue so far up in my pussy that it felt like a dick. As the doctor tongue screwed me, he stuck a finger in my asshole and fingered it. Just as I was about to come, Dr. Curry stood up, unzipped his pants, and reached for one of the flimsy rubbers that shoulda been used to do an internal sonogram. Within seconds, he'd strapped up and pushed his dick inside of me.

"Oh …oooooooohhhhh! Harder, doctor, harder! Pound it!"

The doctor was more than happy to oblige. At this point, both of us were moaning like crazy and didn't care who heard us. It didn't take long for us to get to the point of climaxin'. We were fuckin' like nasty jack rabbits, ripping all the white paper that was beneath me.

"I'm cumming!" he yelled, as he pulled out just in time to bust all over my stomach.

But of course that wasn't enough for me. Not completely content, I grabbed his hand and pulled him to the side of me. I wanted and needed the taste of cum in my mouth. Takin' hold of his semi-hard Johnson, I held it up over my lips. I watched his dick in anticipation as a string of cum hung from the tip.

"Mmmm, hmm," I moaned as I savored the delicious taste of his babies slidin' down my throat. "Delicious," I said with a grin.

After gettin' cleaned up, Dr. Curry did what he was supposed to do in the first place, which is give me a papsmear. It was a fast one; the quickest I'd ever had. After he was done, I walked out of the room and past all the haters who gawked at me, like they'd heard us. I didn't know if Dr. Curry got in trouble or not, but he could examine me anytime.

****

I walked out of the doctor's office feelin' like a new woman. Bustin' a nut was just what I needed to relieve the stress that was startin' to build up on me. Checkin' my cell phone, I saw that I had five missed calls. Knowin' exactly who they were from, I didn't even bother to look at the call log. No doubt it was my mother callin' to chew me out for dropping Candice back off. Well, she wasn't about to fuck up my good mood. I'd call her back when I had the time to listen to her bitch.

As soon as I pulled out of the doctor's office, I got a strange feelin' that I was being followed. I quickly chalked it up to nerves. With everything that had been going on in my life, it was a wonder that I hadn't had a nervous breakdown. But then I looked in the rearview mirror and noticed that there was a white, Chevrolet Impala makin' every turn I was makin'. I made a left on Ivanhoe and the car was right with me. Then I drove across St. Clair and over the bridge.

Again the car was still on my ass. Getting' extremely nervous, I hopped on the freeway at 152nd and sure enough, the Impala followed. With increased speed, I hit the highway hard, driving my ass off. Now, I'm no Mario Andretti, but a bitch can drive. It looked like I'd met my match because no matter what I did the Impala stuck to me like flies to shit.

150

Finally, I'd had enough of the bullshit. I pulled off the freeway on 185th and yanked into the Shell gas station. I figured the best way to get a good look would be to make them come a little closer. I parked in front of the pump closest to the gas station door, walked inside, and bought a pack of gum. I kept peeking through the glass trying to catch a glimpse of my stalker. When I got back outside, I saw that the car that had been followin' me was parked in the front of the pump closest to the street. From a distance, it looked to be a male; my guess only because the hat that was pulled down over the head resembled a guy. In a bold move that even surprised me, I made a beeline straight for the Impala. My hand was already inside my purse palmin' my blade. I got halfway between my car and the Impala when all of a sudden the Impala darted out into the street and took off down the road.

"Fuck you, muthufucka!" I shouted, running into the middle of the street.

20

Essence

Looking into the mirror, I could see that I was starting to lose some of my thickness. I hadn't paid much attention to it before but the doctor was right. I was losing weight. Before long, I was going to have to make a decision about telling Angie and Diamond. I didn't have many friends, but I didn't want to lose the ones that I had over withholding information. That's part of the reason that I wanted to get them together and talk about J-Bone's low down ass. I disliked him so much that I was tempted to give him some of this poison. But not only would that hurt him, but Angie too, and put her life in jeopardy. Even though he's two timing her with Diamond, Angie would still continue to sleep with him. I knew. I just knew she would. I picked up the phone and called Angie. The voice mail immediately picked up.

"Well, I guess that idea is all shot to hell," I said out loud as I pressed end. I had forged a plan to get Angie and Diamond to meet me at Applebee's so we could clear the air. Even though Diamond was dead wrong, I hated to see two good friends at each other's throats over a man. Since Angie wasn't answering her phone, I could only assume that she was still ticked off by what I told her. I also had to assume that since I haven't heard from Diamond, she hadn't heard from Angie either. I decided to give Diamond a call and ask her to meet me at Applebee's anyway. That way if Angie called back, I could tell her to just meet us there.

"What's up, chick," Diamond said when she answered the phone.

"Hey, what are doing right now?"

"I just left the doctor's office," she said, slightly laughing.

"What's so funny," I asked.

"Chick, you don't even want to know." The way that Diamond was snickering, I figured she would just tell me later on anyway.

"You talked to Angie today?" I asked.

"Nope, why?"

"Because I was trying to get a hold of her to see if you two wanted to meet at Applebee's."

"Well, I ain't heard from her but I'm more than down to get some free grub!"

"Free? Who told you that it was free?"

"Yo' invitation told me it was free," she said, smacking her lips.

"Whatever Diamond," I said, annoyed at her it's-all-about-me attitude. "Meet me there in a half an hour."

"Bet chick. See you in thirty."

After disconnecting from Diamond, I tried once again to call Angie, but she still wasn't answering. I reached for the remote to turn off my television and stopped dead in my tracks. My mouth fell open as I saw Maurice and Marcus being led out of a house in handcuffs. I quickly turned the volume up so I could hear what was going on.

Elsewhere in the news, Columbus FBI agents raided a house today and seized more than fifty pounds of marijuana from suspected drug dealers Maurice and Marcus Reynolds. The two brothers are being held without bail pending an investigation.

I just sat there shaking my head. I should have known

when Maurice told me that they had to go out of town on "business" what it was all about. Throwing my hands up at the television, I went into the bathroom, reached into the medicine cabinet, and grabbed my bottles of Viread, Zerit, and Epivir. Then I grabbed a cup from the cupholder and filled it with water. After twisting the cap off of each bottle, I took a pill out of each one and stared at them. "What a screwed up mess I've gotten myself into," I said as I threw all three of them in my mouth and swallowed them with a big gulp of water. After walking back through the living room and clicking the off button, I walked out the house without giving the Maurice and Marcus situation another thought.

Applebee's was more crowded than I thought it would be at four o'clock in the afternoon. I looked at my watch and noticed that Diamond was fifteen minutes late. Not that I was surprised though. She was known to be late for everything. While I was waiting on Diamond, I started to daydream. I thought about how much I was starting to feel Gwen. I knew that she had a girlfriend but to be honest, I didn't care. As long as I could spend time with her, I was good even if it meant that I had to share her for the time being. I kept wondering how Angie and Diamond were going to react when they learned about the two of us. I ordered a Strawberry Martini in honor of Gwen, and took the first sip as Diamond walked in with these oversized shaded on.

"Damn, where mine at?" she asked selfishly.

Without even looking at Diamond yet, I beckoned for the waitress to come back and let Diamond order her drink along with ordering our food. "Girl, what the hell happened to you?" I asked her as I glanced up from the menu and looked at her face more clearly. Her cheek was discolored and swollen. And the fact that she had sunglasses on told me that she probably had a black eye.

"Chick, I don't even wanna talk about it," she said. "It ain't nothin' I can't handle though. I got it under control." My face must've showed concern because Diamond held her hands up and said, "E, I'm fine. Don't worry."

"Okay, whatever you say, Diamond. "You probably fucked somebody's man again. Anyway," I added, waving her off, "sooo, what happened earlier that was so funny?"

"Girlllllllllllll, I was in the doctor's office and….let's just say I had the best check up everrrrrrr!" she shouted.

"Diamond why the hell are you talking so loud? People starting to stare."

She looked around and scrunched up her face. "Shit, fuck them. Anyway," she continued, "When I got back to the examination room, the nurse told me that my regular doctor had to leave because of a family emergency at home. The fill in doctor was fine as fuck girl!"

Diamond, leaned back, crossed her arms and slightly smirked. Now, it was my turn to get loud. I had known Diamond for a long time so I knew what that look meant. "No you didn't, Diamond! No you didn't screw the man right in the office!" Diamond just shrugged her shoulders. "Nasty, nasty, nasty," I said as I shook my head.

"Whateva homegirl! You know I gots ta get mine on!" Just then, the waitress came back with Diamond's drink and our food. "Damn, about time," Diamond said nastily. The waitress eye-balled us and simply walked away.

"Diamond, are you sure you haven't heard from Angie?" I asked in a more serious tone.

"Uh…no! I told you that earlier." Diamond cocked her head to the side and squinted her eyes. "Why do you keep askin' me that shit, chick? You think I'm lyin' or somethin'?"

"Quit tripping D. Didn't nobody say that you were lying."

"Then why the hell do you keep askin' me about Angie's ass?"

"I was just asking."

Unlike Diamond, I had morals. So when I couldn't look her in the eye, she knew that there was something that I wasn't telling her. Diamond then looked up to the ceiling and bit her bottom lip. Then, after letting her eyes drop to me with an evil glare, she popped her lips and rolled her eyes.

"You just couldn't mind your own fuckin' business could you, Essence?"

"What the hell are you talking about?" I was trying to play it off but Diamond had figured it out.

"Bitch you know what the fuck I'm talkin' about! Some kinda way yo' ass found out that me and J-Bone was messing around and you went back and told Angie's ass! That's why you keep askin' me about her 'cause you figurin' that she probably said somethin' to me about it by now!"

Knowing that there was no sense in trying to deny what Diamond had figured out, I decided to just come clean and see what she had to say. "Okay Diamond, look. The night I came by to check on you after the funeral, I left the coolers in the car. When I double backed to give them to you, I saw J-Bone's truck sittin' out front."

"So fuckin' what? Did it ever occur to you that he just came by to check on me Essence? Yo' ass is always jumpin' to conclusions!"

Now, I was pissed. Not only was Diamond insulting my intelligence, but she was loud talking me in front of the whole restaurant.

"Then how come you didn't tell anybody that he came by Diamond," I asked matching her tone.

"I ain't gotta tell y'all my every fuckin' move! Last time I checked, I was grown, bitch!"

"What? Angie's boyfriend was over your house and you didn't feel the need to share that with Angie? Diamond, you sound like a fool!"

"You know, Essence, fuck you! You always act like you know what's best for everybody else! I'm outta this bitch! You and Angie can both go to hell!"

Before I could respond to her rant, Diamond jumped up and stormed out of the restaurant. I thought briefly about going after her, but I wasn't about to kiss her ass. If she wanted to act like that then screw her too. She was dead wrong but acted like I was the one at fault. Now, I was glad that I told Angie. Patrice's advice about cutting Diamond loose played over and over in my mind. I was getting tired of her antics. I ordered another drink, this time an apple martini, and sat at the table, surrounded by all the food we'd ordered. Twenty minutes passed and I was still sipping on my drink and trying to calm down. I allowed my mind to float back to Gwen again and all that I would do to her when I saw her.

My thoughts had me going crazy, so I hopped up, left forty bucks on the table and rushed out of the restaurant. I was two steps away from my truck when a loud, disgruntled voice called my name. I turned to see who it was and got the surprise of my life. Frantically, I fumbled for my keys, and made it inside just as Cedric started banging on my window. He'd picked up weight over the years, so much that I barely recognized him.

"Essence, what the fuck, girl!" he shouted as I started the car.

The nigga was damn near climbing on top of the truck like some big bear. "What do you want?" I shouted back while my heart raced.

"Yo, you got some answering to do. I got this shit, and I think yo ass gave it to me!"

"What are you talking about?" I belted back, pulling off slowly. I made sure to play things off like I had no idea what he was talking about. I haven't seen you in over four years, Cedric."

"Yo, stop the muthafuckin car. I 'ma kill yo ass bitch. I need you to go with me to the doctor. My girl don't have that shit. It's you! It's you!" he kept shouting.

"Go with you to the doctor for what?"

I saw two people exit the restaurant and head our way. I got so nervous that I hit the gas not caring that Cedric was half-way laying on my windshield. He fell off in no time at all, yelling and ranting behind me.

"I'll get your ass, Essence!"

I hit the highway as the tears fell wondering why I never figured all of this would eventually come back on me.

21

Diamond

By the time I pulled up to my house, I was three times as pissed off as I was when I left Applebee's. I jumped out of my car and walked up on my porch mad as fuck! I still couldn't believe that Essence was all up in my business like that. What Angie didn't know wasn't gonna hurt her ass so Essence shoulda just stayed the fuck out of it. Fuckin' stool pigeon ass bitch! I snatched the mail outta my mail box, opened my door, and stomped inside. As usual, I sifted through the bills playing eenie meenie minie moe, choosing, the only two that would get paid for the month. All others would have to wait until the first of November when my unemployment kicked in. I came across a letter with no return address on it. I thought about just throwin' it in the trash but my curiosity got the best of me, so I opened it. Inside was a folded piece of paper. I unfolded it and my blood pressure shot up to stroke level.

Enjoy your last few days on earth bitch!
Signed, Mrs. Sims.

Before I could relax for even a second, my house phone started ringin'. Although the caller ID said incomplete call, I answered it anyway.

"Hello?"

"Hello, bitch! Suck any dick today?"

"Who the fuck is this?"

"Stop playing dumb, bitch! You know who the fuck this is! I guess you thought this shit was over huh, bitch? Well I got some bad news for your slutty ass! It's just beginning! Did you really think you were going to cause the death of my baby brother, cut my girlfriend, and not have to suffer the consequences? You gotta answer to me now, bitch!"

"Let me tell yo' ass somethin', dyke," I screamed. "First of all, I cared about your brother so you can kiss my ass with that blamin' me shit! Second of all, yo' muthafuckin' threats don't scare me, hoe! Now back the fuck up off of me before I really fuck you and ya dyke ass friend up! Last time I checked, I was slicin' arms! Next time, I'm slicin necks!"

"Fuck you bitch," Kellie yelled in my ear.

"Nah, fuck you hoe," I spat back.

There was no way I was gonna give Kellie the satisfaction of gettin' the last word so I pressed end and hung up in her face. I wish she'd just leave me the fuck alone. I know I expected Darius to defend my honor at the club, but how the fuck was I 'spose to know that nigga was gonna pull a gun out and start cappin'.

"Whateva," I mumbled as I rushed into the kitchen and poured the last corner of my Absolute into a glass, taking it straight to the head. I needed some relief in the worse way, so I picked up my cell and dialed J-Bone's number. When it went to voice mail, I left a sexy seductive message that would get his juices flowing.

"Hey, baby. I was wonderin' if you was gonna let me have some of that sweet, juicy dick later on. When you get this message, give me a call so we can arrange somethin', okay?" I started to moan like I was on the verge of comin'. "See how hot I am baby," I said as I walked over to the living room window and looked out. I turned my head to the right and saw Paul gettin' out of his car and walkin' toward his porch.

He mean mugged me as he was walkin' so I decided that since he wanted to stare, I was gonna give his ass a show. I started unbuttonin' the top of my fitted shirt. When I thought it was unbuttoned enough, I reached in and pulled out my left tit. I continued to moan into the phone as I blew kisses toward Paul and massaged my nipple.

Feeling that I had made my point to J-Bone, I hung up the phone and threw it across the room, landing in pieces on the floor. Then I pulled out my other tittie and licked my lips. By this time Paul had stopped walkin'. Apparently this got to him, cause now he was standin' there poundin' his fist into his hand and noddin' his head. After flippin' him the bird, I turned around and pulled down my booty shorts, giving him my entire ass to kiss. Then I turned back to the window and mouthed the words *nigga you gonna pay* through the glass.

This bitch ass nigga had the nerve to grab his crotch, as if he was tellin' me to suck his dick? Not willin' to let that nigga get the best of this little battle, I held up my thumb and forefinger to show him how small I thought his Johnson was. If looks could kill, I woulda died at that moment. When I felt that I had tortured him enough, I turned and switched away from the window laughing, leaving him to look stupid alone.

****

After takin' a short nap and wakin' back up, I was still pissed off that Essence was tryin' to get in my fuckin' business. What was goin' down between me and J-Bone didn't have shit to do with her nosey ass. I didn't need her to tell me how wrong I was. I already knew that shit. I hated the fact that I was fuckin' one of my friend's boyfriends but for some reason, I just couldn't help it. Every time he put that big ass python in my face, I just had to have some of it. I picked up my phone to see if he had returned my call and saw that he had called twice. I quickly picked up the phone and called him back.

"I see you got my message huh," I said when he answered the phone.

"Hell yeah, and we can definitely do that shit. You

ready?"

"You know it. You know what? Let's be a little adventurous this time. Let's go up to Gordon Park."

"Gordon Park?"

"Yeah. Unless yo' ass is scared, nigga."

"Nah, baby girl, I ain't hardly scared. What time do you wanna hook up?"

"Gimme about an hour."

"Okay."

"Alright then nigga, pop you a Viagra and meet me in there in an hour."

Laughin' at my own joke, I hung up before he had a chance to respond. After takin' a hot shower, I picked out a shirt that I would wear as a dress, stopping just below my butt cheeks. It would give J-Bone the easiest access to my pussy. Wearin' panties tonight would be a no-no since I knew they were gonna be comin' off as soon as I got there. After slidin' the shirt over my smooth legs and clean pussy, I stood in the mirror and admired my body. That's when I decided that I wasn't going to wear a bra either. Like most men, J-Bone was a big tittie man, so maybe I could get him to suck them real good.

After gettin' my hair together, grabbin' my purse, and checkin' to make sure that I had my blade in it, I headed out the door. I didn't even make it past the threshhold before my house phone rang. Figurin' that it was probably that bitch Kellie again, I ignored it and kept on walkin'. I still didn't know how the fuck she got my number though. After checkin' myself one last time, I walked out of my house with my hand inside my purse daring that Impala to pull up. I was ready for whateva popped off.

I didn't know if Paul was watchin' or not, but I didn't wanna take a chance on him attackin' me again. I had a surprise waiting for his ass. I glanced toward his house and when I saw that the coast was clear, I hopped into my ride and pulled out of the driveway. I didn't know why but for some strange reason I was nervous as hell. Thoughts of Kellie, Mrs. Sims, and the unknown person in the Impala kept fucking with my mind. Even though I had quit smoking over a year ago, now was the perfect time for me to light one up. I stopped at the 7-Eleven and picked up a couple of loose cigarettes to calm my nerves. As soon as I stepped out of my car, I got the strangest feeling that I was being watched. I swiftly looked around. Not seein'anything out of the ordinary, my body shook it off. Luckily, there wasn't a long line, and I was back in the car within minutes.

After hopping onto the freeway, and watching for any cars following me,I felt at ease again. I took a deep breath and shook·my head as guilt started to creep in. Everything that Essence said was right and I knew it. "After this, I ain't fuckin' with this nigga no damn more," I mumbled to myself, even though I only halfway believed it. Havin' that strange feeling of bein' followed again, I looked in the rearview mirror and did a double take. The white, Chevy Impala was about three car lengths behind me. I panicked.

"I know this bitch ain't followin' me," I mumbled to myself, thinkin' that it was probably Kellie. I pulled off at the next exit with the Impala right behind me. Then, I pulled back on to the highway real fast, pulling a street move. Just like I thought, so did the Impala, only this time I was able to get a quick look. Indeed it was a woman, but I couldn't make out her face.

"What the fuck? Now, I wish that I had my gun instead of my knife. If bitches wanted me to bring out the hood Diamond, then I would. I slowed down, ready for war. But the confrontation would never come since the dumb bitch got pulled over by a cop. I looked down at my speedometer and saw that I was doing eighty miles an hour. "Deuces, hoe," I said, throwing up two fingers and sped off.

****

With my nipples hard and my pussy wet, I pulled into Gordon Park ready for some stiff dick. After searchin' around for a few minutes, I spotted J-Bone's Tahoe. I pulled up beside it and quickly jumped out of mine. Not one to waste time when it came to getting my freak on, I reached for his dick as soon as I got in the truck.

"Damn, girl, it's like that already?"

"Nigga, you know how I get down."

In less than five seconds, his dick became fully erect. Saliva dripped from the corner of my mouth and landed on the tip of his magic stick, causing it to throb. Supreme satisfaction overtook me as I engulfed his entire shaft and let it slide down my throat. I moaned in ecstasy as the tip tickled my tonsils. Then I grabbed his hand and shoved it under my dress so that he could play with my panty less crotch. I moaned even louder as he stuck two fingers inside my hole.

"Girl, I gotta have some o' this pussy now!" he screamed. Wantin' to feel his manhood inside of me, I un-wrapped my mouth from around his pipe and hopped into the back seat.

"Come on nigga! What you waitin' on?"

J-Bone got out of the driver's side with his dick stickin' straight out. We were both so horny that we didn't give a damn if anybody saw us or not. When J-Bone opened the door, I made sure that the first thing he saw was pussy staring him in the face. With my right leg hung over the front seat and my left leg hung over the back one, J-Bone stared with sheer lust in his eyes. And when I reached down and spread my soaked lips, revealin' the hot pink center of paradise, that nigga lost it. He dove head first into my vagina like he was captain of the swim team.

"That's it nigga, eat that pussy!" He flicked his tongue across my clit so hard that it only took a few seconds for me to get my first nut. "Oh my God," I screamed as I dug my finger nails into his leather seats. I was still cummin' when J-Bone pounced on top of me and shoved his massive meat inside.

I tried to scoot my ass back against the door to relieve some of the poundin' but J-Bone wasn't havin' that shit. He grabbed my hips, forcefully yanked my ass back toward him and continued to assault my helpless womb. This nigga was punishin' the fuck outta my pussy.

"Oohhh yesss!" I yelled as I squirted for the second time.

"I'm about to cum," he declared as he shot an endless stream of semen into my love nest. J-Bone fell backwards onto the door and smiled, knowin' that he had just beat my pussy to death. Still breathin' heavily, I covered my face with both hands so that he couldn't see the tears that had started to well up on my eyes.

"What's wrong Diamond?"

"My life. It's all fucked up. Nobody would even understand," I told him.

"I would. Tell me."

"It's over, J-Bone. I can't see you anymore. I'm for real."

22

Essence

After the night I had, I couldn't wait to hook up with Gwen. Cedric had put so much fear in my heart that I didn't know what to do. I could still see the anger in his eyes, and had even thought about going over to Angie's to hide out for a few days. I still hadn't heard from Angie but at this point, I had too many issues. All I wanted to do was toss back a few glasses of Moscoto and have an orgasm. After going through my closet and taking out some sex toys, I went into the bathroom and ran myself a steaming hot bubble bath. All kind of sexual thoughts ran through my mind as I waited for the water to get ready. I was just about to get into the tub when my cell phone rang. When I looked at the screen and saw private, I let it go to voice mail. It rang two more times while I was in the tub, and a third time once I got out. I was getting tired of hearing it. The fourth time, that it rang I snatched it up to my ear with as much attitude as I could muster.

"Hello." Whoever was calling was seriously screwing up my groove. When no one said anything, it made me angry. "Who the fuck is this?" I screamed.

"Hey, honey."

My heart fluttered. I never expected to hear his voice. Between him and my sister, my sexual identity was all screwed up. "Dad?"

"Yeah, Essence, it's me."

My heart sank slightly. I hadn't talked to my dad in over three months. Yet hearing his voice again caused me to miss him dearly. Although he'd been locked up, away from me most of my life, he'd made it perfectly clear that no matter what the situation was, he would always love me, and would always be there for me. He wanted to make up for lost time.

"Hi honey. How are you doing?" he asked in a concerned voice.

"I'm fine dad," I answered, my voice cracking. He didn't buy it for a second. He could always tell when something was wrong with me.

"Essence honey, don't lie to me. You know you can't pull nothing over on your old man."

I could almost see his toothy grin on the other end of the phone. A single tear rolled down my face as I shook my head and smiled at the fact that my father knew me so well. He was, if fact, the only man on earth that I could honestly say that I still cared about.

"Your health is holding up since we last talked, right?"

"Sorta."

"Sorta? That doesn't sound good. What's wrong?"

"I don't know dad. I guess it's just a combination of things. My two best friends are at each other's throats. I think I've turned into a full-fledged lesbian. And oh, there's this little HIV thing that might turn into AIDS that I'm worried about."

"Are you taking your medication regularly honey?" he asked ignoring my lesbian comment.

"Yes," I replied, making him feel better.

"Just follow the doctor's instructions and everything will work out."

My dad and I had a very open relationship so I felt that I could talk to him about anything. Besides, he'd known about me having HIV for over two years now. "Dad," I said, ready to confess to him about death that I'd been dishing out, "I've been doing something so terrible, I don't think even God would forgive me for it." I went on to tell my father about how I'd been sleeping with every man that I could, trying to infect them with the deadly virus.

"Oh, God! No, baby!"

His words made me feel awful. I simply lowered my head.

"Essence, that's something that you really shouldn't be doing," he said sorrowfully. "Let me put it this way. What if you ever found out that the guy you got it from was doing the same thing that you are doing just because someone gave it to him and you just happened to get caught up in his web? Would you think that he was justified? Or would you hate him for making you pay for someone else's sins?"

As usual, my father had given me something to think about. After admitting to him and myself that he was right, I went on and told him about the mess between Diamond and Angie. Then I got on Tierra. He knew my feelings about my older sister, and what she'd done to me while he was locked down. My father listened with the patience of a licensed shrink. I guess that's why we got along so well. When I finished talking, my father did something that I never expected him to do.

"Essence, I'm sorry," he said.

"Sorry? For what Dad?"

"For not being there for you. I feel like a lot of this is my fault. If I had been a better father to you, then things wouldn't be going bad for you now. Maybe if I would have paid more attention to you two when you were coming up, you and Tierra would have a better relationship."

"No, Dad," I said, stopping him from blaming himself before it went too far. "Don't even blame yourself for the poor choices that I've made throughout my life. There is only one person to blame for this and I see her every time I look in the mirror. And as far as Tierra goes, she did that to me, not you."

Even in his silence, I could tell that my father still harbored some of the blame; mostly for being absent through my

171

younger years.

"I have an idea," he said. "Why don't you come stay with me for a little while? You know, get away from things, clear your head."

"Come on, Dad," I said slightly smiling. "I'm a grown woman and I can't be running home to daddy every time something bothers me."

"Well, okay honey, I won't push you. But you know that you are always welcome in my house."

"I know. Thanks Dad.

"Just do me one favor."

"What's that?"

"Stop infecting people. Practice safe sex. Or just don't have sex at all. I don't wanna lose you."

I smiled. "I love you, Dad."

"I love you too, Essence. Goodbye."

Talking to my father made me feel better. But the simple fact of the matter was that I was so ashamed of my condition that I had inadvertently stepped away from the one person who had always loved me. My mind shifted to Angie for some reason. I still hadn't heard from her. I dialed her number and once again was sent to her voice mail.

"Okay Angie, I'm getting a little nervous now. I've been trying to call you for the last few days. Please call me when you get this message." I pressed end and laid my phone on the sink, hoping to hear from her.

Suddenly, I felt like being spontaneous, living my life to the fullest, like the doctor said. In a dash, I threw on a sexy, black, backless dress that I'd never even worn. I sprayed on some strawberry scented spray to make me smell nice and sweet, and threw a few sex toys in my bag. I headed out the door ready to surprise Gwen. I smiled all the way over to her house thinking about the fun that we were going to have. By the time I got to her house, my coochie was throbbing. I walked up to her door and rang the bell. When Gwen opened the door, her mouth fell open.

"Surprise!" I yelled as I walked right past her and into her living room. As soon as I got there it was my turn to be surprised. A very, dominant looking woman was laying on the couch dressed in nothing but a G-string. I could only assume that it was her girlfriend. "Oh, hello," I said. Even though Gwen had told me that she had a girlfriend, the sight of another woman lying there on her couch still got me a little heated, but I played it off real good. I studied the competition carefully. She was okay looking, just not feminine at all; especially with the boyish hair-cut.

"Essence, what are you doing here?"

"I thought I would come over and surprise you, but it looks like I'm the one who got the surprise."

"I like surprises," the other woman said.

"Essence, this is my girlfriend, Kellie...Kellie this is Essence," she said, introducing us both.

Kellie got up and strutted over to me with a smile on her face, and her small tits shaking. At that moment, I was sure I could steal Gwen away from her. She didn't have shit on me.

"Well, hello Essence," she said seductively. "I've heard a lot about your talents." She tried to grab my hand to lead me over to the couch but I pulled away from her.

"You know, I think I'm going to go," I said, not feeling the group thing.

"Oh baby, you're more than welcome to stay," Kellie said. Then she walked back to the couch, sat down, and spread her legs, giving me a perfect view of her love patch.

"Essence, I told you that I had a girlfriend and if you woulda called, you wouldn't be standing there all pissed off."

"I'm not pissed off," I lied. "I'll call you tomorrow," I said, walking toward the door.

Gwen twisted her lips and folded her arms while Kellie said something that left me spellbound. "Do you know everything there is to know about your girl Diamond? That girl is deadly."

Thoughts immediately began to play ping pong inside

my mind. How did she know Diamond? How did Kellie know that I knew Diamond? Was Diamond gay, too? What the fuck? I was all messed up?

"I'm gone Gwen," I blurted as I opened her front door.
"Fine."

Gwen closed the door behind me like she didn't give a fuck. My heart sank knowing that my new love was about to get pleased by another woman. And my mind continued to race, trying to figure out Diamond and Kellie's affiliation. I quickly hopped into my truck and peeled rubber down the street.

23

Diamond

Thankfully, I ducked just in time. The booming sound of my front window being shattering and glass flying everywhere had me holding my chest and running for cover. Somebody wanted me dead. As soon as the red brick landed on my living room floor, I jetted out front like a cheetah determined to catch the culprit. I was tired of bitches fuckin' with me…tired of being taken for a joke. As soon as my bare feet hit the front lawn, I heard the tires screech. My neck swiveled in every possible direction until I laid eyes on a green, Grand Prix peeling off, running from the scene of the crime. I started shouting, and chasing behind the car like an Olympic runner at top speed. The fact that Mrs. Sims thought she would throw a brick through my window and get away with it was beyond me.

"Come back here, bitch!" I shouted, now running bare foot on the cold pavement.

A few neighbors were out looking at me like some alien running through the streets in grey sweats, with half my ass showing. But I didn't give a damn. My goal was to catch Mrs. Sims' white ass, and beat her to a pulp. But those thoughts were useless. She'd gotten at least a third of a mile ahead of me, and I barely had enough breath to make it back. Finally, I stopped. I huffed for minutes, kneeling down and grabbing my knees wondering why nobody tried to help me.

"Y'all ain't worth shit!" I shouted. "That- that- bitch-threw a-a- a-a a- rock –through- through- my window," I told the bystanders.

I still only received stares. No help. It took nearly five minutes for me to get back to my house where I contemplated calling the police.

I began pacing the floor trying to map out my lies and what I'd actually tell the police when they arrived. I thought about calling Jason until my cell phone vibrated. I looked at the caller ID and started not to answer it. But knowin' my mother like I did, she would just keep calling back. Shit was gettin' hectic. Too hectic for me to handle.

"Ma, what is it?" I snapped.

"What the hell is wrong with you dropping this child off over here? I wasn't even at home and you drop a twelve year old off in a house by herself?"

I huffed. "I'm sorry. I just had something real important to do yesterday. I'ma be by later on and pick her up."

"What time?"

"Gimme about half an hour, I got some crazy stuff going on right now."

"That's it. One hour," she said hangin' up in my face.

After hangin' up from my mother, I spent thirty minutes taking the plastic wrapping off my clothes from the cleaners and using it to cover the hole in my window. It took me damn near a whole roll of duct tape to tape it securely. It still looked a hot mess, but would have to do until I could afford to have the glass replaced. But that bitch was gonna pay, I told myself.

On the way to my mom's house, I started thinkin' about the things that I had gone through in my life that shaped who I turned out to be. The day my Uncle violated me was the day that my life was ruined. Instead of learnin' about how love and sex go together, all I learned was how to love sex. If my mother was any kind of a mother she woulda put a bullet in his head when he got me pregnant. While it is true that I didn't resist at the

176

time because I was a little hot ass, I was still a damn minor. Hell if I had my way, Candice would never be here.

Why the hell would I want a child fathered by my uncle? That was the main reason that I never told anyone about her. I decided today was the day I would confront my mother. I pulled up into her driveway and took a deep breath. This was not gonna be pleasant. In my mind, my mother was just as much at fault as I was. If she woulda done a better job of raisin' me when my dad died then I wouldn't be this way. I hopped out and walked up to the house with my game face on. I prayed to God that Candice was in her room because I didn't want to discuss this in front of her. When and if my mother and I came to an agreement, then we would talk to her about it. Usin' the key that I had been usin' since I was young, I opened the door and strolled into the house. My mother was stiitin' on the couch with a Virginia Slims cigarette hangin' out of her mouth.

"Where's Candice?" I asked dryly.

"Outside with her friends."

"Good."

"There's nothing good about you Diamond, " she said as she looked at her watch and frowned.

"What? What was that comment for?"

"Girl, you was supposed to be here a half hour ago."

"Well, I'm here now." My mother just glared at me for a minute before shakin' her head. "I don't know why you shakin' your head like that. You act like I ain't got nothin' else to do."

"Diamond, you need to start makin' this child a priority in your life."

"Like you did in mine?"

"What the hell is that supposed to mean?"

"You know exactly what it means, Ma. When I was growin' up, I don't remember you spendin' a lot of time with me when dad died."

"Diamond please. Didn't nobody have the energy to be chasin' your hot ass around."

"Oh really?"

"Yeah really! You never listened to nothing nobody had to say, girl!"

"Well, maybe if you woulda took the time to listen to me, instead of gallopin' around with ya boyfriend all the time it woulda made a difference in my damn life!"

"Oh, is that why you chose to try and screw my man? Because you felt that I wasn't listening to you?"

"I was tryin' to get yo' attention, Mama! That's what unwanted little girls do!"

"No, you were trying to get fucked! And now you wanna bring your ass in here and blame me because you're a fucked up mother? You got a lot of fucking nerve!"

"I wouldn't even be a damn mother if you woulda let me get an abortion!"

"Abortion is murder, Diamond, and I didn't want any part of that!"

"Damn, Ma, you act like you was the one havin' the abortion! This ain't yo' body, it's mine! And besides, if I ever did decide to have a baby, I wouldn't want to have one by my damn uncle!"

My mother opened her mouth, but nothin' came out. Stunned silence filled the room.

"You ain't got nothin' to say about that, do you Mama?"

Ignoring the statement about her brother for the moment, my mother bent down and picked up a card from the table. Tears suddenly filled her eyes as she looked at the card and then back at me.

"Diamond, I am truly sorry about that. I had no idea that my brother was molesting you and Charmaine until years later. If I would've known that…"

"Whoa, hol' up! Charmaine? He was fuckin' Charmaine, too?" My mother rubbed her temples as if that was somethin' that she had never intended to let me find out. "Let me get this straight," I said. "He was screwin' both of us and you didn't even have a clue?"

My mother scowled at me.

178

"I didn't know about Charmaine until later," she said through gritted teeth.

"Ooohhh, so I'm not the only nympho in the family, huh," I said, makin' quotation signs with my fingers as I said nympho.

"You know what Diamond? All that shit you're talking has nothing to do with you becoming more active in this child's life! We agreed that when Candice became twelve, you would let her move in with you! Diamond, do you want this child to have a better life or not?"

"Yeah Mama I do, but…"

"Then take this card," she said shovin' it in my hand.

"What the hell is this?" I took the card, looked at it, and started laughin'.

"You know you trippin', right? You want me to go see a sex therapist?"

"Yes."

"And just how the hell is this supposed to help Candice have a better life?"

"Because before you can help her, you need to get yourself together first!"

I opened my mouth, but nothin' came out. For the first time since I had been there, I was at a loss for words. I looked at the card and then back at my mother. After slidin' it into my back pocket, I looked back at my mother and said, "You see, this is why I wanted to get a damn abortion in the first place! I knew having a damn child would bring havoc on my life! Things woulda been much easier if you…"

Before I could say another word, I heard Candice sniflin' from the kitchen. She musta came in through the back door because when me and my mother went to the kitchen she was standin' near the sink cryin'.

"Oh God," I said, rushin' over to her. "Candice baby, I'm sorry. I…"

"Get offa me!" she screamed. "Just leave me alone!"

Candice ran past me and my mother and bolted up the

stairs. I called after her, but she didn't stop. I started up the stair case as Candice ran into her room and slammed the door.

"Damn! How much do you think she heard?" I asked my mother. When she didn't answer, I turned around to see her lookin' at me with a heated expression on her face.

"What? I know damn well you ain't about to blame me for that shit that just happened!"

"Who the hell else am I going to blame," she spat.

"Yo' damn self!"

"What?"

"You the one who asked me to come over here, so you just as much to blame as me!" My mother walked up so close to me that I could smell what she had for breakfast.

"You're a fucked up, sorry excuse for a mother. You know that?"

"Well, I learned from the best!"

Apparently, I went too far 'cause my mother reared back and slapped the taste outta my mouth. But what she didn't know was that I was tired of her shit, too. As soon as my head swung back around, my hand followed it as I returned her slap, with a slap of my own.

"Are you fucking crazy putting your hands on me, Diamond? Girl, I raised your ass!"

"That don't give yo' ass the right to assault me!"

"Get the fuck out!!"

"Gladly mother! You just stay the fuck outta my life!"

I walked out and slammed the door as hard as I could. With Candice on my mind, I cried all the way home.

24

Diamond

I tossed and turned all night thinkin' about Candice; her face, her smile…that innocent look in her eyes. I guess that as long as I wasn't spendin' that much time wit' her, I didn't have to worry about my feelin's gettin' involved. But seein' her run up the steps cryin' like that did somethin' to my soul. Deep inside, I knew that it wasn't my mother's fault. I just didn't want to place the blame where it really lies…on me. "I gotta do a better job of bein' a mother to Candice," I said to myself. I thought about callin' my mother and apologizin' for what went down at her house, but decided against it. It was too early in the mornin' so I promised myself that I would just call her later.

Reachin' over on my dresser, I picked up the card that my mother gave to me. **Dr. Judy Barnett, Therapist.** I took a deep breath and picked up the phone. Quickly, I punched in the numbers before I lost my nerve. It rang several times before someone answered.

"Dr. Barnett's office, may I help you?"

I froze.

"Hello? Whoever you are, it's ok. Take your time. We are here to help."

Apparently I wasn't the first person to freeze up when they answered the phone. Her tone did make me feel a lot better about things though. It gave me the sense that she cared.

"Hi...uh, my name is Diamond Robinson and I got your card from a friend of mine," I lied, "and I was wonderin' if I could make an appointment to see Dr. Barnett."

"Sure. Let me get some information from you and I will pass it on to her. She has three appointments today so she may not be able to call you until tomorrow."

"Okay, thank you."

I gave her the info and hung up. After that, I thought about Essence and Angie. I hadn't talked to Essence in two days, I hadn't talked to Angie since our blowup. I really needed to apologize to both of them too, but especially Angie. I decided I would go over to her house to make amends.

As soon as I got dressed my cell rang. I look at the screen to see some weird number. I wasn't in the mood to be arguin' with Kellie's psychotic ass this mornin' so I let it got to voice mail. She'd been calling throughout the night, causing me to make a mental note to change my number as soon as I got a moment. I walked out the door, closed it, and turned to lock it with my key. At that moment I wanted to find Kellie and break her fuckin' neck. I stood stiff for seconds. Spray painted on my nice, clean door in black spray paint was the sentence '*A slut lives here!*' The bitch had a nerve to sign her name like she was an artist or something.

"Are you fuckin' serious," I screamed. Knowing there was nothin' that I could do about it at this moment, I gritted my teeth and headed to the car. It seemed like the whole world was suddenly against me.

My whole mood had changed. I wanted revenge on Kellie, but had no idea where she lived, so I decided to make a deal with Mr. Sims instead...if he gave me my job back then I wouldn't kill his wife. It took me about twenty minutes flat to get there. My music blasted the entire way listening to every hard core, fuck a bitch up rap song I could find. When I pulled into the lot, I listened to the end of a Nicki Minaj cut with my adrenaline pumping.

I got out, walked into the place like I owned it. "Sup Tracy," I said to the receptionist as I switched by. I could feel her starin' me down from behind so I slowed down to give her a chance to hate just a little bit longer. I hopped on the elevator and rolled my eyes at the corny elevator music that was playin' over the speakers. When I got to my floor and got off, everyone was starin' at me like I didn't belong. I walked over to my cubicle arrogantly, like I couldn't be affected by their sneers. Soon, the smile completely disappeared from my face. All of my shit, from my ink pens to my stapler was packed neatly inside an open box.

"Who touched my shit?" I yelled.

The girl who sat in the cubicle next to me came around and whispered, "I think someone called security on you a few seconds ago."

Without sayin' another word, I quickly stormed into Mr. Sim's office ready to bargain for my job back. I slammed the door shut when he turned to see the anger in my eyes.

"I need my job back and you're going to give it to me!"

"First of all, don't come in here screaming like you've lost your damn mind, Diamond!" I looked around and noticed that some of his shit was packed up, too. "What, Diamond? Did you really think that what happened here last time wasn't going to get back to my boss? I didn't fire you Diamond, he did! And he suspended my ass, pendin' an investigation!"

"Suspended," I screamed. "Ain't that a bitch? Yo' ass gets suspended and I get fired! They probably gonna call yo' ass back, but I guess I'm just shit outta luck, huh?"

"What do yo want me to do, Diamond? Go up there and tell my boss that if he fired you, he's gonna have to fire me, too? I can't do that! I have a family!"

"Oh, so for all that shit that yo' wife talked, I guess she ain't gonna divorce yo' ass huh? You basically get a fuckin' vacation and I just end up gettin' fucked in the ass, again!"

"Diamond I don't know what to fuckin' tell you! I'm sorry that this shit happened but there isn't anything that we can do about it now!"

"Oh it's somethin' I can do about this shit alright!"I walked up to him and lowered my voice so that if anybody was eavesdroppin', they wouldn't be able to hear my threat. "The way I see it, Mr. Sims, is that I was forced to have sex with you at the threat of losin' my job." I stepped back, folded my arms and smirked. Mr. Sims looked at me and just shook his head.

"You would really do that, wouldn't you?" My smile got broader as I raised my eyebrows and shrugged my shoulders.

"Besides, I'm gonna press charges on your wife if you don't help me get my job back. The bitch threw a brick through my front window this morning. I saw her!" I shouted, taking two steps forward. "And she's been following me."

"Well, you know what, Diamond? Do what you gotta do," he said firmly. "So, as of now Diamond you're still fired. Now as for you suing the company, go right ahead. That's between you, the company, and their high powered lawyers."

"I guess so," I said. I wasn't fazed in the least at the mention of lawyers. I was smart enough to know that they would probably settle out of court long before a trial date. Plus from what I'd heard, their unemployment pay was pretty good. Just as Mr. Sims was about to open his mouth and say somethin' else, the door flew open and three guards barged inside. One of the security guards hit me with an upper cut, and the other drug me toward the door.

"Get off me! Get the fuck offa me!"

I finally calmed down when the guard pushed me toward the elevator. The girl that sat next to me brought me my purse and asked me if I was okay.

"Hell yeah, I'm ok! But ain't no way I'ma let these muthufuckas get away with this. I'll see you white muthufuckas in court!"

****

After cussin' out the receptionist, I jumped into my car

and banged my head against the steerin' wheel. Quickly, I leaned back against the headrest and slowly started to realize how my sexual addiction was ruinin' my life. I'd lost my job, my daughter, my friends, and so much more. As much as it hurt to realize, I was in some way responsible for Darius' death. I didn't pull the trigger, but I did put him in a position where he had to defend me. That alone put his life in danger. That didn't mean that I would take Kellie and her mother's shit, but I did feel fucked up about it now.

Tears started to run down my cheeks as I shook my head from side to side. I pulled out of the parkin' lot wonderin' if my life could get any worse. I needed someone to talk to so I decided to call Essence. I was still heated with her for snitchin' on me to Angie, but I really needed a friend at the moment.

"Hello," she said dryly after answerin'.

"Hey, E. What you doin'?

"Nothin'. What do you want Diamond?"

"Well I was wonderin' if I could come over and…"

"Diamond, I really don't want to be bothered with you right now."

I was super shocked; I couldn't even speak.

"Uh…okay, chick…I…"

"Look Diamond. I really don't appreciate the way you acted at Applebee's. And I really don't like who you've become. You embarrassed me in front of the whole damn restaurant! Did you actually think that I was going to let you off the hook this easily?"

"Hol' up, Essence. You snitched on me, remember?"

"Yeah I remember! But that still doesn't give you the right to…You know what Diamond? I don't have the time nor the energy to go through this with you! Goodbye!"

"No Essence wait, please don't hang up! There are some things that I want to tell you!" I thought that she had hung up until I heard her sigh.

"What Diamond? What do you have to tell me?"

"First of all, Essence I want to say that I'm sorry. I was

185

totally wrong for goin' off on you the way that I did. I know now that this whole situation is my fault. Can I please come over? There are a lot more things that I have to get off my chest and I could really use a friend right now."

After a brief pause, Essence answered with a huff. "Diamond, I swear if you ever do that to me again…"

"I won't E. I promise."

Essence made another annoying sound. "What time did you want to come over Diamond?"

"Any time you pick is fine with me E."

"Okay, give me a couple of hours."

"Thanks, oh and could you call Angie and tell her to come, too. I want to apologize to her face to face."

"I'll try. But I still haven't been able to reach her."

****

After hangin' up from Essence, I felt slightly relieved. I couldn't wait to get over to her house and pour my heart and soul out about everything that was happenin' in my life; even the secret that I vowed to tell no one, taking it to my grave. Essence was a true friend and I was gonna make sure that I never hurt her again. After makin' a right off of Warrensville Center Road onto Mayfield, I drove a few blocks and did a double take when I saw Candice at a bus stop sittin' on some boy's lap. He was a short guy, with rough looking braids, appearing to be much older. Her tongue was so far down his throat, she coulda licked his adam's apple. They were in one corner of the bus stop and another young couple in the opposite corner.

"Ah hell nah!" I hung a short right into the parkin' lot of Mr. Hero's and jumped out of my car steamin'. Candice was so wrapped up into the thug, she never even saw me comin'. Now, I knew I hadn't been the best role model for her, but I wasn't about to let her go down the same path that I went down.

"Candice! Girl what the fuck you doin' sittin' on some nigga's lap at a fuckin' bus stop? Yo' ass is supposed to be at school!" Candice jumped up off of thug boy and straightened her clothes. The dude had a hard on and wasn't embarrassed in the least.

"Mom! What are you doin' here?"

"What am I doin' here? What the fuck are you doing here? Ain't yo' little ass supposed to be in school!"

"Don't you know," she said foldin' her arms.

"Girl, who in the fuck do you think you talkin' to like that? Don't get yo' ass beat in front of ya little friend here!"

"I'm just sayin, Ma. You don't really want me. You don't ever ask me how I'm doin' in school or nothin', now all of a sudden when you see me out here instead of being where you think I'm supposed to be you wanna embarrass me."

"What the hell do you mean where you supposed to be? You supposed ta be in school!"

"No, Ma. They're having some kinda meeting today, so we only had to go for half a day."

The boy that was with her put his hand over his mouth and snickered, makin' me feel like a jack ass. I gave his ass a death stare and he quickly cut off his laughter. The other couple pretended to play around on a cell phone.

"Well, if you don't have school then where the hell are you going?"

"To the mall."

"Does your grandmother know that?"

"Yes. She told me that I could go after I got out of school."

"Does she know that you got out of school early?" Her silence told me all I needed to know. "Yeah, that's what I thought." Candice snickered and shook her head, causin' me to lose my temper completely.

"What the fuck is so funny? You disrespect me one more time out here and I'll send you to the mall with a broken leg! Don't try to talk shit to me in front off yo' little friend cause he'll see you get yo' ass beat out here!" The boy acted like he wanted to say somethin', but I shot that shit down real quick.

187

"You are my muthafuckin' daughter and you will respect me! Do you fuckin' understand?" I looked back to see the bus approachin'.

"Yes, Ma, I understand."

Candice then did somethin' that I didn't have an answer for. She walked up on me and leaned in close. "All I'm doing is going to the mall to get me some new shoes. That's all. You know *mother*," she emphasized in an even lower voice, "If you are going to be a mother in public, could you find it somewhere in your heart to be a mother in private, too?"

My daughter then hopped on the bus with her friends. It was at that moment that I realized just how much she needed me.

⦚25

Essence

After hanging up from Diamond, I tried to call Gwen to get a handle on our situation. I was hoping that I could get her to come over for a little while, which is why I told Diamond a couple of hours. Even though I knew Gwen had a girlfriend, my heart wasn't trying to hear that. I wanted her all to myself and I needed to find some way to make that happen. I didn't know if Diamond and Angie would understand or not, and I really didn't care. I was in love and would do what made me happy. Gwen didn't answer so I left her a message.

"Hi, Gwen. I just wanted to call and apologize for the way I acted last night. You did tell me that you had a girlfriend and it was childish and immature of me to behave that way. Let me make it up to you. Give me a call when you get this message."

Two minutes later a text message came through.

'Thank u 4 apologizing. I was a lil put off by the way you acted last nite. Don't even no if me n Kellie will last. Let's have fun 4 now n let the chips fall where they fall. I'll call after work.

I was still slightly jealous of Kellie but if I wanted to continue to see Gwen then I was going to have to hide the fact that I was. Hell, I was just happy that she said that she would call me later. I hated to admit it, but Gwen had turned me all the way out. I no longer had any interest in men….didn't even want to infect them anymore. The only thing that a man could do for me now was introduce me to his gay sister. I texted her back and told her that she didn't have to worry about me getting jealous anymore and that I would be looking forward to her call. As soon as I sat my phone back down, Diamond called sounding frantic.

"Chick, I know you told me a couple of hours but I need to come over now!"

"Huh? What's wrong Diamond?"

"Girl, I just…Essence I just need someone to talk to before I fuckin' explode. I just got the craziest call and you the only one that I feel comfortable talkin' to about my business like this." Hearing Diamond talk like this had me a little concerned.

"Okay, girl, come on now."

"Thanks. I'm on my way."

I had no idea what the hell was going on with Diamond but whatever it was had her spooked. I went to the refrigerator and poured us both a glass of wine. From the way Diamond was sounding, she needed something for her nerves. When Diamond arrived she kept twisting up her face and shaking her head.

"Okay, Diamond, tell me what's going on," I said, giving her the glass of wine. Diamond took a deep breath, drank some of the wine and started talking.

"Let me start off easy. Then I'll tell you what's really troubling me."

"So talk."

After Diamond told me the story of how she set it up for her boss to get caught screwing her, I asked her the obvious question. "Diamond, why would you do some dumb shit like that?" My friend had gotten way too reckless with her lifestyle and it was starting to piss me off. The stuff that she was doing just wasn't making any sense.

"I honestly don't know what I thought Essence. I know

190

that it was stupid on my part. I mean, at the time, all I was thinkin' about was how excitin' it would be to play with fire." For the first time since I had known Diamond, I started to pity her.

"Diamond, I don't know what to say."

"I know, right?" I sat there for a minute waiting to see if she was going to tell me the big news. She's the one who wanted to come over so I figured she wasn't about to get quiet now.

"Diamond." She held up her finger indicating that she wanted me to give her a minute. Apparently coming clean was harder than she thought it would be.

"Essence, it's a lotta shit that you and Angie don't know about me. For one…I have a sister."

"A sister," I said trying to act surprised.

"Yeah, her name is Charmaine. She's a few years older than me."

"Wow, Diamond, how come you've never told me and Angie about her?"

"Cause we don't get along and plus it never came up. I hate her ass with a passion and the feeling is mutual." She paused before saying, "I also have a child."

"Whoa, wait a minute Diamond, what did you say? Did you just say that you have a child?"

"Yeah, I did."

I was trying to look surprised, but I didn't think that I was doing a very good job. I was glad that Diamond's head was down or she would've seen my guilt. We both sat there quiet for a few seconds. Then I figured that if I wanted to know anything about this child, I'd better ask.

"What's her name?"

"Candice," she said softly.

"That's a pretty name." Diamond smiled at my comment. "How old is she?" This question seemed to wipe the smile off of Diamond's face.

"She's twelve."

"Twelve," I repeated. *Now, that I didn't know.*

"Yeah, I had her when I was thirteen."

"Damn, D!"

"Yeah, I know."

"Well, I still don't quite understand why you didn't tell us that you had a sister, or about Candice."

"Actually, it's because of her father."

"Oh, he must be an asshole."

"It goes deepa than that."

"Spit it out."

"Essence, before I tell you this, you have to promise not to judge me."

"Diamond, I'm not in any position to be judging any-one," I said, thinking about my secret lifestyle.

"Whew." She paused and took a deep breath. "My daughter's father is my uncle, my mother's brother."

I was speechless for seconds. Then I had to ask her again to make sure that I had heard her right.

"Your uncle? Your blood uncle? As in your mother's brother?" Tears rolled down Diamond's face as she silently nod-ded. "Oh my God!"

"That's not all E. I got this crazy call earlier, from this guy's family who I used to date. They told me he died E."

I couldn't make the connection but could tell from the fear in Diamond's eyes that she had something to do with it. "I don't understand, Diamond. You gotta tell me everything."

Just then, somebody knocked on my door. Startled by the knock, Diamond jumped, causing her purse to fall out of her lap and onto the floor. I did a double take when I saw the familiar bottle of pills roll across the floor. Diamond tried to hurry and pick them up, but I had already seen the label. My mouth got as dry as the Sahara when I saw the medication name Viread in the bottle. My eyes popped to the front of my lids. I was shocked. Spellbound, I had at least twenty questions for her. I stormed over to the door ready to tell whoever was at the door that they were going to have to come back. I was so shaken at seeing that bottle, that I didn't even bother to look out the peephole.

When I opened the door, J-Bone walked straight in. I was so out of it from seeing those pills roll around on the floor, that I didn't even think to ask J-Bone why he was there. I was still staring into space when Diamond came out of the bathroom, and J-Bone began speaking. She probably had no idea that I knew what that medication was for.

"I...I got a call a few hours ago from the Police Department. They told me that they were calling my phone because it was the last number that was dialed from Angie's phone." Water glistened up in the corners of J-Bone's eyes. "They told me that Angie had been in a car accident. She gone E. Angie is dead."

Diamond started shaking so badly that J-Bone had to sit her down on the love seat.

"Oh God no! Oh God no!" She looked over at E, shaking uncontrollably.

J-Bone reached down and grabbed her. My head started to spin as I was being hit with a double dose. I still hadn't wrapped my mind around the fact that one of my best friends had HIV like me, and my other one was gone forever. I shook my head slowly from side to side trying to come to grips with what was going on. After the shock subsided, all three of us sat in my living room mourning the loss of our dear friend. I looked up at J-Bone and saw that he had a strange look in his face.

"You know, the Police said something about being sorry for both of my losses. I was in shock about Angie at the time so it didn't click in mind to ask him about it." Diamond and I looked at each other and she broke down crying again. I walked over to J-Bone and placed my hand on his shoulder. There was no easy way to tell him what I was about to tell him.

"I'm so sorry, J-Bone. When the officer said he was sorry for both of your losses, he was talking about Angie and her unborn child. She was pregnant with your baby J."

"Oh God," J-Bone cried out as he put his head in his hands.

Tears flowed down my face as I did my best to hold him

and Diamond together. Diamond started beating on the arm of the love seat screaming, "I'm sorry Angie." As bad as I felt for J-Bone, I had to go over and comfort Diamond. She was really starting to lose it.

"It's cool, D," I said softly.

"No, you don't understand," she said. "A couple of days ago, we got into a big argument. She stormed out of my house really upset."

I didn't say a word. I knew exactly why she was upset, but now was not the time to be bringing it up. Diamond got up and walked over to J-Bone and put her hand on his shoulder. Something told me that it was a bad idea for her to do that, so I walked over beside her.

"J-Bone, I'm sorry. I'm so…"

"Get the fuck offa me!"

Diamond jumped back as J-Bone started after her.

"J-Bone don't," I screamed as I got in between them. "Let's all calm down. We're all hurting," I said through light sniffles.

"You know what bitch?" J-Bone pointed at Diamond. "All of this shit is your fault! Stay the fuck away from me Diamond!" J-Bone then forcefully pushed me out of the way and grabbed Diamond by the collar.

"And when I say stay away from me Diamond, I fuckin' mean it!"

I tried to pull J-Bone's arm off of her, but he was like a raging bull.

"I swear to God Diamond, if you ever come around me again, I'ma break yo' fuckin' neck! I swear! I really mean it!" J-Bone then stormed out, leaving Diamond crying and gasping for air.

26

Diamond

I hadn't slept even thirty minutes all night. Right after I left Essence's house yesterday, I called my mother and told her that Candice would have to stay over there for the night. I told her that it was truly an emergency and I would explain it to her in the morning. Of course she didn't believe me, and called me every name but a child of God.

I put my mother out of my mind for a while. All I could think about was Angie. Every time I closed my eyes, I saw her face, repeatedly asking me why. Why did I violate her friendship, she wanted to know. It was killing me. The worse part of all was that, in a sense, J-Bone was right. I was somewhat responsible for her death. Maybe if I woulda came clean with her when she came over and confronted me about me and J-Bone, then this tragedy would not have happened. We mighta got into a bigger fight, but at least she would have still been alive. My sexual addiction was startin' to cost me everything that I loved. If I knew all this shit was gonna happen, I woulda tried to get some help a long time ago. But I honestly fooled myself into thinkin' that what I was I doin' was harmless. I honestly thought that I was only having a little fun. That no one would get hurt.

And now, because of my screw-up's, Angie was no

longer alive. Sittin' up on the edge of the bed, I used my arms to steady myself. Then I stood up and made my way to the bathroom. It felt like my legs were going to give out on me. After makin' it to the bathroom, I leaned against the sink and stared into the mirror. For the first time in my life, I hated my own reflection. The fact that my face became puffy and swollen from cryin' had nothin' to do with it either. For the first time in my life I saw the reflection of a manipulative monster. After washin' my face, I went back to the bedroom and took the first step toward makin' me a betta person. Pickin' up the card that my mother gave me, I stared at it for a second. Then I picked up my house phone and dialed the number to the therapist. I know the receptionist told me that she would give the Doctor my info and have her get back to me, but I was desperate to start gettin' my life turned around.

"Judy Barnett's office," the polite receptionist answered.

"Yes, my name is Diamond Robinson and I called yesterday to see about makin' an appointment to see Dr. Barnett."

"Yes, Miss. Robinson, I remember you. The Doctor will be here in about ten minutes. I see here that you are the first call on her list, so she will more than likely be giving you a call in the next twenty minutes or so. I've given her your information and she's read over it but she will probably still want to ask you a few questions over the phone before she sets up an appointment for you to come in."

"Sounds good," I said. "I'll wait for her call."

After hangin' up, I noticed that my stomach was growlin'. I hadn't had anything to eat in over fourteen hours and my stomach was startin' to let me know it. After fixin' me a bowl of Frosted Flakes, I plopped down on the couch. I turned the television on and the commercial that was playin' caused me to burst into tears. A Johnson and Johnson baby powder advertisement was showin' and just seein' that made me think about Angie's unborn baby. I immediately changed the channel, tryin' to find anything that would take my mind off of losin' Angie for the moment. The room was kinda dark so I went to the window and opened up the curtains. Bright sunlight splashed through and into my face. I glanced to the left and saw Paul about to get into his car. He stopped when he saw me standin' in the window. I had on a silver night gown that showed off my hips and tits so I knew exactly what his ass was thinkin'.

He shot me a weird look, just standing and staring like a robot. I was gonna give his ass a nice little peep show. I started by rubbin' my right hand between my legs and pinchin' my nipple through my gown with the left one. Paul became mesmerized, like he was frozen in that one spot. Then I opened my gown ever so slightly so he could get just a glimpse of my treasure chest.

After finger fuckin' myself for couple of seconds, I raised my hand to my mouth and rubbed it around on my lips just before insertin' it into my mouth. I could almost see his hard on pokin' through the other side of his car. The phone rang and snapped me out of my nymphomaniac state. I cursed for allowin' myself to lose control like that. The goal was to leave all that mess behind.

"Oh man, I gotta do a betta job of controllin' my urges," I mumbled to myself. I picked up the phone and was pleased to see that the doctor had called me back so soon. I know the receptionist said the next twenty minutes but I really wasn't expectin' it.

"Hello, Miss Robinson. This is Doctor Judy Barnett. How are you doing today?"

"To tell you the truth, I'm not doin' so good." Dr. Barnett didn't sound at all like I thought she would sound. I expected her voice to be much lower than it was, sorta sexy since she was a sex therapist. Just the opposite, her voice was a high pitched soprano.

"Oh, I'm sorry to hear that Miss. Robinson. I have looked over your info and normally I would conduct a phone interview but I really don't see a need for it. I have an opening tomorrow at one o' clock. Do you think you can make it?"

"Yes, I can make it."

"Good. I will see you then."

I hung up the phone feelin' much betta about myself. This was the first step to gainin' back control of my life. And hopefully my sexual urges, too. The next thing that I had to do was call my mother and apologize to her for disrespectin' her. Now that I had got the call to the therapist out of the way, callin' my mother seemed much easier. "Hey Ma," I said with as much sorrow in my voice as I could when she answered the phone. I wanted her to know right off the bat how sorry I was for what happened. My mother hesitated for a second before acknowledgin' that it was me on the other end.

"Hey," she said, dryly.

"Ma, I just wanted to apologize to you for what happened the other day. I realize now how my addiction is screwin' up my life and everybody around me and I just wanted to let you know that I called the number you gave me and talked to the therapist."

"You did?" My mother seemed to perk up when I told her that.

"Yeah. I made an appointment to see her tomorrow. I'm going to try to do better, Ma. I swear."

"That's great Diamond! Now you can start being the mother to your child that she deserves!"

I got quiet for a few seconds as my thoughts drifted to Angie.

"Diamond? You there honey?"

"Huh? Oh yeah, I'm here. I was just thinkin' about my friend Angie."

"Who?" As soon as she asked that question, I knew right then that me and my mother needed to be more involved in each other's life. I know that she had seen Angie before 'cause I remember her being there twice when my mother dropped by. But the fact that she didn't know her well told me we didn't interact enough.

"Angie. She was there when you came over the last time."

"I'm sorry, Diamond, I don't remember her. What about her though?"

"She was killed in a car crash a few days ago. That was the emergency I had the other day.

"Oh my God, Diamond, I'm so sorry! Why didn't you tell me that the other day?"

"I didn't find out until yesterday."

"Oh my God. Honey I'm so sorry. Have you heard anything about the arrangements yet?"

"Not yet. Angie's parent's live out of town, so I just have to wait and see how they wanna handle it."

"Oh My Goodness. This is awful." There was a slight pause and then my mother dropped something on me. "Honey, I know that we have been at odds lately, but why didn't you tell me that Darius had gotten killed?"

Now, I was speechless. It's not like I was tryin' to keep that from my mother, it's just that we didn't have that kind of relationship where I felt like I wanted to talk to her about it. Talkin' to my friends about it was all I needed.

"I'm sorry, Ma. Wit' everything that was happening between us, I just didn't bring it up. How'd you find out?"

"His mother stopped by here and…"

A lump formed in my throat.

"Ma! Did you say his mother stopped by your house?"

"Yes. Is there something wrong? I mean, I know you two dated back when you were younger, so when she asked for your number I didn't see the harm in giving it to her. She asked for your address, too."

Now, I knew how Kellie got my phone number. "Damn, my address," I mumbled with frustration. If I wanted to turn my life around completely then I was gonna have to start being honest about everything with my mother. "Hol' on one second ma," I said as my other line beeped.

"Hello?"

"Hello Diamond?"

"Yes?"

"Hi, this is Doctor Wright. How are you doing today?"

"I'm fine," I said after hesitating a little. I knew why she was calling but I honestly didn't want to hear it.

"Listen Diamond, you really need to come in. Your CD4 blood cells have fallen to dangerous levels.

"Yeah alright," I said with a tude, "I'll come through tomorrow." Then I hung up so they couldn't say anything else. I had what the fuck I had and there wasn't shit I could do about...so why worry about it. Rememberin' that I had my mother on the other line, I clicked back over.

"Ma, there are some things that I think you should know, but I don't wanna tell you over the phone, okay? I'ma stop by later and tell you."

"Uh...okay, honey," my mother said, soundin' nervous. "Be careful out there."

27

Essence

Every time I closed my eyes, I saw Angie's face. There was no way in the world that I was going to be able to work like this. If I stayed here I was going to end up making a mistake that could cost someone their health. I went to my supervisor and told her that I was sick and that I needed to go home. She immediately told me to leave.

"Off the record, I really don't know why you came in today, Essence. If it was me, I would've called off," my boss told me. Then she gave me a hug and told me to take care of myself. Whispering in my ear, she said "Since you and Angie were cousins, you know you can stay off tomorrow too if you want. She stepped back and gave me a quick wink of the eye followed by a smile.

"Thanks, Regina."

On the way out people who I didn't see when I came to work, stopped me and told me how sorry they were about my friend. The news seemed to be traveling fast and I wanted to get out of there before I broke down again. Just as I was about to get on the elevator, Jennifer, one of my long time co-workers told me she had been calling my extension all morning.

"What's up?" I asked, attempting to press the down button again.

"My brother told me to tell you he needs to talk to you ASAP."

I stalled for moments. "Ahhhhhh, about what?"

Jennifer shrugged her shoulders and I just got quiet. Her brother and I had fucked about two years ago, so I hoped it had nothing to do with him and HIV. "Just call him," she ended as I hopped on the elevator.

I got downstairs, and hopped in my truck as fast as I could crying my eyes out. It seemed like all my bad deeds were beginning to come back to haunt me. I called Diamond to check on her and to get some sympathy. I didn't call this morning because I wanted to give her some time to mourn alone.

"Hey, chick," she said, answering the phone.

"Hey, Diamond. Are you okay?"

"Not really, but I'm getting' there. Have you heard anything else from J-bone regarding the funeral?"

"No, I haven't." An awkward silence filled the line as my mind went back to J-Bone attacking Diamond. It was clear that he blamed her.

"Essence?"

"I'm here, D."

"Essence, I don't care what happened the last time I saw him, I'm going to that funeral whether he likes it or not."

"I know, D. But listen, we really need to talk. I just left work and I was wondering if you wanted to meet me at my house so we can toast to our dear friend."

"That's a good idea, E. I'm on my way with a bottle now." Right then I knew I'd take the opportunity to question Diamond about the bottle that dropped out of her purse.

"D, you know…we have so much more in common than just the loss of Angie."

"What do you mean?"

"I mean we got the same problems," I hinted. I paused trying to figure out the best way to convey my thoughts. Diamond, what kind of pills fell out of your purse the other day?"

"Oh, that wasn't nothing, girl."

202

"Really? What were they for," I pressed.

"I'll tell you later, girl."

"Diamond… I mean we are friends and you would tell me if you were really sick, right?"

"Quit playin', you know I would tell you."

Although I was pissed at her dishonesty, I decided to let it drop for the moment. "Okay, I'll meet you at the house."

After hanging up from Diamond, Gwen sent me a text message telling me that she wanted to come by when she got off from work. I made a mental note to try and have Diamond gone before she got there. With all that was going on, now wasn't the time to reveal my alternate lifestyle to her. Ten minutes later, I pulled up in my driveway. No sooner had I gotten out of my truck, I saw Diamond coming down the street, balling like she was headed to put out a fire. I waited for her to get out of her car and as soon as she walked up to me, we embraced each other in a sisterly hug. We needed each other badly.

"How you be chick?" she asked.

"I'm alright, what about you?"

Diamond just shrugged her shoulders, letting me know that she could be doing better. We walked into the house and Diamond plopped down on the couch.

"Let me go get us some glasses and something to mix that with," I said. I came back into the living room and Diamond looked as if she was in a daze. Then she dropped her head and a tear hit the floor.

"E, do you think that Angie knew that I loved her?"

"I know she did D. We may have had our differences, but we always got through them and this was going to be no exception."

I didn't have the heart to tell Diamond what Angie had told me when I blew the whistle on her. That she hated her guts and that they would never ever be friends again. The betrayal had hurt Angie much more than it made her angry. I poured both of us some vodka in a glass but when I got ready to mix the cranberry juice with it, Diamond took her glass to the head. She didn't cough or nothing. She just held out her glass for a refill. When she tried to toss it back again, I stopped her.

"No, Diamond. You don't need to be drinking that stuff straight like that." I poured some cranberry juice into her glass and for the first time since Angie's death, I could clearly see the guilt etched on her face. My cell phone rang and a number came up that I didn't recognize. I took a chance and answered it anyway.

"Hoe, you know I found out where you work," the voice belted.

I hopped up and began pacing the floor. My chest heaved up and down as I asked the question, "Who is this?"

"Bitch, this Cedric, the man your nasty ass decided to fuck and give HIV to."

"I think there's been a mistake," I said calmly.

"Nah bitch. The mistake was you not letting me know what you had."

I rushed into my back bedroom so Diamond couldn't hear me. "Cedric, you gotta know that I didn't know. I mean that."

The next thing I knew the line went dead and Diamond was calling my name.

"What?" I asked her when I waltzed back into the living room. Suddenly, my phone rang again. I shrieked then looked down at the number. I recognized it this time.

"Hey, what's up Essence? How you doing?"

In my eyes, J-Bone was just as responsible for Angie's death as Diamond was. "Fine, and you," I responded.

"I'm makin' it. Look the reason that I called you was to let you know that Angie's mother flew her body back to her home town and had her cremated."

"What?"

"Yeah, she called me today and told me. I asked her how come she didn't let us know that she was gonna do that and she went the fuck off. Told me that it was all of our faults in the first place that her daughter and grandchild were dead. It took everything in me to keep from cussin' her ass out!"

And it's taking everything in me to keep from cussing you out, I thought to myself. The only thing that was keeping me from doing that was that I knew that he was suffering, too.

"Okay. Thanks for telling me."

J-Bone went on rambling about how Angie's mother had talked to him, but I had tuned him out. I kept thinking about the previous caller and how my life was now in danger. Finally, J-Bone said he had to go but would come by later. *Thank God he was getting off but I prayed he wouldn't come by!* I politely hung up the phone and moved closer to Diamond. The minute I sat down beside her, she could tell that something was wrong. I placed my arm around her neck.

"What's goin' on E?"

"That was J-Bone." My facial expression saddened. "He said that Angie's mother flew Angie's body back to her home-town and had her cremated."

"What!" You mean to tell me that we ain't even gonna get a chance to say goodbye to our friend?"

I couldn't even speak. I just shook my head. Diamond burst into tears. I grabbed Diamond and wrapped my arms around her tightly, squeezing her to the point that she felt un-comfortable. I had no idea what to say to her. It was obvious that she was feeling guilty about Angie's death. I held her for the better part of five minutes as she cried and called Angie's name. When she was done, she sat up and wiped her tear-stained face.

"Hey, go get them pictures we took when we went to the club a couple of months ago," Diamond said smiling. Her sad memories seemed to be replaced by memories of joy. I got up and went to my bedroom. When I came back, I had six photos of me, Angie, and Diamond kicking it at the Mirage nightclub in downtown Cleveland.

"Damn, chick, why you keeping 'em in yo' bedroom?"

"No particular reason. I just took them in there the other night and laid them on the dresser. I'm definitely going to put them out here now though." As Diamond was looking at the pictures, I thought about the secrets that had come between the three of us and how they had destroyed our friendship. Then I thought about all the stuff that Diamond had told me about her past life and figured that now would be the perfect time to tell her about my alternative lifestyle. Grabbing the pictures from her hand, I sat them on the table and looked at her.

"Diamond, there's something that I have to tell you about me. But when I'm done you have to tell me everything there is to know about you. Everything."

"Bet."

"We have to start being real, true friends...but I'll start. I'm in a new relationship, D."

Diamond's mouth flew open at my news. "You bitch! Been gettin' you some new dick huh?"

"Not exactly," I said as I stood up slowly, pacing back and forth.

"Not exactly? What the fuck does that mean?"

Gathering up all the courage that I could muster, I stopped pacing put my hands on my hips and spit it out. "Diamond, I'm bi-sexual!"

Diamond closed her eyes and shook her head from side to side. "Excuse me?"

"I said I was bi-sexual."

"As in you eat pussy now?"

"Yes, Diamond. I eat pussy, carpet munch, deep sea dive, whatever you want to call it, ok?"

"What the fuck," she said gazing at me like I had two heads.

Neither of us said a word for a few seconds. Diamond was just sitting there staring at me, and I stared right back. If Diamond wanted to remain friends then she was going to have to accept the choice that I had made.

"Wait, wait, wait! What I wanna know is…what bitch pussy you been eatin'," she said as she burst out laughing. "Hol' up. Before you answer that, I gotta go pee."

Diamond got up and started walking to the bathroom.

She looked almost zombie-like as she walked toward the back. As soon as she closed the bathroom door, I looked at the picture of me, Diamond, and Angie with our arms draped around each other and the tears that I had been holding for the last couple of hours came cascading down. I jumped when I heard the door bell ring. It rang back to back a few times. Thinking that it was J-Bone, I got up more than prepared to tell him that he wasn't invited to our mourn Angie session. I know he was hurting too, but this was for me and Diamond. I opened the door and was shocked to see Gwen standing there.

"Hey, baby," she said, strolling inside without an invite. Seeing my reddened face, she asked me if I was okay. Right then it occurred to me that I hadn't had a chance to tell Gwen about Angie.

"No, not really," I said completely forgetting about Diamond for the moment. "A very good friend of mine got killed a few days ago."

"Oh my god, Essence I'm sorry to hear that." She leaned in to kiss me on the lips. I pulled back, walking away slightly.

"Yeah. it's really been rough on me and my other friend." Still holding the picture in my hand, I walked over to Gwen and held it up.

"Yep, these are my girls."

Instantaneously, Gwen's whole expression changed. Her nostrils flared and her back stiffened. Simultaneously, I heard the toilet flush. Gwen looked at me with fire in her eyes.

"Is something wrong?" I asked, leaning back.

All of a sudden, Gwen looked like she was ready for war. I didn't know what was going on and didn't want to take any chances, so I backed up a little bit. Gwen quickly put her finger on the picture and drug it back and forth between Diamond and Angie. "These two bitches are your fuckin' friends?"

"Uh…yeah, do you know them?"

Just then Diamond walked back into the living room. She took one look at Gwen and stopped dead in her tracks. "Ah hell nah," she screamed. "What the fuck this bitch doin' in here?"

"No, what the fuck are you doing in here?"

The two women started toward each other and I quickly stepped in between them. "Hold up! What the he'll is going on here?" I asked them both.

"This here is one of the bitches me and Angie got into it with at Darius' funeral!"

"And this is the bitch that cut me! Bitch, I'm about to fuck you up!"

My eyes grew so wide they almost popped from my head. *How could I have been so stupid*, I asked myself. I started banging on my own forehead thinking about the many times that Diamond mentioned Darius's sister Kellie. Then I thought back to when I met Kellie at Gwen's. I just never put the two together. So…so…so stupid, I kept saying as Gwen began inching her way toward Diamond.

Diamond finally kicked off her shoes. "Don't talk me to death! Essence, let that bitch go!"

"Fuck you hoe," Gwen spat as I pushed her back against the wall. "Gwen hold up. I was at the club the night Darius got shot. It wasn't Diamond's fault," I said calmly, hoping to talk some sense into her.

"Essence, I know that. But Kellie is my girlfriend and I gotta ride with her. She think's that Diamond is at fault so what am I supposed to do?"

"Wait a minute," I said, backtracking the years. "Me and Diamond were friends when she was dating Darius and I don't remember him having a sister."

"That's because she didn't stay with them. She stayed with their father." Gwen then stared into my eyes. My heart started to break because I had feeling that I knew what she was about to say.

"Essence…"

"Gwen baby, don't say it. We can work this out."

Gwen just shook her head. "Essence, maybe it's best if we just don't see each other…"

"No, Gwen!"

"Essence look… Ahhhh, shit!" Before she could get the last word out of her mouth, Diamond had reached around me and slashed her across the arm.

"Diamond, stop! What the hell are you doing?"

Gwen attempted to run for the door, but Diamond stuck her leg out and tripped her before I could react. Before Gwen could get up, Diamond was on her. I panicked then rushed toward them both. I saw a rage in Diamonds eyes that I had never seen before. Knowing that if I didn't do something soon, Gwen would more than likely get stabbed multiple times.

The struggle went on for minutes until Gwen rolled over on her back just in time to see Diamond pounce on top of her, pinning her down. Dreadfully, Diamond stuck the knife up to Gwen's neck. Gwen caught her arm just as the blade started to press down against her skin. My feet felt as heavy as cement as I made my way between the tussling women. Blood had begun to trickle down Gwen's neck. Diamond kept pushing the blade deeper, scaring the shit outta me. She had snapped. She was going to kill Gwen.

"Diamond, get the fuck off of her! Please don't do this! Please!

I grabbed Diamond around the neck and forcefully pulled her off of Gwen. With all the strength I had in my body, I slung Diamond to the floor.

She hopped up with her shoulders back, and her chest heaving up and down. "Oh so it's like that now, chick? You gon' take this bitches' side over mine?"

"Diamond, calm the fuck down! What the hell was I supposed to do, let you kill her?"

"Hell muthafuckin' yeah! Fuck that bitch!"

I looked into Diamond's eyes and saw a total stranger. I didn't know who the hell I was looking at but I didn't want to know this person at all. "Diamond…Get out."

"Oh fo' real? You gon' dis me over a piece of pussy. You just started lickin' this bitch. We been down for years."

"Diamond, get your crazy ass the fuck out of my house!"

"You know what, fuck you then! And this ain't over with bitch!" she told Gwen who was still stretched out on the floor. "If I see yo' ass on the street, I'm fuckin' you up! Believe that!"

Diamond stormed out the door. I knew right then that I had lost another friend for life.

28

Diamond

Ain't this a bitch? How the fuck Essence gon' side with that bitch over one of her home girls? After I told her ass how them tramps tried to play me and Angie at Darius' funeral, she shoulda been helpin' me kill that bitch. My mind flipped back to when I saw that bitch in Essence's living room. I just snapped. All the frustration and pain that I been feelin' the last few days just came the fuck out. I knew one thing... I would give Essence one more shot, but she was gonna have to make a choice. Either she gonna be cool with me or cool with them hoes.

Just thinking about Kellie and Gwen got me even more stressed than I already was. Knowing just what I needed to calm my nerves, I grabbed my cell phone off the night stand to call J-Bone, hoping he'd answer my call. Images of his dick popped into my head, makin' me weak. Throwin' my head back, I reached between my legs and rubbed my pussy. I picked up my cell and dialed his number. He didn't answer at first, so I called back. And again. I needed to get off in the worst way, and I did-n't feel like doin' it myself.

"Yeah," he answered.

"Hey, sweet thang. I was wonderin' if you felt like givin' a bitch some of that dick today. I'm hot as fuck over here."

When he didn't say anything, I smiled. Usually, he would

hesitate 'cause he wanted me to beg a little. As horny as I was, I was glad to oblige him. "Baby, I know I told you we were done, but I didn't mean that shit. You know I didn't. Please baby. I feel like swallowing today," I said nastily.

"Bitch! The only thing I feel like givin' yo' muthafuckin' ass is a bullet! And I thought I told you to leave me the fuck alone! You the reason that I'm not gonna be a father! What, you though I was fuckin' playin' when I told you to stay away from me? Well I wasn't Diamond! I told you to leave me the fuck alone and I meant it! Fuck you and fuck ya' dry ass pussy. Now stay the fuck away from me before I fuck you up!"

J-Bone hung up in my face and left me speechless. I couldn't believe that he talked to me like that. I knew that I had a meeting with the therapist later, but my pussy was so hot, it was burning my leg. I ran back into the bedroom and grabbed the biggest vibrator I had in my closet. Then I jumped on the bed and spread my legs wide.

"Oooo, now that's what I'm talkin' 'bout," I moaned out loud as I plunged the black twelve inch substitute dick into my womb. My pussy had a level 10 fire going on. I thought it would melt the rubber. I hadn't bust a nut in a couple of days and was way overdue. I knew that I needed to change my ways but at least I wasn't out ridin' some random dick. It didn't take long as my sweet love juice drowned the sheets. Feelin' satisfied, I laid back and took a nap until it was time for me to go see the therapist.

****

The first thing that stood out to me when I got to Dr. Barnett's office was the Mercedes Benz that was parked in the front. *Damn, this bitch must be makin' big paper*, I thought.

I walked into the ranch style office and looked around. The place was spotless with wall to wall beige carpet, two cream colored leather recliners and a leather couch of the same color. The walls were decorated with plagues of Dr. Barnett's achievements. The receptionist had her back turned to me as she was searchin' through a file cabinet. When she turned back around and saw me, she gave me a warm smile. I loved the fact that she'd colored her hair bright red. Instantly, I felt like this was the place that I needed to be.

"Hello, may I help you?"

"Yes, I'm Diamond Robinson. I talked to Dr. Barnett earlier. She told me that she had an openin' in her schedule today."

"Oh yes, Miss. Robinson. It's nice to finally meet you. I'm Lacey. Please have a seat and fill this out for me."

She handed me a clipboard and a pen. On the clipboard was a sex addiction quiz entitled *'Are you a Sex Addict'*. Shit, I didn't need no fuckin' test to tell me what I already knew. But if I had to take it, fuck it. The first question was: How often do you think about sex? All the fuckin' time, was my answer. The next one was embarrassin'. *Have you ever had unprotected sex with someone and you didn't know their name?* Sadly my answer was yes, more than I care to remember. The next question was, *If you are in a stable relationship do you masturbate more than twice a day?* Hell yes, I wrote down. How many sex partners have you had in life? Damn, I didn't have enough fingers, toes, or limbs to keep track. My guess was 250, but I wrote 150 just to tone it down a bit. There were twelve questions in all so I kept going, determined to start turning my life around.

Some of them were embarrassin' but most of them were just to gather information. After I finished anwerin' the questions, I handed the clipboard back to Lacey and took a seat. I knew that I was probably in for a little bit of a wait so I grabbed a magazine off the table and started flippin' through it. To my surprise, the doctor came out to get me in a matter of minutes.

Dr. Barnett was a short, fat, dark skinned woman with small wire-framed glasses hangin' off the end of her odd nose. They looked like they were gonna fall off any second. I walked into her office and the first thing that I noticed was how plain it was. No pictures on the wall, no decorations, nothin' but a damn couch and chair.

"I see that you are looking at the many decorations in my

office," she said and smiled at her own weak ass joke. Tryin' to be polite, I gave the doc a shit eatin' grin like I thought the joke was at least half way funny. "Please have a seat on the couch, Miss. Robinson."

While I sat down and made myself comfortable, Dr. Barnett picked up a pen and pad. "I'm ready," I told her proudly.

She laughed. "So, Miss. Robinson, I have read your chart, but I want you to tell me in your own words, why you are here."

Is this bitch serious? I'm here because dick controls me.

"Well, Dr Barnett, it's like this. I can't get enough sex. I want and need it all the time. It doesn't matter if it's with the neighbor, someone else's man, or even the cable repair man. When the urge hits me, I just gotta have it."

While I was talkin', Dr. Barnett was writin' somethin' down on the pad. She'd scribble a few lines then look up at me. When she was done she handed it to me. *'Nymphomaniac: Excessive sexual desire in and behavior by a female.'*

"Does that describe you, Miss. Robinson?"

"To a fuckin' T," I blurted out. "Oh, I'm sorry."

Dr. Barnett held up her hand indicatin' that my bad language was excused. After that we got into a discussion about when I first experienced these feelins' and did I think that it was just normal to feel this way. Then when she asked me what in my life had led me to realize that I need help, I poured my soul out to her. I told her everything, from the incident in the club to Angie's death. Time flew by as she let me cleanse my soul. Before I knew it, the hour was up and it was time for me to leave.

"Well, in my opinion, this has been a productive session. Next time we'll talk about some of the things that you can do to help overcome your addiction." I asked her if it was possible if I could start comin' to her, twice a week. That seemed to impress her but I wasn't being totally honest wit' her ass. I did want to get help, but a bigger reason was because my insurance through Progressive would only last through the month.

I walked out of Dr. Barnett's office feelin' like a weight

had been lifted off of my shoulders. She told me that just bein'
able to admit that I had a problem was a big step toward bein'
able to conquer my addiction and that I should be proud of the
fact that I was able to do that. She also told me that in some cir-
cles, being a nymphomaniac is classified as bein' a mental disease. I don't like the sound of that shit but I guess you could say
that I was crazy for cock. Excited that I was finally doin' somethin' that was gonna help me and my daughter, I called my
mother. I was disappointed that she didn't answer so I just left
her a message.

"Hey, Ma, it's me. I just wanted to let you know that I
just left the therapist's office. Today was my first session and I
feel betta already. I was gonna stop by but I see you ain't at
home. I'll call you later. Love you, bye."

Then I hung up and smiled all the way home.

29

Diamond

After unlockin' my front door and rushin' inside, I felt a heavy push in my lower back. My purse went one way and I went the other as I fell to the floor. I looked into Paul's sneerin' face. Dressed in a white wife beater and joggin' pants, Paul looked like a Greek God. *Damn, this nigga look like he been workin' out fo' real*, I thought. My mouth started to water as I looked at his rock hard abs cuttin' through his shirt. Okay, I need to get this nigga the fuck outta here. Ain't no way in the hell I'm gonna be able to resist him if he stays longer.

"Paul, I don't know why you pushed my but I think you should leave." Paul just looked at me and smiled. As hard as I tried, I couldn't keep my eyes off of his dick.

"So, you wanna tease muthafuckas, huh?"

Damn, this nigga was sexy as fuck! Terry Crews didn't have shit on him today. Paul grabbed his dick and I almost came on myself. At first I thought that he was just tryin' to turn me on wit' the shit he was doin'. But my horniness soon turned to fear as Paul stormed across the room and snatched my ass off the floor. Apparently he had been waitin' for me to get home so he could make his move.

"Paul, what the hell are you…"

Slap! Paul backhanded me and knocked me back onto the floor. "Paul, stop please!"

"Shut up, bitch! I'ma teach yo' ass a lesson about disrespectin' me!"

I tried to get up and run but Paul kicked me in the ribs and knocked the air out of me. I was terrified as Paul reached down and ripped my shirt off. God he was strong. Although I did have a bra on, I instinctively tried to cover up my breast. This only seemed to make Paul madder.

"Ain't that a bitch. I know yo' sluttly ass ain't tryin' ta cover them titties up now! Bring yo' ass here!"

Paul grabbed the pants I had on and tried to rip them from my hips, leaving burn marks on both sides. He literally had me upside down as he shook my pants off. When he finally did get them off, my legs fell to the floor. That's when he jumped on top of me and tried to spread my legs with his knees. Somehow I managed to work my knee inside of his legs and jam it into his balls. For a split second I thought I was gonna get to my nightstand in my bedroom. That's where I keep my gun. If I could get to it, Paul was a dead muthafucka. But as soon as I thought I was free, Paul reached out and grabbed my ankle. I responded by kickin' him in the mouth but that still didn't get him to release my leg. With one quick yank, I was right back on the floor. I reached up and grabbed a handful of his flesh, diggin' my nails into his cheek.

"Bitch!" Paul yelled, right before he reached back and punched me in the face.

He hit me so hard that the back of my head bounced off the floor. The double impact nearly caused me to black out. Paul then raised his fist to hit me again, but decided not to when my body went simi-limp. Paul then grabbed me by my hair and dragged me across the room like a caveman. The pain was excruciating. It felt like my hair was being torn away from the scalp. Once he got me to the bedroom, Paul picked me up and threw me on the bed. If I could just muster up the energy to get to my gun, this nigga was screwed. But Paul had beat me silly.

My lip was split, my eye was black, and I know I felt a knot formin' on the back of my head. Looking down on me with a vicious sneer, Paul unzipped his pants and took out his dick. For the first time in my life, I was afraid of a penis.

"Paul please, please don't do this," I staggered to say.

"Didn't I tell yo' ass to shut up," he replied as he reached down and wrapped his hand around my throat. "Now be quiet, hoe!"

I was too weak to fight as Paul turned me over on my stomach. After a few smacks to the back of the head, Paul rammed his dick in my ass. The length and width of his meat combined with my dry asshole hole caused me to wince and cry out in pain.

"Pleeeeassse stopppp," I cried.

"Shut up, bitch! You know you like it!"

When I felt Paul stiffen I felt a sense of relief 'cause I knew he was about to cum and it would be over. But instead of coming in my ass, on my ass, or even in my mouth, Paul did something that had only happened to me before by accident. After pulling his dick out, he crawled around to the side of my face. Then he reached down, pulled my eyelid up, and came directly in my eye. It burned like crazy! I tried to turn my head but Paul held it there. After emptying the rest of his nut into my face, Paul got up and zipped his pants back up. Then after spittin' in my face, he called me a filthy hoe and walked out.

****

I laid there for twenty minutes before I had the strength to move. When I finally did, I went straight to the bathroom and jumped in the shower. My asshole was killin' me and my eye was red. Because my other eye was black, I was gonna have to wear shades for a week. The hot water was my best friend as it massaged and soothed my beat up body. Tears welled up in my eyes as I recounted the brutal way Paul raped me. Later on I was gonna go to the police station. Ain't no way in hell I was gonna let Paul or any other man get away wit' rapin' me. After I got out of the shower, I called Essence to let her know what had happened. I really needed a friend right now and I was hopin' that she would meet me at the Police Station. This was some-thin' that I didn't want to do by myself.

"What?" she asked, answerin' the phone wit' an attitude.

"Damn, chick, what's wrong wit' you?"

"Diamond, what do you want?" It was obvious that Essence was still pissed off at me for goin' off at her house.

"Look, E, I'm sorry I got carried away at your house but…"

"Carried away? Diamond you were trying to kill her! If I hadn't pulled you off of her, you would be facing a murder charge right now!"

"I know and I'm sorry about that. But when I saw her I just snapped."

"Get to the point of why you called Diamond."

"E, I just got raped. Paul just raped me." An awkward si-lence filled the air. "Essence, did you hear me?"

"Yeah, I heard you," she said, nonchalantly.

"Well damn, E, don't sound too concerned," I said, a lit-tle put off by her attitude.

"What do you want me to say Diamond? You want to hear me say that I feel sorry for you? You want me to give you some sympathy? I'm sorry that this happened to you, and no woman deserves to be raped under any circumstance but can you honestly tell me that you had absolutely nothing to do with it? You didn't tease Paul some kind of way? You didn't provoke him any?"

I couldn't say nothin'. All I had in the way of a come-back was "So, what you sayin' that I deserved to be raped?"

"Diamond, are you even fucking listening to me," she said soundin' irritated. "Didn't you just hear me say that no woman deserves to get raped? And I can tell by the way you avoided the question that you did do something to provoke him!"

220

"Essence, I just need you to stand by my side as a friend right now."

"Diamond, I'm sorry, but I can't do this with you anymore. I'm sorry about what happened to you, but we need some time apart from each other. I need some space."

"Space? Why? Because I beat ya little dyke, girlfriend's ass?" As soon as it left my mouth I wanted to take it back.

"Diamond, if you call yourself trying to make me choose between you and Gwen don't, because I'm not going to do that. You act like I said that I don't ever want to see you again. We just need some separation from each other right now. Whatever other stuff you've got going on in your life, you need to take care of it. But for right now, we need some time away from each other. Later chick."

Essence hung up on me, leaving me speechless. And in the process, crushed my heart.

****

Almost an hour later and I was still heated, shocked from Essence's words. My whole world seemed to be crashin' down around me. The only thing holdin' me together was the fact that I'd reconnected' wit' Candice. What she said to me at the bus stop may have been a little disrespectful but it was the truth, which is the only reason I didn't snatch a knot in her ass.

There I was trying to chastise her in public like I had been the perfect mother. Hell, I hadn't even been a good mother. And although I was ashamed of her father, I shouldn't have abandoned her like that. I should have been involved in her life from the start. Tears snaked their way down my face as I thought about how I had neglected her over the years. But all that was about to change, I told myself. My daughter was now the most important thing in the world to me. I was gonna teach her things that would make her a much betta woman than I ever was. I took a deep breath, got up, and limped my sore ass to the mirror.

I looked fucked up. Along with rapin' me, Paul had also beat the shit outta me once again. Lookin' down at my night stand drawer, I seriously thought about grabbing my gun, going next door, and blowin' his muthafuckin' brains out. But then I thought about Candice and the fact that I needed to be in her life. So, beatin' back the urge to do a one eighty seven, I started gettin' dressed to go to the Police Station. I was just gettin' ready to walk out the door when my house phone rang.

Thinkin' that it was probably that crazy bitch Kellie, I ignored it. I was still kinda leery about Paul's earlier attack so I kept my hand in my purse just in case. By the time I got to my car my cell phone had started ringin'. Seein' that it was my mother made me smile. Thinkin' that she just wanted to chit chat, I let it go to voice mail. I wanted to get the Police Station as soon as I could so I could put Paul's rapist ass in jail.

****

My ribs were sore as hell as I got out of the car. Luckily for me, the Cleveland Heights Station didn't have no damn steps for me to have to climb up. I walked inside and strolled up to the counter, where the old grey haired receptionist was sittin' reading the Cleveland Plain Dealer.

"May I help you miss," she said without even lookin' up.

"Yes. I'd like to report a rape."

"Oh my God," she said after finally lookin' up. "Are you the victim?"

Nah hoe, I look like this on a daily basis, I wanted to say. "Yes."

The old woman walked around the desk and threw her arms around me. If I didn't know better, I would think this bitch was tryin' to hit on me. "Come over here and sit down dear." She led me over to the cold bench and sat down beside me. "Dear let me go get a detective to talk to you." She then got up and walked to the back of the station. Ten minutes later, a very handsome detective came out and walked over to me. He was

222

slim but muscular and had a thin moustache that was connected to a salt and peppery goatee.

"Hello Miss Robinson. My name is Detective Byrd. Do you need to see a doctor before we talk?"

"No, I'm okay."

"Well, to make this an official rape Miss. Robinson, you will have to see a doctor so it can be confirmed."

"Okay," I said sighin'. I really didn't feel like goin' to the doctor but felt a little better when he told me that I could go to-morrow.

"Let's go back to my office so I can take your report."

The officer then led me back to his office and took my statement. I gave him my address and told him that Paul stayed next to me. He then asked me if there was anywhere else that I could go for a few hours until they went to pick Paul up. After tellin' him that I would find somewhere to go, he assured me that he would get right on it, and that Paul would be taken into custody. I left the station knowing that Paul was gonna get what he had comin' to him. As soon as I got outside of the station, my cell phone started to go off again. Seeing that it was my mother, I smiled and answered the call. The news she gave me wiped the smile from my face in a hurry.

30

Diamond

As soon as I walked into my mother's house the smell of Virginia Slims slapped me in the face like a strong wind. The odor did nothin' to calm my pissed off disposition. Of all the fucked up things that coulda happened to my daughter, this was the thing that I feared the most. I honestly didn't know who to be more pissed off at, the nasty ass boy who did this to her or myself for not being there and letttin' this bullshit happen. Candice was sittin' on the couch with her knees pulled up to her chest. Whimperin' softly, she looked up, saw me and dropped her head back down to the floor. My mother was pacin' back and forth across the floor like this was a national tragedy. No sooner had she finished smokin' one cancer stick, she didn't hesitate to fire up another one. Ignorin' my mother's death wish I walked over to Candice and sat down.

"Are you okay, Candy?"

"Candy?" my mother asked.

"I don't know," I said shrugging my shoulders. "It just came to me." The name popped into my head because Candice looked so sweet and innocent sittin' there. Turnin' my head back to my daughter, I wrapped my arm around her and asked her again if she was okay.

"Yeah Mama, I'm fine"

"Baby, what the hell were you thinkin'?"

"That's just it," my mother yelled. "Her little ass wasn't thinkin'! I don't know how many times I've told her that...Diamond what the hell happened to your face?" When my mother told me that Candice had Chlamydia, the fact that I had been raped had to take a back seat.

"It's a long story, Ma."

"Anyway, I didn't want to bother you because I know that you've been going through some things but this girl has really been gettin' out of control lately!"

"Candice, what's goin' on wit you?"

"Oh, please! It ain't like y'all care," Candice jumped up and tried to run upstairs.

"Candice Robinson, get yo' ass back down these stairs," I screamed at her. She was so shocked that she almost tripped coming back down the steps. When she got to the bottom step, I ran up to her and put my finger in her face. "Let me tell you somethin' girl! Don't get it twisted because I let you get some shit off yo' chest when I saw you at the bus stop! I am still your damn mother whether you like it or not! Now I'ma ask you one more damn time and after that I'ma start kickin' off in yo' ass until you feel like talkin'! What the hell is goin' on wit you? Why are you runnin' around here havin' unprotected sex? Hell, why are you even havin' sex in the first place?"

Candice dropped her head. I reached down, cupped her chin and picked it back up. "Candy, we on your side baby girl. But in order for us to help you, you gotta let us know what is goin' on." Candice looked up at me with her big brown eyes and my soul melted. My heart broke into a thousand pieces when a single tear ran down her face.

"I just feel so lonely sometimes, Mama." I looked at my mother and without sayin' a word she told me that this one was all on me. I walked Candice over to the couch and sat her down. Then I grabbed her face and turned it toward mine.

"Candice, I'm so sorry that I haven't been there for you. This is just as much my fault as it is yours. But from now on, I promise you that mama gon' be here to take care of you, okay?"

"Okay," Candice said, looking at me skeptically. "Does this mean that I can spend the weekend with you sometimes?" An extra layer of guilt splashed down on me. She had asked me a couple of weeks ago if she could come and stay the weekend with me, but of course I was too busy chasin' behind a dick.

"What that means baby is that you can come and live with me if you want to." Candice's eyes lit up like neon lights.

"Fo' real Mama?"

"Yep," I looked at my mother and tears of joy were runnin' down her face.

She walked over to where we were sittin' and the three of us hugged for ten minutes. This was the feeling that I had been missin' out on for far too long, and I hoped that it would never leave. "Candice, I swear from now on, I'm gonna make you the number one priority in my life."

"Okay," she said, then looked at me skeptically.

I know she had her doubts and with the way I'd treated her, I couldn't blame her. But I was determined to make them go away. "Tomorrow, I'm comin' to get you for good," I told her. "Gather everything that you want to take with you and pack it up." Candice flew up the stairs, smiling every step of the way. Then I turned to my mother, who had tears of joy in her eyes. "Ma, I wanna thank you for everything that you done did for me. I love you," I said, hugging her.

Although I knew I wasn't gonna be on this earth long, I decided to make the best of my time with Candice. One day soon, I knew I would have to tell my mother the truth about my health. But this moment was too happy to ruin.

31

Diamond

When I left my mother's house, I was floatin' on cloud nine. The fact that I had made up wit my daughter made me feel like a whole different person. I started makin' plans for me and Candice in my head. Later on I was gonna call and make us appointments to get manicures and pedicures. Until I got another job, I was gonna have to be careful wit my cash but spendin' the day wit Candice would be priceless. I thought about celebratin' by goin' out and gettin' laid, but I quickly put that thought out of my mind. If I was ever gonna get well, I had to stop thinkin' about sex all the time.

My thoughts drifted to Essence. I was really gonna miss her as a friend, I told myself turning the corner and turning up the music. I didn't give a damn about her being bi-sexual. I just think that it's fucked up the way she ended our friendship. Angie was gone forever. I didn't want to lose Essence too. I decided to call her and try to make up, but as soon as I picked up the phone it started vibratin'. It was the Cleveland Heights Police Station. I held my breath hopin' that the detective was about to tell me that they got that rapist muthafucka Paul in custody.

"Hello."

"Hi Miss. Robinson. This is Detective Byrd. I was calling to give you an update on the case. We went by your neighbor's house to arrest him but he wasn't there. Apparently he has moved out. We had a warrant so we didn't have to wait for someone to open the door. When we went inside, the entire apartment was empty. I assure you though that we will continue to look for him and we will not stop until we find the son of a bitch."

I didn't know how to feel about what he'd just told me. I was glad that the asshole didn't stay next to me no more, but I wanted the bastard behind bars, not roamin' the streets. "So, you ain't got no idea where he could be?"

"No ma'am, but like I said we won't rest until we have him in jail."

"Could you please tell me when you catch him?"

"Sure thing ma'am. We will notify you as soon as he is in custody."

I hung up wonderin' if I was gonna have to look over my shoulder for the rest of my life. I ain't a scary person but Paul's attack left me feelin' unsure of my safety. I was gonna make damn sure that my gun was in my reach at all times. I decided to stop at the convenient store and pick up a bottle of wine. The good in my life was startin' to outweigh the bad. I flipped open my phone and called Essence. This bullshit had gone on long enough. I needed to talk to her and see where we stood wit' each other. I had no idea what I was gonna say to her but we needed to have a conversation.

"Yeah Diamond," she said as soon as she answered.

"Okay, Essence I think me and you need to talk about some shit. We been friends way too long for us to just flush that down the toliet. I mean..." I stopped when I heard a voice in the background.

"Is that bitch over there again?"

"No, Essence, I'm over her house, but so what? You ready to hang up now?"

"Essence I'm just sayin. I don't understand how you can be screwin' somebody that's the enemy of yo' best friend."

"That's because you don't love anybody except yourself

Diamond. Me on the other hand, I have feelings for other people and that includes Gwen. I love her Diamond and I'm sorry if you can't understand that."

"I understand about being in love, E. I just don't see how you can just stop givin' a fuck about our friendship."

"I never said I did. I just said that I thought we needed some space away from each other."

"Essence, you act like I started that shit at the funeral. I didn't. All I did was defend myself. Why can't you understand that shit?"

"I do understand that. But you are the one that's trying to make me choose and I'm not going to do that." I didn't know what to say. I wasn't ready to lose Essence as a friend, but I didn't think that I would ever be able to be around her little girlfriend.

"Look, Diamond, I have to go. We can talk about this later, ok?"

"The fuck you mean you gotta go," I snapped. "We been friends all this time and now you ain't got time to fuckin' talk?" Silence filled the line for a second before my other line beeped. I ignored it then gave Essence a piece of my mind. "You know what! Fuck you, Essence!"

"No, fuck you, Diamond! You acting like somebody owe your ass something! You want to talk about something heifer, let's talk about how you got HIV and haven't said anything about it! How the hell you got that death package and didn't tell your friends about it? I saw very clearly what the name of that medication was! Did you forget that I work in a hospital Diamond?"

I was stunned. I'd tried to snatch my medication up as fast as I could but I guess I'd been too late.

"Say something, Diamond."

After weighing my options, I felt that it was best that I went ahead and told Essence the truth. With Angie gone, I really didn't want to lose my other best friend.

"Okay Essence. You right. I do have HIV. I'm sorry that I

didn't tell you before, but I didn't want to lose you as a friend."

"Diamond, that shit is still foul! You should've told us!"

"I know Essence. I'm sorry." The phone went dead for so long, I thought that she had hung up.

"How long have you been sick, Diamond?"

"Around seven years."

"Have you been protecting yourself with condoms while fuckin' everything that moves?"

My mind went blank for a moment. Essence did have a good point. I'd gotten so crazy, wanting and needing sex every ten minutes that most times I hadn't worn a condom.

"The reason I'm asking Diamond…is because….well because I have HIV too, but I've been infecting niggas with it. Purposely. I just hate them." She started whimpering and getting all emotional.

"Oh my God! Essence, I wish I had known girl. Having this shit is rough and we coulda been helping each other all this time. *I just couldn't believe Essence had it too.* Shit, I only wish I could find that asshole Trevon and…"

"Wait! Diamond! What did you just say?"

"I said I wish I could find that asshole Trevon and cut his throat!" For some reason, Essence got deathly quiet.

"E? Essence?"

"Diamond, I gotta call you back," she said hanging up.

I really hoped that this wasn't the end of our friendship. I loved Essence like a sister, but it seemed like she really didn't have time for me anymore. At least I had Candice. Minutes later, I rushed into my house and poured myself a glass of wine. Me and the Vodka had ended our relationship. The phone started ringing like crazy, but whoever was callin' would have to wait. I needed a few moments to digest what Essence had told me. How the fuck did we both end up with HIV? And why didn't I act more responsible, wearing a rubber each and every time? My mind flipped to all those I'd fucked bareback; Paul, Rich, Kenneth, J-Bone…the list went on. Damn, I was gonna get in touch with each of them first thing in the morning

32

Essence

As soon as I hung up from Diamond, I dialed Trevon's number. When he didn't answer I went off. "You dirty, low down son of a bitch! You mean to tell me that you fucked two best friends and gave both of us that fucking monster? You piece of shit!! If I ever see you again, I'm gonna cut your dick off!!"

I pressed end and jammed my phone back in my pocket. I did my best to calm down before Gwen got back in the room from taking a shower. Five minutes later, she emerged from the bathroom naked and dripping.

"Everything cool, baby?" she asked, as she sat on my lap. I nodded my head wondering what would become of me and Diamond's friendship. I felt better being over at Gwen's house instead of being at home. The way Diamond had been acting lately, I didn't trust her not to come over my house and act a fool again. I know that I was being a hypocrite by getting mad at her for not telling me that she had HIV when I hadn't told her about me but oh well. I didn't want to lose her friendship, but I wasn't going to let her get in the way of me being happy either. I looked at the bandages on Gwen's arm and wondered what would possess Diamond to snap like that.

"I'm sorry about your arm. I don't know what got into Diamond."

"Jealousy is what got into her ass. But enough about that bitch," Gwen said as she started to caress my breast. "Let's go into the bedroom and have some fun." Gwen got up off of my lap and grabbed my hand.

"So, where is Kellie tonight," I asked with Gwen pulling me into her bedroom.

"Huh? Oh, she had something to do tonight," she said, sounding mysterious. "I won't see her until tomorrow so just relax." There was something about the way she made that statement that made me feel uneasy, but when she pulled me close to her and kissed me on my neck all my cares went away.

"Oooo Gwen, that feels so goood."

"You like that girl? You like to feel this tongue?"

"Mhhmm, I love it."

"Get naked and lay down on the bed honey. I got something special in store for you tonight."

Gwen then walked out of the bed room. I snatched my clothes off as fast as I could in anticipation of a steamy rendezvous. My entire body started to tingle thinking about what Gwen was about to do to it. "There's a bottle of honey oil in the drawer! Take it out and sit it on the night stand for me," Gwen yelled from the kitchen.

I don't know what she was doing in there but I couldn't wait to find out what she had in store. I took the oil out and put it up to my nose. The sweet smell of honey filled my nostrils, causing my nipples to get hard with excitement. When Gwen came back into the room, she had on nothing but a tool belt, a hard hat and had a cooler in her hand.

"Time to go to work," she said seductively. She then unloosened the tool belt and let it fall to the floor. Slowly and sexily she walked over to the bed and started to nibble on my feet. "Tastes good but it needs a little more flavor."

Gwen then walked over to the cooler and opened it. She reached in and pulled out a can of strawberry flavored whipped cream. After walking back over to the bed, Gwen swirled the whip cream on my big toe. Then she leaned down and flicked her tongue across my toe, causing my body to shudder.

After tasting the other four, Gwen then walked over to the night stand and picked up the bottle of honey oil. After squirting some of it in the palm of her hand, Gwen rubbed it over both of my legs. My vagina felt like lava. Gwen then crawled onto the bed and spread my legs apart. Picking up the bottle of whipped cream, Gwen sprayed it down the left side of my leg and up the right one. Then she licked every bit of it off, stopping at my clit to tease me a little.

"Don't stop! Please, don't stop," I begged.

"You ain't seen nothing yet," she said. Gwen then crawled off of the bed and over to her lunch box. She reached in it again and pulled out a cucumber and an ice cube. Sticking the cucumber in her mouth, Gwen came back over to the bed and rubbed the cucumber on my clit, causing me to shake.

"Damn, bitch, what the hell are you doing to me," I said, trembling.

"You know what," she said, "I wanna tap that pussy." I looked at her curiously thinking, *with what?* I guessed she changed her mind about using the cucumber and ice cube because she put them back into the cooler. Then she went to her closet and came back out with a strap on. The stiff rubber dick that stuck out from it had to be eleven inches long.

"What the hell are you going to do with that?"

Flashing a sinister smile, Gwen said, "Turn that juicy ass over so I can hit that pussy from the back!"

Smiling at her demands, I slowly turned over and got on my hands and knees and spread my legs. Gwen got behind me and stuck her face into my dripping cum hole. She licked it so hard I thought I was gonna cum in her mouth right then and there. When she was sure that I was good and wet, she plunged inside.

"Oh yes, Gwen, yes," I squealed as she grabbed my hips and started slamming into my womb. Gwen pounded my pussy like I was her personal bitch.

"Give it here bitch! Gimma this muthafuckin' pussy!"

"Take it Take this pussy!" Gwen was punishing my womb. In some strange way, I think that she was taking Diamond's behavior out on me.

"Cum bitch! You betta cum or I'ma beat this pussy up all night."

All of a sudden, I felt something cold being rubbed on my ass. Apparently I was wrong when I thought that Gwen had put the ice cube back into the cooler. She continued to screw me from behind as she slid the cold cube down the crack of my ass. I was on the brink of busting a nut and when she pushed the ice cube inside my ass hole, I lost all control. A stream of pleasure rushed down my leg as my back arched. I collapsed onto the bed, totally satisfied with what my lover had done to me. We laid there for about ten minutes before she got up to take a shower.

"I'm going to take a shower sweetie. When I come back, be ready for round two," she said, slapping me on the ass.

I laid face down in the bed trying to catch my breath. Gwen had put it on me so good that I didn't care if I ever saw another dick again. I was more than ready for round two. I looked over at the strap on that Gwen had left on the floor and smiled devilishly. Easing out of the bed, I picked it up and put it on. Then I crept toward the bathroom ready to return the favor of her pounding my love hole. I didn't feel like waiting for her to get out of the bathroom. I had never used a strap on before and I wanted to see what it felt like to screw another woman. As I got to the door, I heard her talking on the phone.

I waited patiently for her to get off the phone so I could go in and surprise her. The more I waited the more my smile started to fade. Utter shocked spread across my face when I heard what she was saying. My heart pounded. I began to sweat. I tiptoed back down the hall to her room, and quickly got half-dressed, with my pants still unbuttoned and shirt hanging off my shoulder. Within seconds I'd made my way toward the front door, shoeless. I was halfway there when Gwen's chilling voice cut through the air like scissors.

"Going somewhere Essence?"

I turned around and saw a look in Gwen's eyes that I had never seen before. "Yes. I have to make a run right quick."

"Where to?" she asked, smiling sinisterly.

"Huh? Oh, I just remembered that I didn't set the alarm at my house." It was a weak lie, but it was the only one that I could think of at the moment.

"Bitch, why don't you stop lying!" she snapped. "You're just trying to get out of here so you can go warn that tramp ass friend of yours!" My heart dropped again. I couldn't believe what Gwen was doing. Tears welled up in my eyes as I visualized losing another friend in less than a month's time. "Gwen, please call it off. Please don't let this happen. It would kill me if something happened to Diamond."

Gwen burst out laughing. "I don't give a fuck about that slut or you either for that matter!" Tears rolled down my face. I truly thought that me and Gwen could have something special. As if reading my mind, Gwen put her hands on her hips and laughed some more. "What, bitch you thought I loved you? I never loved your ass! You were just a means to an end! You're not here tonight by accident! You're here so you wouldn't be in the fuckin' way when your slutty ass friend got what was coming to her! So, if you think you can get to her in time, be my guest. And oh yeah, thanks for the good pussy," she said as she walked back to the bedroom laughing.

As much as I wanted to go after her and beat the shit out of her, I had to get to Diamond first. I dashed out the door pressing buttons on my phone, trying desperately to reach my friend. When she didn't answer I dialed 911. I told them what I knew and hopped in my truck. As soon as I turned the ignition, my cell phone rang. Please let it be Diamond I thought as I answered it without looking at the screen. "Hello?"

"Yeah, this Trevon and I don't appreciate you calling my phone with that bullshit!"

"Bullshit? Nigga you the one full of bullshit! How in the hell are you going to fuck two best friends and give both of us

HIV, nigga?"

"What?"

"Motherfucker you heard me!"

"Essence, I don't know what the fuck Diamond been tellin' you, but I didn't give that shit to her. That bitch gave it to me!"

My mouth fell open at Trevon's comment. Absent mindedly, I sat the phone down on the passenger's seat and rubbed my face. I couldn't believe what I had just heard. I sat there for a few minutes trying to wrap my mind around the information that I'd just received when suddenly my window shattered and glass flew into my face. My lap was covered with so many tiny pieces of glass, I was afraid to move.

"Yeah bitch, I told you that I was gonna get yo' muthafuckin' ass!"

Although I hadn't looked around yet, I knew it was Cedric. His unmistakable raspy voice was a dead give a way. Before I could do anything to defend myself, Cedric punched me in the face, dazing me. He then grabbed my hair and yanked my head back toward the head rest.

"It took me a while to find you but I got yo' ass now bitch!"

My eyes got big and fear gripped my entire body as I felt the cold steel of Cedric's switchblade press against my neck. I reached for his arm and tried to pull it away from my neck but he was much too strong.

"Oh God no, please don't!" I screamed with tears now flowing down my face. Piss ran down my leg as the stark realization that I was about to die set in.

"Say goodnight bitch," Cedric said as he started to drag the blade across my neck.

ϟ33

Diamond

"Ughhhh," I grunted as the phone continued to ring like crazy. I got up off the couch and switched my way over to the phone. I looked at the caller ID and saw that it was my mother. My life had really started to come together and havin' them in it was the best thing that coulda happened to a bitch like me, so I answered. My happiness soon turned to utter fright, when I heard my mother yellin' like a wild woman.

"Diamond! Oh my God, Diamond, what have you done?" she wailed.

"Huh? Ma, what are you talkin' about?"

"There's a man here who says his name is Hank claiming that you made him sick!"

My heart instantly sank to the pit of my stomach. I knew exactly who Hank was.

"He says that…"

"Gimme the phone, bitch," I heard him say. "Now you…Shut the fuck up, you lil slut," he yelled at Candice, who I heard crying loudly in the background. "Like I was saying, bitch! My beef ain't with them, it's with yo' nasty, disease passin' ass! And if you ain't ova here in thirty minutes, I'ma shoot yo' old-ass momma, then I'ma body that lil slut you call a daughter, then I'ma rape this big tittie sister of yours right before I blow her fuckin' brains out! Your life or theirs! You got thirty minutes!"

"Hank, please don't do this!" I shouted while bending and holding my stomach. I became sick at the thought of what I'd done. I knew there would be consequences, but damn!

"You think I'm playin, don't you?"

"No, Hank. I'm…."

I was cut off by the loud sounds of gun fire. Bile rose up in my gut. And I threw up. POW! POW! He shot two more times.

"Thirty minutes lil slut!"

I was crying and sniveling so hard I could barely hear him talking to someone in the background. It seemed as though Candice was in the back crying even harder than I was. I knew I needed to get there to help my baby.

"If you don't shut the fuck up, I swear to God I'ma stick my dick in yo…"

That's all I heard before he hung up and left me praying to God. Within seconds, I'd grabbed my car keys, ready to jet out the door, but had a strange feelin' that somebody was watchin' me. I took two steps toward the front door when some-body appeared, tripped me purposely, and caused me to fall on the floor. Instinctively, I turned around and saw a silhouette standin' there.

"Hello, bitch! I've been waitin' a long time for this!"

Quickly, I tried to reach for my purse that had fallen on the floor, but the impact slammed me against the wall. My auto-graphed pictures of Darius leapt off the screws and shattered onto the floor. My life flashed before my eyes as I screamed out in agony. I thought back to all the lives I'd ruined and the mar-riages that had been wrecked because of me. The loud thunder clapping through the skies drowned out my call for help.

Pow! The first bullet got me. The red hot slug from the .357 Magnum ripped through my right shoulder blade, shred-ding tissue and bone along the way. I scrambled my way along the floor hoping for a way to defend myself. Finally, my fingertips touched the tip of my purse lying ten inches away. I sighed and pulled it my way, praying to God, he'd help me make it out alive. I stuck my hand down inside reaching for the .25 automatic. To my surprise, it wasn't there. I looked up through tear soaked eyes and saw my assailant holding the missing pistol.

"Looking for this?"

The shooter's haunting laugh sent chills up and down my spine. Bleeding profusely, I struggled to stand up.

"Who the fuck is you? What the fuck is this shit all about?"

"You've stolen something from me that I can't get back, and now it's time to pay the piper," the cold voice responded.

I was sure that I'd heard that voice before, but couldn't quite place it. The shooter was dressed in black jeans, a black pullover hoodie, and black boots with a black fedora hat pulled down over one eye. I still didn't have a clue. Suddenly, I looked at the floor in amazement as the .25 slid across the floor and stopped in front of me.

"Go ahead, bitch. Pick it up."

Foolishly, I snatched the gun up, pointed it, and pulled the trigger. The hooded gunman's sinister laugh resonated throughout the room.

"And all this time I thought you were smart. You're a dumb bitch. You really think I would give your ass a loaded gun? All that cum you've been swallowing has made your ass retarded."

I threw the gun down in disgust. "Fuck!"

"Yep bitch! That's exactly what you are! Fucked!"

"Fucked?"As hard as I tried, I just couldn't get a clear read on the voice that wanted me dead. There was no slurred speech or slang to connect them with the hood. There was no deep, baritone voice that said it was a seasoned killer. In fact, the voice seemed light, telling me that it could've been a woman. "What the fuck is that 'spose ta mean?" I asked.

"It means, you illiterate hoe… it's payback time. You took away my life and now I'm going to return the favor.

It was a woman, I told myself. Took their life away? I tried to think back but I'd fucked so many men during that time that I couldn't be sure whose wife stood before me. I flinched when my assailant reached into her back pocket. With a flick of the wrist, a picture sailed across the floor toward my feet. Reaching down with my good arm, I picked it up and stared at it.

"I don't even know this fuckin' kid!"

"Well, maybe you should meet him then. The assassin walked stealthily toward me with the barrel pointed at my head. When the hat and glasses were removed, a look of terror filled my heart. Then it hit me. It was Darius' baby picture.

"Oh my God! It's you, bitch! It's..."

"Your worse fuckin' nightmare hoe! Not only was my son killed because of you...but you were probably the tramp who gave him that poison." Her voice slowed, and softened. "I would tell you to say hello to him, but he's in heaven. And you're on your way to hell."

White light flashed in my face as a hollow point bullet sprinted through my brain. Darius' mother then walked over to me as I lay gasping for air, bleeding profusely. She spit, then quickly walked out the front door where Kellie stood telling her, their work was done. Darius would be proud.

Words from the Author

To my readers and fans,

I hope my novel **Next Door Nympho** has entertained you. Although I presented you with a work of fiction, my goal was to open up the eyes and ears of people who aren't one hundred percent clear on how to protect themselves sexually, nor on ways to prevent AIDS. My book highlighted the consequences of having unprotected sex. The focus was put on young adults, but we're all affected. The one thing we must all remember about AIDS and HIV is that this disease does not discriminate. It doesn't care what color you are, how old you are, or how much money you have. One time people! It only takes one time to have unprotected sex in order to contract AIDS. It can only be contracted through the exchange of bodily fluids through blood transfusions, unprotected sex, or previously used needles.

Although scientists and doctors are working hard to find a cure, for now; once you get it, you've got it! So, please use a condom. If you have had unprotected sex within the last five years, please get tested. At the end of 2009, there were 33.3 million adults living with HIV/AIDS. To date over 230,000 African-Americans have died of AIDS, and nearly half of the people living with the disease in the U.S. are African-American. Let's all wake-up and promote AIDs prevention. Contact Aids info@ 1-800-448-0440; Center for Disease Control and Prevention @404-639-3311, or the Teen AIDS Hotline @ 1-800-283-2473.

Peace,
C.J. Hudson...The Keyboard Assassin

ORDER FORM

MAIL TO:
PO Box 423
Brandywine, MD 20613
301-362-6508

FAX TO:
301-579-9913

Ship to:

Address:

Date: _____ Phone: _____

Email: _____

City & State: _____ Zip: _____

Make all money orders and cashiers checks payable to: **Life Changing Books**

Qty.	ISBN	Title	Release Date	Price
	0-9741394-2-4	Bruised by Azarel	Jul-05	$ 15.00
	0-9741394-7-5	Bruised 2: The Ultimate Revenge by Azarel	Oct-06	$ 15.00
	0-9741394-3-2	Secrets of a Housewife by J. Tremble	Feb-06	$ 15.00
	0-9741394-6-7	The Millionaire Mistress by Tiphani	Nov-06	$ 15.00
	1-934230-99-5	More Secrets More Lies by J. Tremble	Feb-07	$ 15.00
	1-934230-98-7	Young Assassin by Mike G.	Mar-07	$ 15.00
	1-934230-95-2	A Private Affair by Mike Warren	May-07	$ 15.00
	1-934230-94-4	All That Glitters by Ericka M. Williams	Jul-07	$ 15.00
	1-934230-93-6	Deep by Danette Majette	Jul-07	$ 15.00
	1-934230-96-0	Flexin & Sexin Volume 1	Jun-07	$ 15.00
	1-934230-92-8	Talk of the Town by Tonya Ridley	Jul-07	$ 15.00
	1-934230-89-8	Still a Mistress by Tiphani	Nov-07	$ 15.00
	1-934230-91-X	Daddy's House by Azarel	Nov-07	$ 15.00
	1-934230-88-X	Naughty Little Angel by J. Tremble	Feb-08	$ 15.00
	1-934230847	In Those Jeans by Chantel Jolie	Jun-08	$ 15.00
	1-934230855	Marked by Capone	Jul-08	$ 15.00
	1-934230820	Rich Girls by Kendall Banks	Oct-08	$ 15.00
	1-934230839	Expensive Taste by Tiphani	Nov-08	$ 15.00
	1-934230782	Brooklyn Brothel by C. Stecko	Jan-09	$ 15.00
	1-934230669	Good Girl Gone bad by Danette Majette	Mar-09	$ 15.00
	1-934230804	From Hood to Hollywood by Sasha Raye	Mar-09	$ 15.00
	1-934230707	Sweet Swagger by Mike Warren	Jun-09	$ 15.00
	1-934230677	Carbon Copy by Azarel	Jul-09	$ 15.00
	1-934230723	Millionaire Mistress 3 by Tiphani	Nov-09	$ 15.00
	1-934230715	A Woman Scorned by Ericka Williams	Nov-09	$ 15.00
	1-934230685	My Man Her Son by J. Tremble	Feb-10	$ 15.00
	1-924230731	Love Heist by Jackie D.	Mar-10	$ 15.00
	1-934230812	Flexin & Sexin Volume 2	Apr-10	$ 15.00
	1-934230748	The Dirty Divorce by Miss KP	May-10	$ 15.00
	1-934230758	Chedda Boyz by CJ Hudson	Jul-10	$ 15.00
	1-934230766	Snitch by VegasClarke	Oct-10	$ 15.00
	1-934230693	Money Maker by Tonya Ridley	Oct-10	$ 15.00
	1-934230774	The Dirty Divorce Part 2 by Miss KP	Nov-10	$ 15.00
	1-934230170	The Available Wife by Carla Pennington	Jan-11	$ 15.00
	1-934230774	One Night Stand by Kendall Banks	Feb-11	$ 15.00
	1-934230278	Bitter by Danette Majette	Feb-11	$ 15.00
	1-934230299	Married to a Balla by Jackie Davis	Mar-11	$ 15.00
			Total for Books	$
			Shipping Charges (add $4.95 for 1-4 books*)	$
			Total Enclosed (add lines)	$

* Prison Orders- Please allow up to three (3) weeks for delivery.

Please Note: We are not held responsible for returned prison orders. Make sure the facility will receive books before ordering.

*Shipping and Handling of 5-10 books is $6.95, please contact us if your order is more than 10 books.
(301)362-6508